PAINTED LADY

A James P. Dandy Elderhostel Mystery

Peter Abresch

INTRIGUE PRESS | DENVER

First Printing, March 2003
Intrigue Press, an imprint of Corvus Publishing Group

Book layout and design by Speck Design, www.speck-design.com

ISBN 1-890768-47-2
Library of Congress Control Number: 2002116914

Printed and bound in the United States of America.

1 2 3 4 5 6 7 8 9 10

ACKNOWLEDGMENTS

To my publisher Derek Lawrence for picking up the Elderhostel mystery series. My freelance editor Dorrie O'Brien, who isn't free, but is very good. Wayne Sundberg and Joan Day who did such a fine job of coordinating the Santa Fe Trail Elderhostel.

My wife Annemarie, who took all the research pictures and who put up with my grumbling when things weren't going right.

In memory of John Lindsey, who told me how this book would have to end and whose advice I surely miss.

For the Sisters In Crime, Denver Chapter, for maintaining the hospitality room at Bouchercon 2001.

To all the folks at *Elderhostel Inc.*
11 Avenue de Lafayette, Boston, MA 02111-1746
http://www.Elderhostel.org
who have treated me so generously.

On all the *Elderhostels* I have attended I have found nothing but fun, camaraderie, and adventurous spirits, and nary a body. . .yet.

Peter E. Abresch
Peter@elderhostelmysteries.com
www.elderhostelmysteries.com

For all who have helped
me on my faith journey,
especially those who are often overlooked:

the Reverends
James Finan, Peter Alliata, John Brady,
Martin Casey, Bill Cleary, John Courtney, Peter Daly,
James Downs, Paul Dudziak, Ray Kemp,
Lawrence Gatti, Paul Hill, Joseph Naughton,
Ray Wadas, and Francis Walsh

ONE

Jim Dandy popped a bite-sized éclair into his mouth, savoring the vanilla cream wrapped in flaky dough and topped with chocolate. Other goodies lay scattered across the white tablecloth—bagels, cream cheese, donut holes, various cheeses—but he preferred to camp out with the éclairs.

Probably not a good thing for a sixty-plusser to be scarfing down, but, damnit, he deserved some compensation for being left in the lurch on his own.

What the hell was he doing here, stuck in a hospitality room of a Denver hotel with a bunch of people he didn't know, didn't want to know, authors and fans of mystery novels at a convention called Bouchercon?

What the hell was a Bouchercon?

"Bouchercon is from a man's name; the title means the Boucher Conference," a woman at the far end of the table said, addressing a group of people standing in the center of the room. They had apparently gotten curious about the conference and simply asked the hospitality room's hostess what the title meant.

1

He popped another bite-sized eclair into his mouth and drifted down to eavesdrop.

"Anthony Boucher wrote a weekly column about books in the New York Times in the fifties and sixties. He was the leading Unite d States authority on mystery authors and their heroes, if not the world. He was an author himself, spoke seven languages, wrote opera reviews, did everything, but he's mostly remembered as a mentor to fellow authors."

Sounded like she was just getting wound up.

He retreated to his end of the table where a woman interloper was threatening to take his spot by the éclairs.

"This is a lovely spread, isn't it?"

He glanced around to see that only the two of them were in conversational range, which meant the plump, fortyish interloper was talking to him.

Great, just great.

She picked up a cheese cube and motioned with it for him to take in the large room with two conversational groupings of easy chairs and couches. "It's really nice of the Denver Sisters in Crime chapter to put this on for us."

"I'm not part of us."

Dark brown eyes in a chubby face blinked at him, as if wondering on whose authority he was scarfing up the éclairs.

"I mean, you know, I'm not with the group."

"You're not with Bouchercon?"

"My girlfriend is. She's an artist. Illustrated a book cover for someone."

"Really? Which one?"

He shrugged. "A mystery to me."

"What's her name?"

2

What was she doing, giving him the third degree?

"I might want her to illustrate my next book," she said.

"Oh. Dodee Swisher." Never hurts to give out a little PR. Unless the woman had just wanted to sneak in the fact she was an author.

"Is she here?" the interloper asked, turning to the people in the room.

He shook his head. "She's finishing a painting of the two big horse statues down in the lobby."

"And when she's finished? You have to forgive me, I'm a mystery author and I have to know all the details."

"When she's finished?" He grabbed a paper plate, turned his back on the woman, and pretended to study the snacks at the other end of the table.

"Yes, when you're finished . . .?"

"We're heading out for an Elderhostel."

"What are they, like a trip or something?"

"Sort of."

"Sort of?"

He turned back to her, took a breath, and let it out. "They're learning adventures for those over fifty-five, each one with a theme. This one's on the Santa Fe Trail."

"Really? My last book took place in Santa Fe."

"Uh-huh."

He loaded his plate with five éclairs and walked to a corner window seven feet away. He set the goodies on the deep sill and stared down five floors at the intersection of Denver's Sixteenth Street Mall and Court Place, bright in the high-altitude sun.

"I think you'd like it," the woman said, barging into his space and setting her plate next to his, like old friends sharing an alcove.

Great, just absolutely great.

"My novel, you'd like it."

He turned back to gaze across the street at the black-tarred flat roofs of the buildings facing out onto Court Place.

"It got terrific reviews."

A silver utility penthouse perched on one of them, about twenty feet square, and as he watched, a woman in a tan dress emerged, came around to his side, and flattened against the wall as if she were catching the mid-morning sun.

"Some really, incredibly fantastic reviews."

Wasn't she ever going to shut up?

"It's called *Pick Your Friends, But Not Their Noses.*"

Jim rolled his eyes, popped an éclair into his mouth, and returned to watching the woman in the tan dress.

"You see, it's a play on words, and it contains a lot of humorous episodes, if I do say so myself."

"I don't read mysteries."

"Oh, you'd like this one, even so."

He turned from the window and searched the large room for a head covered with wheat-colored curls.

Where the hell was Dodee?

First she makes him come all the way in from the airport when they're only going all the way back out again, then she gives him a peck on the cheek and abandons him to the mercies of babbling mystery writers roaming the hospitality room.

"You can buy one downstairs in the convention sales area and I'll autograph it for you."

This after not seeing him for a couple of months.

"See, it starts out in Santa Fe."

4

Did she think he was having fun?

"My heroine, Penelope Pentalope, meets Bixby Boyd in the Plaza."

Maybe he should pack an emergency ration of éclairs and bug out. Except the damn woman would probably follow him even if he went into a men's room.

"Oh, my God! My God. Oh my God!"

He whirled around to the window and caught a fast glance of the woman on the roof going over the ledge, arms flailing and tan dress billowing out as she disappeared down into the canyon of Court Place.

"She was pushed," the woman said.

He swung back to her. "Call nine-one-one."

"Oh, yes, she was pushed—"

"Call nine-one-one."

"I saw her, she was—"

Jim grabbed her and gave her a little shake. "Call nine-one-one!"

Then he raced across the room, threading his way through the milling people, banging into a man as he reached the hall. He turned left and ran for the elevators, found the stairs and took them two and three at a time, breathing hard, and bounced out into the lobby.

He shouted at Dodee standing at her easel. "Stay there until I get back!" Then he barged through an outside door, darted between honking cars, and charged down Court Place.

5

Two

His charge down the street degenerated into a stagger by the time he passed under the Duffy's Restaurant canopy and stumbled over to the woman sprawled on the other side. He bent over her, hands on his knees as air wheezed in and out of his lungs and spots danced before his eyes.

Sonofabitch, he needed someone to call 911 for him.

He wiped his face with his handkerchief, then dropped to one knee and felt her wrist for a pulse as blood pooled about her.

Nothing.

A door slammed and he turned to a man rushing out of the arched entrance of the building behind him.

The man pulled up short, green eyes staring at Jim over a black handlebar mustache worthy of an old-time speakeasy bartender. "You a doctor?"

"EMT." He turned back to the woman and leaned his handkerchief-filled hand on the pavement. "Emergency medical technician," he said, still gasping as he eased aside a gold chain that had bunched up around her neck.

"Don't take that," the man with the handlebar mustache said.

Jim placed a finger on the woman's jugular.

No pulse there either.

"Oh," Handlebar said behind him, "sorry."

What would he have done if he had found one?

He wiped his face with the handkerchief again, then leaned on all fours on the sidewalk and tried to catch his breath.

God, he was getting old.

Or was it Denver's altitude working on his Eastern seaboard lungs?

He looked down on an olive-colored face framed by two long braids of black hair and said a silent prayer.

The tan dress turned out to be buckskin with leather fringes hanging from her sleeves and across the breast. One foot was covered by a homemade moccasin with leather tongs tied above her ankle. A second moccasin rested on its side inches from her bare foot, the spreading blood threatening to engulf it. He picked it up and a soft insole slipped out.

"What's that?" Handlebar asked.

Jim placed the moccasin on the sidewalk beside his handkerchief-filled hand, retrieved the insole, and replaced it in the moccasin.

"What fell out of the shoe?"

Jim pocketed his handkerchief and stood up.

Black eyebrows knitted over the green eyes of the mid-forties man, and a lock of curly hair hung down over his forehead. "Sorry, about the neck chain, I mean." Handlebar brushed back the stray curl. "I thought"—he shrugged—"I didn't realize you were—" He shrugged again. "What fell out of her shoe?"

The wail of klaxons broke into the Court Place canyon

as an ambulance raced down the street, a police car close behind. Jim waved them down and stood aside as a woman in a white coat raced toward him.

"Stand back. We'll need some room here."

"I think it's too late," Jim said.

"You a doctor?" White Coat asked as she knelt beside the woman and touched her neck for a pulse.

"EMT. She fell off the roof." He watched White Coat shake her head and sit back on her haunches. "Either that or she was pushed."

"What's this about being pushed?"

He turned to a new face, deeply tanned, marred by a pale scar running between his eyebrows, head covered with a Denver Police cap. He looked young enough to be in high school, but then, people were looking younger all the time, and the gun strapped on the man's hip probably meant he was no teenager.

"What's this about being pushed?" the cop asked again, a rectangular tag over the left pocket with the name of Sundown.

Jim motioned up the street. "I was in the Mark Adams Hotel—"

"The Adams Mark, sir?"

"Huh? Oh yeah, right, the Adams Mark."

The woman in the white coat came up. "She's expired. What do you want us to do?"

"Better leave her," Sundown said. "We'll wait for the coroner. Would you ask my partner to call it in and bring the tape?" He turned back to Jim. "You were saying?"

"I was looking out a window of the Adams Mark, about five floors up, and I saw her come out on the roof."

"The deceased?"

"Right. There's a silver utility penthouse up there and I saw her come out. She stood around the side like she was sunning herself, but she could have been hiding from someone."

"Uh-huh. Then what?"

"Then I turned away—"

"You said someone pushed her off?"

"I don't know that. I turned away and a woman author next to me said something like, 'Good grief,' or 'What the hell,' and I looked out the window just as the woman went over the side."

"What about being pushed?"

"That's what this woman said. All I could think of was getting down here to see if I could help."

"Are you a doctor?"

"Emergency medic—an EMT—back in Maryland. I just arrived this morning. I'm also a physical therapist. I thought I might be able to help, but of course when I got here I couldn't find a pulse."

A second policeman came up to them carrying a yellow tape. "Whassup?"

"Possible homicide. You call it in?" The second cop nodded. "Okay, we better tape off this area and see if we have any witnesses over there," he said, nodding to a small crowd standing by the corner of the building. Then he pulled out a notebook and turned back to Jim. "So you didn't see anything? Someone can vouch for you being in the hotel at the time the woman went off the roof?"

"Well, yeah, I was in a room full of people and talking to that woman author. And those who witnessed it here," he said, motioning to the same people Sundown had, "they'll tell you that I came running down the street after the woman hit the ground. And also this man—" He turned toward the arched doorway of the building, but Handlebar had disappeared.

"What's the name of this author?"

"I don't know."

"Then how do you know—"

"They're having some kind of mystery convention at the hotel, Bouchercon I think it is, and we just got to talking. I can tell you the name of her book. It's called *Pick Your Friends, But Not Their Noses.*"

A frown screwed up the lips on the young policeman's tanned face.

Jim nodded. "Yeah, I thought it was crazy myself, but that's what she said. You should be able to find her name from that."

The cop wrote in his notebook, then looked up. "Your name, sir?"

"James P. Dandy."

"And you're staying at the Adams Mark?"

"No, I just came to pick up my friend. We're spending the night at, ah"—he searched in his pockets and came out with a piece of paper he had brought from home—"the Comfort Inn out near the airport."

The man wrote in the notebook again and looked up. "We can reach you there if we have more questions?"

"Until tomorrow morning. We're leaving on an Elderhostel, that's like a learning adventure."

"Yes, sir, my mother goes on them all the time."

Jim revised the cop's age up from mid-twenties to at least low-thirties. He turned back to the woman on the ground. "Can I ask you something? The way she's dressed, and with the olive-colored skin, is she a Native American?"

Officer Sundown nodded. "Although I don't know why she's in native dress." He tapped his pen against his notebook a couple of times, then pulled out a card and handed it to Jim. "Thank you for your cooperation, Mr. Dandy. We appreciate you trying to help. If you can think of anything else, please give us a call. And I hope this beginning is not indicative of your stay here. Welcome to Colorado."

THREE

All systems—heart, lungs, and testicles—had returned to normal by the time he trudged back to the pair of bronze-colored horse statues in the Adams Mark lobby. They stood six feet at the shoulders, heads high, each with a raised foreleg curled in mid-prance.

Only one thing was missing.

He scanned the area, bustling with people, half with convention tags hanging around their necks.

Where the hell was Dodee?

Didn't he order her to stay here?

Oh, yeah, like that would make an impression.

Then he saw her, loose curls of wheaten hair, trim body dressed in a light-blue pantsuit, loafers on her feet, coming around the corner from the elevators. A flat, black sketchbook case hung on one shoulder, a light-weight, collapsible aluminum easel strapped to it, her wheeled valise trailing along behind like a reluctant dog. A smile crinkled her cornflower-blue eyes as she walked straight up to him until their toes touched and her peach-blossom perfume lured him into its realm. She dropped the strap of her suitcase, wrapped one arm around his neck, pulled his head down to hers, and gave him a kiss that carried the promise of secret delights to come.

He stared into her big blues. "I suppose you think that makes up for me coming in from the airport—"

She kissed him again, carrying the promise of lewd and carnal pleasures.

"I suppose you think that makes up for deserting me in the hospitality room—"

She kissed him once more, carrying not the promise, but real-time, right-now, down and dirty lust.

He sighed. "Okay, I suppose it does, but you better stop this before I have to hold your sketchbook case in front me to keep from being embarrassed."

Her smile broadened. "Always bragging, sweetheart. I'm ready to go. Where are your bags?"

"I checked them in at the bellhop's station." He shook his head. "I don't understand why I had to come all the way down here when I could have waited for you at the airport hotel."

"I wanted you to meet my friend who commissioned me to do her book cover. It's up for an award. The book cover." She waved toward the horse statues. "She also commissioned me to paint these."

"Finished?"

"Enough. I couldn't work any longer when I knew how antsy you were."

"Well, I'm here, you might as well introduce me—"

"Can't now. Maybe at the end of the Elderhostel. She's speaking on a panel right now, and then has to do a signing. If you hadn't been in such a hurry when you flew across the lobby—what was that all about?"

"A woman fell off the roof of a building and I thought I might be able to help."

Her eyebrows arched. "Fell off?"

"Or was pushed"—oh shit—"no, fell off—"

"Pushed? Who—?"

"Fell off, Dodee, damnit. Either way, it's not our business—"

"But if she was pushed—"

He put his hand across her mouth. "Listen to me, lady. It is not our business. The police are investigating it. It's their job. They do not need your help." He felt her tongue lick the palm of his hand and he removed it. "You are a wanton woman."

He retrieved his bag and jacket and followed Dodee out the main entrance. They stood in the cool shade of the late September day while a taxi driver loaded their things in the trunk, then they headed out of Denver toward the airport. Dodee cuddled up next to him as they passed the domed Pepsi Center, her peach perfume now taking on overtones of lilies-of-the-valley. She wrapped both her arms around one of his, slipping her smooth hand into his. "What about the woman who was pushed—"

"Fell."

"Okay, fell off the roof."

"Promise to let it drop when I'm finished?"

She made a little cross on her left breast.

So he told her, finishing off with how he'd damned near killed himself running down the street.

"Probably the altitude. We're five thousand feet above sea level." She turned to him. "She was dressed in buckskin and moccasins? Was she an Indian?"

"The policeman said she was."

14

"What else did he say?"

"I'm finished."

She leaned forward and focused her big blues on him. "What?"

"You promised to let it drop when I finished. I'm—"

"You're not finished. You haven't told me—"

"I am finished. I told you everything I know. Ask me a million questions and I'll give you a million 'I don't knows.'"

She continued to stare for a moment, then sat back and snuggled in. Sometime later the Denver International Airport peeked over the horizon like white teepees against the Colorado-blue sky.

"What do you think of it?" she asked.

"I'm impressed. All the shops and the artwork, the trees and greenery in the atrium—I was ready to move in. How about you?"

"I love it. But I don't live here."

"What does that mean?"

"I think from an artist's viewpoint. To me it's beautiful architecture. But people here either love it or hate it."

"Yeah, but we didn't need it," the driver said.

Dodee glanced up at Jim and arched her eyebrows as if to say, "See what I mean?"

The taxi turned off the highway miles from the airport and cut across a flat, brown-grass prairie on a two-lane road. They came to a U-shaped drive in the middle of Nowheresville with three motels bordering the outside rim. A chrome-and-glass restaurant, the Moonlight Diner, occupied the open-ended middle.

Jim followed Dodee through two sets of double doors into the Comfort Inn's lobby. A conversational area—easy chairs, settee, a cocktail table with a vase of fresh roses—centered around a raised hearth fireplace on the left. Opposite it was the front desk.

Jim dropped their bags and leaned on the counter. "Is it too early to check in for the Elderhostel?"

A young, blond-haired woman smiled at him. "You're right on time, but you have to sign in at the Elderhostel desk," she said and motioned to the hospitality room straight ahead.

He picked up the bags and they continued through to a bright room filled with four-person tables, two of which had been pulled together and covered with manila folders. A man with sand colored hair sat at an angle behind them, buried in a mystery novel, *The Case of the Rabson Lock*. He looked up as they approached and a smile pinched laugh lines around alert blue eyes set in a ruddy face.

"Ah, two more victims—I mean, Elderhostelers—for the Santa Fe Trail, I presume." He stood up, five feet eight inches, a paunchy stomach that looked like it hadn't missed many meals. "I'm Ace Rudavsky, your coordinator for the week."

Jim shook his hand. "I'm James P. Dandy and this is Dodee Swisher."

"Oh, yes," he said and started thumbing through the folders. "Just saw your names here."

"Ace? That a nickname?"

"Yep." He pulled out two folders and handed them across, along with two motel registration cards. "Real name's Fred, well, Federico Rudavsky. Now you know why everyone calls me Ace."

Jim collected the folders and handed the registration cards to Dodee, who stared back at him. "I want these?"

"I don't have a pen."

She continued to stare for a moment, then shook her head and started filling them out. "You owe me."

"Add it to the list."

"Dinner's at five," Ace Rudavsky said.

"Where?" Jim asked

"Right here." He pointed to a long counter with a coffee urn at one end. "The hotel has no dining facilities, so we're having it catered." He handed across two plastic water bottles with plastic straws. "The air is dry here and you'll dehydrate before you know it. Fill these up, keep them with you, drink from them often. Welcome to Colorado."

"What about that nickname?"

"I just told you."

"People suddenly started calling you Ace because it was easier than Federico? Why Ace?"

"Long story."

Jim motioned to the empty lobby. "No one's rushing us."

Federico Ace Rudavsky let out a sigh and shot a quick glance at the ceiling. "Okay. I was a tank gunner in the military and one day on maneuvers in North Carolina I accidentally blasted a cow all over a farmer's field."

Jim smiled. "I guess that would do it."

"That was just the start." He grinned. "In Alaska, I accidentally leaned against a gun and it blasted a moose to smithereens. I reinforced that in Southeast Asia when my gun went off on its own and blasted a water buffalo into oblivion." Ace held out his arms and shrugged.

They took the elevator to the second floor, and marched down the hall to room 202. Bathroom immediately to the right, closet to the left. A king-size bed faced a dresser with

17

a television on top and a mirror behind. Opposite the door, by a window with the drapes closed, a desk with a chair and a couch formed a small alcove to give it the appearance of a suite.

"This is nice," Dodee said, slipping off her jacket.

Jim opened the drapes, flooding the room with light.

Dodee's arm slipped around his waist as she huddled to his side.

He put his arm around her and nodded at a prairie falcon skimming over the brown-grass plain that went on for fourteen million miles, broken only by the two-lane blacktop road they had come in on. "Makes you think what it must have been like a couple or three hundred years ago."

"No paved road for one thing," she said. "No forty-minute taxi ride from Denver."

"No Denver. We'd have come in covered wagons making sixty miles a day from Kansas City rather than sixty miles an hour from Denver."

"Did they make sixty miles a day?"

"Whatever. One of the things I suppose we'll learn."

"How did they know which way to go?"

"Oh, no problem. GPS."

"GPS?"

"Global Positioning Satellites—uh," he grunted as she poked him in the side.

"Don't be smart, sweetheart."

"I don't know how they found their way. Followed the setting sun, I guess. There certainly were no road signs."

"But it was a simpler life, filled with adventure."

"Think so?" He brushed back a wheat-colored curl that had strayed over her smooth brow. "No spray to keep your hair tidy. No wrinkle-free clothes. No time for aerobics classes to keep you nice and trim."

"No time to sit around and become couch potatoes."

"No e-mail and telephones to keep you in touch."

"No televisions and newspapers to stress you out."

"No comfortable motel rooms to loll about in."

"No money to pay out to cuddle up in your own covered wagon."

"No soft bed to fool around in."

"No . . ." She glanced at the bed and back to him. "That's true."

"No Moonlight Diner in case you wanted to get a late lunch."

"That's also true."

"Speaking of which?"

She put her arms around his neck. "How casually you worked those two things in. Fooling around and food." She pulled his head down and kissed him. "So what's your priority?" she asked, her lips brushing his.

"Hard choice." He kissed her back. "I guess you wouldn't go for fooling around in a booth while we're waiting for our food order?"

She tilted back her head and glared at him.

He shook his head. "No, I thought not. Besides, fooling around in a booth at my age I'd probably throw my back out. But that late lunch sounds pretty good."

"And the other?"

"Tonight's the night."

Four

Jim remembered the Moonlight Diner.

Not that he had ever been there before, but because it was like ten or twenty other diners he had visited with his father, from New York to Florida, before the Interstate highway system and McDonald's made them obsolete. It resembled a chrome railroad car without wheels. A long counter with red stools lived across the aisle from booths beside three-foot-high windows to let in plenty of light. Dodee led him down the counter to one of four side-by-side booths at the end.

A heavy-set waitress with a pencil sticking out of her hair dropped off two menus and continued on to bus the next table.

Jim slipped on his reading glasses, gave it a quick glance, and looked up. "I'm having a buffalo burger."

Dodee raised her eyebrows. "Just like that. You're not even going to look over the menu?"

"Buffalo burger."

"You don't want a salad? We're going to eat dinner in two hours, at five o'clock."

"Buffalo burger, buffalo burger, buffalo burger." He

closed the menu and slapped it on the table. "And maybe French fries."

She smiled and shook her head.

"Buffalo burger. Never had one, gonna try it." He replaced his reading glasses in his pocket. "And definitely French fries. Cholesterol City. I'm on vacation."

"I don't see how you keep so slim."

"Because I watch what I eat."

She snorted. "Yes, sweetheart, you watch it right into your mouth."

"I watch what I eat when I'm home. And I exercise five days a week and take a brisk walk all seven. But this is vacation."

She went back to her menu.

"Pardon me," came a squeaky voice from the booth across the aisle. A pair of thick glasses magnified two watery blues eyes set in a tanned, leathery face full of Grand Canyon crevasses, and, by design or circumstances, a head completely denuded of hair. A wrinkled cue ball with glasses. "Pardon me," he said again, crossing long legs sticking out of a lanky body, "you two wouldn't happen to be with the Elderhostel?"

"We're going on one," Jim said, "if that's what you mean."

"Santa Fe Trail?"

Jim nodded. "That's us."

"Me too." The man stuck out a large hand. "Maxwell Solnim's the name. Glad to meet you."

"Jim—James P. Dandy." He shook the man's hand and motioned to Dodee. "This is my girlfriend, Dodee Swisher."

"Glad to meet you, too," he said, nodding at her.

"Looks like we'll be ridin' the bus together, learning about the Indians. I'm looking forward to it."

The waitress came back and Jim and Dodee put in their orders, he for his buffalo burger and she for a small salad.

"No, on second thought," she said, biting her lip as she glanced at Jim, "I think I'll have the buffalo burger, too."

"Ah ha, see."

"I want to try it and I know you'll gobble up every last bit of yours. Finish mine if I can't?"

"Absolutely. If not now, we'll take a doggy bag for a midnight snack." Jim turned to the hairless man after the waitress left. "I think it should be . . . Maxwell, is it?"

"Yes, Maxwell, but I don't hold on to such formality, so it's Max."

"I think it should be fun, Max. I don't know much about the history out here in the west."

"Where are you from?" he asked.

"I'm from Maryland and Dodee's from Kansas City. She's an artist and has her own studio. How about you?"

"I'm from Massachusetts. Heard you mention you exercise a lot. Thought you might like to go out and do some huff and puffs with me in the morning. Say a mile or so and back, get the blood flowing. You're welcome along, young lady."

Dodee smiled. "It's been a long time since someone's called me a young lady. But, thank you, no, I'm going to snuggle in as long as I can."

"I could have told him that," Jim said.

She raised her nose. "I'm on vacation."

He turned back to Max Solnim. "Care to join us?"

"No, no, I have to be getting back. Time for my afternoon siesta. This your first Elderhostel?"

Dodee turned to Jim. "Number four?" He nodded.

"You always do them together?"

"Not the first one," Jim said. "Dodee was there with her aunt and I was alone."

"And you hooked up? That's wonderful. I know two other couples who met that way."

"How about you?" Dodee asked. "You've been on Elderhostels before?"

"Yes, indeed. This is number two hundred and twenty-seven, I think."

"Wow." Jim shook his head. "I've heard of people who've been on over two hundred, but this is the first time I've met one in the flesh."

Max smiled. "They keep me young."

"You don't look that old," Dodee said.

"How old do you think I am?"

She shrugged, and finally, when it became obvious that Max was waiting for an answer, squinted her big blues and guessed. "Seventy-five?"

Max's smile broadened to show even white teeth. "Thank you, ma'am, thank you kindly."

"You're younger?"

"You're much too flattering. I'm ninety-three."

"Wow," Jim said again, shaking his head, "you really don't look it. I guess these Elderhostels do keep you young."

"I enjoy the studies, especially since we don't have to take any tests." He cackled at that. "Besides, I'm alone in the world. Where else can I go and enjoy good company, learn lots of stuff, get three squares a day, and all for a reasonable price?"

"Easy to see you're enjoying your retirement," Dodee said.

"Well." Max drained his coffee cup. "I'm only semi-retired."

"That's like Jim."

"Really?" Max's brow furrowed, ridges among the crevasses in his face. "What do you do?"

"I'm a physical therapist, part-time now. How about you?"

"I used to be an anthropology professor. Retired from teaching, but I'm still doing research for articles and a couple of books. I'm starting a new one about Indians. Native Americans and the white man's trek west. That's one of the reasons I signed on for this trip."

The waitress brought the burgers and Jim's fries.

"Well, I'll let you folks eat in peace," Max said. "Good meetin' you. See you at dinner."

Jim waved as Max left and dug into his buffalo burger. "Um, great. I think it's leaner than beef."

"Your French fries will make up for that," Dodee said, taking a bite out of hers. "What do you think of Max?"

He turned and glanced out the window at the lanky figure striding toward the Comfort Inn. "I hope I look that good when I'm ninety-three."

"Did he say what kind of history books he's written?"

"Nope." He stuffed some fries into his mouth. "The new one is about Indians."

"Think we'll see any on our trip?"

"Yeah, I'd say it's a definite possibility."

They left the diner with half of Dodee's buffalo burger in a Styrofoam container. He looked up at the sky as they crossed the road. "Clouds rolling in."

"My friend says they do in the afternoon, but the days start out clear blue." She pulled her cell phone out of her pocketbook. "I have to call her. Do you mind?"

"No, go ahead."

She dialed, spoke for a few moments, and replaced it in her bag. "I got her answering service and left our room number. I told you I'm staying with her for a few days? You're leaving the Thursday afternoon we get back, right?"

He nodded. "That's the plan."

She adjusted the collar of her blouse. "Did you bring warm clothes?"

"Yep, as you told me, even though it's only September." The crisp, dry afternoon begged for short sleeves, but the first hint of sundown offered a contradiction. He stared out at the dry grassland, stretching on toward the front range with hardly a roll or a dip to mar its surface. "I guess it could get cold in the mountains."

"Lonely, isn't it," she said, making a sweep of her arm to take in the landscape. "Wonder how the pioneers felt about it, day after day with nothing to break it up?"

"They were probably grateful just to see the flat prairie without it being cluttered up with Indians in war paint."

He held the motel door for her. A small gas-log fire now burned in the lobby. A couple sat drinking coffee at one of the four-person tables in the hospitality room, but Ace Rudavsky had apparently passed out all his Elderhostel folders and decamped.

"What would you like to do?" Jim asked.

"You probably want to take a nap, don't you?"

He shrugged. "I was tired earlier, but I've woken up. Two hours' difference in East coast time, I guess."

"I'd like to get my pencils and try to capture the mood of the flat grassland out there," she said, nodding toward the back windows.

"You've got the same view from our room."

"Wrong perspective. I want to get down close to the ground. Do you mind?"

"Want me to get your sketchbook case?"

"No, I'll get it." She took the Styrofoam container with the remains of the buffalo burger. "I need to check what's there anyway."

He walked over to a coffee urn sitting on a long counter, poured himself a cup, added some creamer, and turned to see a woman with clear brown eyes standing next to him.

"Real or decaf?" he asked.

"The real stuff, I think. Can I pour you one?"

"Oh, what the heck." Plump and short, at most five feet, she had auburn hair with an inch-wide streak of gray running straight back from her right temple. "I've had enough to float a battleship already. One more won't kill me. I hope."

He poured her a cup. "Are you here for the Elderhostel?"

"Uh-huh. I'm waiting for my roommate to show up."

He took a sip. "Where's she coming from?"

"I don't know. I haven't met her. I just signed up by myself and Elderhostel matched us up. A lot cheaper than having a single room and I usually enjoy the company. How about you?"

"I brought my own roommate."

"No, I meant are you here for the Elderhostel?"

"Uh-huh. James P. Dandy."

"I'm Betty Baskins. Glad to meet you, Jim."

"Here's my roommate now,"he said as Dodee rounded the corner and handed him her case. "Dodee Swisher, Betty Baskins."

"Hi," Dodee said to the woman, then turned to him. "I forgot my pencils."

"You forgot—"

"My girlfriend called and I forgot. I have to call her on Sunday. Don't let me forget."

"Don't forget to call her."

"Remind me on Sunday."

"Don't forget to call her on Sunday."

She shook her head and then rushed off.

He turned to the plump Betty Baskins. "She's an artist. Wants to sketch the landscape out back."

Betty blinked. "There's nothing out there."

"That's what I told her. I think that's what she wants to capture."

He unzipped her black case. The sketchbook was in the front compartment along with a zippered opening to a second pocket behind that. He unzipped it only to find two, square plastic stiffeners that gave the case its shape. He zipped it back up and pulled the sketchbook from the forward section. "She painted a picture of a couple of horse statues this morning."

"Oh, I'd like to see."

He flipped over a couple of pencil drawings until he came to the painting, and held it up to capture the light.

Two identically posed horse statues, bronzy in color, stood with three legs down and a fourth curled up in a prance. But instead of the Adams Mark backdrop, she had painted in an imaginary field with mountains off in the distance. And instead of just the barebacked horses, a woman in an Indian dress sat on the near one.

"That looks like a medicine woman," Betty said, pointing to the woman on the horse.

He nodded.

More than that. Even though it was slightly out of

focus, like an impressionist painting, she was a dead ringer for the woman who had fallen from the roof.

Or was pushed.

He continued to gape until a male voice burst upon his consciousness and he turned to see two uniformed policemen enter through the lobby's double glass doors. One he recognized as Officer Sundown from earlier in the day. On the sidewalk in downtown Denver. Beside the mangled body of the medicine woman.

FIVE

Jim slapped the pages of the sketchbook together, keeping an eye on the police officers as they stopped at the front desk.

Dodee hadn't told him she knew the dead woman.

Then again, he hadn't told her what the dead woman looked like.

"She's very good," Betty Baskins said. "Does she do this professionally?"

He slipped the sketchbook back in the case and zipped it shut. "She has a studio in Kansas City."

Dodee came around the corner from the elevator, holding up a handful of pencils for him to see.

Whatever her reason for painting the dead woman, now was not the time to be asking about it.

Officer Sundown turned, raised his head in recognition, then tapped his partner on the arm and crossed the lobby. "Mr. Dandy? We met outside Duffy's Restaurant earlier today. I wonder if we could ask you a few more questions about the accident this morning?"

Oh shit. He felt Dodee perk up at that.

Sundown looked around, then motioned to the easy

chairs and couch clustered around the fireplace. "Maybe over there."

Jim strode to the couch, hoping Dodee wouldn't follow, but that was a forlorn hope from the start. She tagged along and sat next to him while the officers took the easy chairs.

"Is that an Native American name?" Dodee asked. "Sundown?"

The officer shifted a vase of roses on the cocktail table out of his line of sight. "And you are, ma'am?"

"Dodee Swisher," Jim answered for her, and took her hand in his. He didn't want her there, but damnit, he wasn't letting the cop dismiss her. "My girlfriend."

Sundown's brows knitted at the discolored scar between his eyes, then he took out his notebook, and glanced through it. "Yes, sir, I just wanted to clear up a few points. You said you saw the woman on the roof before she fell?"

"That's right, at the Adams Mark. I was in the hospitality room—I think it's on the fifth floor—looking out the window when she came onto the roof."

"And the woman author was there with you?"

"Yes, that's right."

"And she said the woman was pushed off the roof?"

He felt Dodee stir at his side. See, that's what he didn't want her to hear.

"That's what she said."

"And you didn't get her name?"

"I didn't get her name, but I told you the name of her book. *Pick Your Friends, But Not Their Noses,* I think she said."

Dodee held out her hand. "I can vouch for Jim being there. He came running across the lobby while I was doing a painting of the horse statues."

Oh, great.

And now what happens if the guy wants to see it?

"We found the author," Sundown said and leafed back through his book. "Tiffany Jewels. She remembered talking to you when the shaman, ah, went over the side."

"Shaman?" Jim studied him. "The dead woman?"

Sundown pressed his lips together, as if he'd like to take the word back, then nodded. "It's been reported Moondance Wolf was an Indian shaman. The clothes she was wearing might even have been those of a shaman."

Dodee leaned forward in her seat. "Really?"

Jim forced himself not to glance at her sketchbook case. "Is that anything like a medicine woman?"

Sundown shrugged. "Tiffany Jewels said someone pushed her off?"

"In fact, I think she said it about three times, kept saying it while I was trying to get her to call nine-one-one."

"But you didn't see that?"

Jim shook his head.

"And you didn't see anyone else up on the roof?"

"I saw the woman falling off the roof and immediately went into rescue mode. I told the author to call—well, as I said, nine-one-one—and then I raced for the stairs." He smiled. "Damned near killed myself doing it."

Sundown wrote in his book without smiling back. "One more thing, Mr. Dandy. You were the first on the scene?"

"I think so. There were other people there, but no one had gone over to check her out. At least, not to my knowledge."

"And you left everything as it was?"

He held out his hands in an open gesture. "I don't think I touched anything. I moved her neck chain out of the way and I felt for a pulse."

"You didn't pick up a moccasin?"

"Oh, yes, I did. Blood was seeping toward it so I moved it."

"Something inside?"

"Right, an insole liner fell out. I put it back in."

"You didn't put it in your pocket?"

"Why would I want to do that?" He chewed on the inside of his lip for a moment. "Oh, my handkerchief." He reached in his back pocket and brought it out. "I wiped my face with it and when I stood up I stuffed it back in."

Sundown nodded and made another note in his book.

Dodee leaned forward again. "Why? Is the insole missing?"

Jim put his hands on Dodee's shoulders and pulled her back against him. "You have to forgive my friend. When it comes to police affairs, she has a lively curiosity—that is to say, she's nosey."

Sundown smiled for the first time since the interview started. "I think I'll stay out of that one, Mr. Dandy." He pressed his lips together. "Did you see a small notebook at the scene?"

Jim ran the picture back through his mind, trying to be more careful this time, then shook his head. "No. I'm not saying one wasn't there, but I didn't see it."

Sundown nodded, then closed his book. "I guess that's it. I gave you a card, right? Please give me a call if you think of something else."

Jim watched them out the door and into their police car before picking up the sketchbook case and leading

Dodee by the arm to the elevator.

"I know," she said, making a stop traffic hand signal, "you want us to stay the hell out of police business."

"No, I—well, that too, but I have another question to ask you when we get up to the room."

She gave him a smug smile. "Oh, really. In the middle of the afternoon?"

"Not that either, although it's not a bad idea." They got off the elevator and started down the hall.

"And we have to go back to the room for you to ask it?"

He opened the door, ushered her in, and shut the door behind him. "You knew that Indian shaman?"

"What Indian—"

"The one in the painting."

"What painting—"

"Damnit, Dodee, the woman who fell off the building. She's the same woman in your painting."

Her big blues leveled at him, eyebrows arched, jaw slack.

He unzipped the black case. "The woman in your painting." He pulled out the sketchbook, flipped the pages to the painting of the twin horses, and held it up for her to see. "That's the same woman who fell or jumped or was pushed off the building."

Now the big blues locked onto the painting.

"Sweetheart, I didn't paint that woman on the horse."

He glanced at it. "But she's right there."

"I can see that, but I didn't put her there."

"Then how—"

"I don't know."

He propped the sketchbook on the dresser next to the

33

television and stepped back. She put her arm around his and stared at it.

"You didn't paint her?"

"When I painted in that rough background and put the sketchpad into the case, no one was sitting on top of the horse. Take a look. Even the style and the brushstrokes are different."

"Did you put it somewhere—"

"It wasn't out of my sight."

"How about when you went up to get your suitcase?"

"I took it with me. And carried it down when I met you."

"So you're saying someone broke in here and changed it while we were having lunch?" She shrugged. He motioned to the painting. "Had to be. It was the only time we didn't have it. But why? And who? The only ones who knew we were here were the police." He turned to her. "Speaking of the police, I don't want you to mention this."

"To the police?"

"To anyone. If someone connects it to the shaman who fell off—"

"Or was pushed."

"All right, all right. Pushed, fell, jumped, whatever—don't tell anyone. If the police think you knew the dead woman, you can forget about leaving tomorrow for the Santa Fe Trail." He turned back and stared at it some more. "What about that hairless guy we met at lunch, what's-his-name."

"Max Solnim."

"Right, Max Solnim. He could have done it while we were eating our buffalo burgers. Except, why?"

She turned and fixed her big blues on him.

He frowned. "I don't think I want to hear this."

She kept staring at him, as if deep in thought.

"I said I don't think I want to hear it."

She shrugged and turned back to the painting.

He glanced at it and back to her.

Of course she'd tell him sooner or later. Whether he wanted her to or not. Probably struggling to hold it back—

"All right, all right, I want to hear it."

A faint smiled played on her lips as she reached up to run her hand through his gray hair.

"Are you going to tell me or not?"

"Who was it who fell, jumped, or was pushed off the roof?"

"How do I know—oh, you mean an Indian? Oh," he grimaced "you mean a shaman."

"A shaman." She nodded. "Like wizard or priest or medicine woman."

"I don't think I want to hear anymore—what are you saying?"

"This woman fell to her death at the same time I was painting." She held out an open hand. "Maybe her spirit put it there?"

He stared at her until she crossed her eyes.

"Yeah, right."

But he didn't have another explanation.

This was some weird shit.

Yeah, buddy.

SIX

When they went down for dinner they were no closer to solving the shaman-in-the-painting question than when they'd started. Dodee led the way to a table beside the far wall and Jim sat down with his back to it.

Others drifted in by ones and twos. Betty Baskins was talking to a statuesque woman with almond-shaped eyes, pale olive skin, and black hair hanging loose to her breasts. The hairless Max Solnim came in with a couple he had befriended somewhere along the way.

Jim watched them all, a group of strangers sizing each other up. Would he end up friendly with any of them? Right now he was ready to give them all a pass.

"May we join you?"

He looked up to see a short, trim man standing beside his table. A lot of pale skin showed through his brown hair, and brown eyes stared out of a pale pink face. A short woman stood next to him, five two maybe, also trim, with blonde hair cut in a bob. She had glassy, pale gray eyes and a winsome smile.

"Oh, yes," Dodee said, "please do. I'm Dodee Swisher and this is my friend, James P. Dandy."

"And we're the Martins," the male partner said "Martin and Helen."

"I'm Helen," she said, smiling again as she sat.

"I guess we're all here for the Santa Fe Trail," Martin said. "I don't think the hotel has another group of people meeting here."

Dodee glanced around. "I don't know, I just assumed everyone's with us."

Martin turned toward Jim. "You must have the same kind of parents I had."

"How's that?"

"With a name like Dandy they named you Jim. You must get a lot of Jim Dandy ribbing."

"I've heard them all."

"I know. With a last name like Martin, my parents named me Martin. I can't figure that out, either."

"Your name is Martin Martin?"

"Actually, Martin James Martin. If Helen isn't along so I can say we're the Martins, I introduce myself as M.J. Martin."

Jim smiled. "I introduce myself as James P. No sense in making it obvious from the top." He turned as Ace Rudavsky and three other men came in carrying foil-covered aluminum pans.

"I wonder what they're having for dinner," Helen said. "We only had a light sandwich coming in on the plane."

"Know how you feel. I came in this morning and all they gave me was a sweet roll."

"You must be starved," Martin Martin said.

"I am."

Dodee shook her head. "Don't let him kid you. He had a buffalo burger two hours ago—"

"Two and a half hours."

"And French fries, and then ate half of my burger when I brought it back to the room."

"You couldn't finish it."

They brought in another round of pans and Ace turned to them as the men removed the foil tops.

"Okay, I think we're ready for dinner. Rather than have a mad rush, we'll come up by tables, and start with the first table by the window," Ace said and motioned to his right. "Then we'll go down row by row. Okay, folks, let's eat."

When Jim and Dodee's turn came, they picked up foam plates and plastic utensils and moved through a line of fried chicken, roast beef with gravy, potatoes, green beans, salad, and rolls, ending up with cans of soft drinks and foam cups of coffee.

Jim loaded his plate and followed Dodee to the table to see the Martins with their heads bowed.

"We'll get in on that," Jim said, sitting down.

"We're just saying a short prayer," Martin said.

"I didn't think you were taking a nap."

Martin smiled. "Lord, we ask You to bless this food to our good and thank You for this nourishment that we take into our bodies. Amen."

"And for new friends, amen," Jim said. He forked up a mouth-sized portion of potatoes and gravy. "Where are you from?"

"Indiana. Near Terre Haute."

Helen cut a piece of roast beef. "We ran a hardware store there for twenty-five years."

"In Boggs Corner," Martin said, "a small town near Terre Haute. Most of the small stores have disappeared since the Wal-Marts and the Kmarts came in, but we were lucky. After we had the store for a few years we bought the property around it—"

"It's a prime location."

"I was going to tell them that, dear. Anyway, when Wal-Mart came in they bought it from us."

"So now you're retired?" Dodee asked.

Martin nodded. "Four years and six Elderhostels ago. How about you?"

Jim shifted a bite of chicken into his cheek. "Semi-retired physical therapist. Dodee's an artist."

"Really." Helen turned to her. "Like a painter or a sculptor?"

"Mostly painting, although I occasionally sculpt when I'm inspired."

"Do you show? Or how does that work?"

"I own an art studio in Kansas City, so I can always squeeze in one or two of my paintings among the other artists. My daughter manages the studio for me."

Dessert consisted of sponge-cake squares and when everything was cleared away into trash cans, Ace Rudavsky stood up, banged a knuckle on his table, and called them to order.

"Welcome, folks, to Colorado and the Santa Fe Trail. If anyone's supposed to be in New York City, you're on the wrong Elderhostel."

Laughter rippled through the room.

"This Elderhostel is sponsored by Colorado State University and we'll be following, well, the Santa Fe Trail. I'd like to introduce Dr. Ward Longtree, who is a professor of Native American History and the program manager for Elderhostel at the University. I say I'd like to introduce him" —Ace spread out his arms and grinned—"but he ain't here."

Another ripple of laughter.

"He was detained on some last minute university matter. So on behalf of Dr. Longtree and Colorado State University, I want to welcome you to this program.

"The Santa Fe Trail is unique in that all the other trails heading west were settler or pioneer trails, but the Santa Fe Trail was established for commerce. We'll talk more about that tomorrow evening when we stop in La Junta. But the big thing to take away from all of this, folks, is if you have any complaints"—he held a flat hand to the side of his lips in a secretive gesture and lowered his voice to a stage whisper—"take them up with Dr. Ward Longtree."

Another ripple of laughter, smaller this time.

"Just kidding. If something bothers you along the way, please, let me know and I'll see what I can do. Not always able to change things, but I'll do my best."

He picked up a sheaf of papers and riffled through them.

"Tomorrow after breakfast, which we'll have right here between seven and eight-thirty, we'll board our motor coach and head south. If you could have your bags out front at eight forty-five we'll be able to load up and get away on time. We leave promptly at nine, so if you sleep in, you better be a fast runner. Don't forget to drop off your key. You won't have to sign out; we'll take care of that."

He split the stack of papers between two people at the front table. "Take one and pass the rest along, please. The bus seating works like this: the first seat behind the driver is reserved for me, but everything else is free. When you take your seat, it will be yours for the day. Every morning we'll shift two seats, rotating in a clockwise direction so that everyone will have a chance to rotate around the bus to the better seats, wherever they are. Also, to make it fair, we'll alternate which side gets off the bus first between every stop. Any question so far?"

No one raised a hand.

"Well, that's unusual. Everyone have a paper? I'd like you to take a look at the statements on them. Like the first one is, 'Owns a piece of turquoise jewelry,' and there's an underlined space after it. Everyone see that? What you need to do is to find someone, besides yourself, who owns a piece of turquoise jewelry and get them to sign it."

Jim put on his reading glasses and studied the list of fifteen statements and shook his head.

Oh, yeah, this was going to be fun.

They should have added a throwaway question, like who bludgeoned their Elderhostel coordinator to death.

"When you get all the blanks filled in," Ace said, "bring it up to me and I'll give you a prize."

Jim looked at Martin Martin, who had his hands on the table, rear end half out of his seat, and a smile on his pale face. "Can we start?"

The coordinator held up a fist, then opened one finger, then a second, and then a third. "Go-o-o ger 'em."

"I've got a turquoise belt buckle," Martin said, glancing around the table. "Who has read a book about Santa Fe?"

"I have," Dodee said and they signed each other's papers, and Helen's as well. Then Dodee turned to Jim. "I'll sign yours." He passed her his paper. "You don't seem to be getting in the spirit of the thing, sweetheart."

"Well, it's so much fun—"

But she was gone. Up and moving from table to table to find someone to fill in a blank. Everyone was up and

41

searching for blank-fillers. Was he the only sane person here? This was a childlike—

"Were you born in the thirties?"

He blinked at a man with a big nose, light-blue eyes, and a pale, freckled face under a full head of black hair going to gray at the sides.

"Do you surf the net?" the man asked, reading from his paper. "Have you eaten Rocky Mountain oysters, tossed a cow pie—"

"I was born in the thirties," Jim said.

"Ah," he said, flicking his dark eyebrows a couple of times, "born in the same decade as me. Number seven, would you sign?"

"Sure, and you mine." Jim exchanged papers, signed it, and exchanged again, glancing down to read the name aloud. "John Walsh?"

"In person. Gotta find someone who's eaten Rocky Mountain oysters."

"I have," a woman at the next table said, raising her hand.

"Hurrah. That's got to be the toughest one on the list."

Jim followed John Walsh, giving his paper to a hazel-eyed woman with thick glasses and frizzy red hair shooting out at odd angles as if she had just been zapped with lightning. She signed both papers with a meaty hand and a delicate pen, "Erynn Sunflower."

"Were you born in the forties?" Erynn asked Jim.

"In the thirties."

"How about, have you ever tossed a cow patty?"

"Yes, as a matter-of-fact," he said and signed her paper. He glanced around at the milling and laughing people.

"Who has four grandchildren?"

"I do," came a woman's voice and a raised hand across the room.

It took him twenty-five minutes, but he got all the spaces filled and Ace Rudavsky rewarded him a miniature Hershey bar.

Awright.

He pocketed his reading glasses, searched for Dodee, and found her in a conversational group of three women and two men.

He sidled up to her. "Got everything filled in. How about you?"

"Uh-huh. Broke the ice, didn't it?"

He glanced around to see everyone in similar conversational groups and shook his head.

What had happened here?

All they did was exchange signatures, like high school classmates with a yearbook, yet half an hour later everyone was laughing and talking and acting like they had known each other for years, something that sure in hell wouldn't have happened in high school.

He panned the room again.

In high school they would have been too worried about what others thought about them, were they dressed in the right clothes, hair in the latest style, were they cool.

Here, no one gave a damn. They had earned their stripes and wrinkles and gray hair, and people could accept them or not. What made the instant friendship work is that they all wanted the same things, to learn a little more about history and life, and to have a good time. The safety of traveling the road together for a short, finite time allowed them to glue into a community. It was the difference between getting on a spaceship full of strangers, and the camaraderie of an Elderhostel.

Then the plump Betty Baskins, she with the streak of gray in her auburn hair, waddled over to Dodee and lobbed in a bomb. "I saw your picture of the Indian medicine woman."

Oh, shit, he had forgotten about her when he'd urged Dodee not to tell anyone about the painting.

SEVEN

"Your painting with the horses," Betty said to Dodee.
"Jim showed it to me this afternoon."

"Oh, he did," she said, swinging her big blues onto him.

"What's this about a painting?" asked the woman with the long black hair and statuesque figure.

Betty nodded. "Dodee did a watercolor painting."

The woman turned to Dodee. Her almond-shaped eyes gave an oriental flavor to her high cheekbones and pale-olive skin, which was marred by a small scar on her jaw line. "Are you an artist?" she asked and held out her hand. "I'm Claire Renquist."

"Dodee Swisher. And this is my friend"—she grit her teeth—"Jim Dandy."

Ah yes, the lady was not happy.

"Claire's my roommate," Betty said, looking up at the tall woman from her five-foot height. "I guess you could say we're the long and the short of it."

Jim shook Claire's firm hand. "To answer your question, Dodee is an artist. Has her own studio in Kansas City."

"Really?" Claire turned back to Dodee. "I manage an art studio in Florida. You heard of Maggie's Gallery? It's

45

famous all over the Eastern seaboard. I would love to see your work sometime."

"It's not really finished."

"Looked finished to me," Betty said. "Two horses with an Indian medicine woman sitting on one of them."

"What's this about an Indian medicine woman?" Ace Rudavsky asked, the short, paunchy coordinator joining the group.

"Dodee's painted one," Betty said.

"It's really not a medicine woman," Jim said.

"Looked like one to me."

Dodee shrugged. "It's just a painting."

"Well, if you like to paint Indian medicine women," Ace said, "we'll probably find some in Santa Fe."

Big-nose John Walsh drifted over. "What's this about Indian paint in Santa Fe?"

Now the hairless head of Max Solnim turned to them from an adjoining group. "No," he said in his squeaky voice, "they only paint themselves up for ceremonies and dances. Doubt if we'll see that in Santa Fe."

"Not painted Indians," Ace said, "Indian paintings."

Max rearranged the wrinkles on his face. "Better chance of finding them on the walls of Mesa Verde."

"You know a lot about Indians?" John Walsh asked.

"I'm researching a new book about Native Americans and the white man's trek west."

"What did you think about that Indian shaman on the news tonight?"

"What news?" Jim asked.

"On television," John said. "A woman shaman jumped off the roof of a five-story building."

Ace's eyebrows rose. "On local television?"

"Downtown Denver."

"An Indian shaman woman?" Claire asked. "Would that be the same as a medicine woman?"

Betty turned to Dodee. "Like in your painting."

"When did you see this?" Ace asked.

John shrugged. "Just before I came to dinner. It's under investigation."

Betty turned back to Dodee. "Is that the same woman in your picture?"

"No. It's just a painting."

Max Solnim stifled a yawn. "Well, if I'm going for a brisk walk before breakfast, I better get to bed. How about it, Jim?" The watery blue eyes were magnified by his thick glasses. "Join me for huff and puffs in the morning?"

"Maybe, but if you don't see me, carry on." He motioned to Dodee. "Ready to go up?"

They took the elevator and Dodee's big blues locked on him as soon as the doors slid shut.

"I thought we weren't supposed to mention the woman on the horse to anyone."

"I forgot about her. I opened the sketchbook to see what you'd painted, and what's-her-name—-"

"Betty Baskins."

"—was right there. That's the first thing she said. 'Look at the medicine woman.'"

"Well, now everyone knows about it."

"They don't know it's the same woman."

The doors slid open and he held them until she got off, and stood there chewing the inside of his lip.

"What?" she asked.

"We're going to be pestered about the painting for the

whole trip. How would you feel about leaving it at the desk until we get back?"

She shrugged.

He let the doors go. "Be right back."

He waded through the first-floor crowd trying to get on the elevator, passed the emptying hospitality room, and pinged a small service bell on the front desk. A dark-haired man, looking freshly shaven, hurried out from behind a back partition.

"Hi, I'm with the Elderhostel, room two-oh-two. Could I leave something here for the week and pick it up when we return? It's a painting. You wouldn't happen to have a tube or something to protect it?"

"You can leave it here, but as for protecting it"—his brow wrinkled, then his face brightened—"well, you know, I might have something," he said, and retreated behind the partition.

A van pulled up outside the double glass doors and a petite Chinese woman with long black hair climbed out of the passenger seat, showing well-shaped legs beneath her hiked-up skirt.

"How about this?" The desk clerk held up a long flower box and nodded across to the vase of wilting roses on the cocktail table. "Some newlyweds caught an early morning flight and left those behind."

"That's perfect."

He took the box, glanced at the beautiful Chinese woman, and headed for the elevator. He pushed the button and heard mechanical sounds of the doors closing on the next floor, intermingled with garbled conversation from the lobby, and stepped on board when the doors slipped open. He reached up to punch the second-floor button, but a small hand caught the door.

"Mr. James Dandy?"

He stared into the dark eyes of the petite Chinese woman, his hand still in midair.

"I'm glad I caught you." She gave him a brilliant, white-toothed smile. "I wonder if you could help me clear up a few questions." Dark eyebrows arched. "About the shaman woman?"

He had been right about one thing that morning; the police were definitely looking younger.

"It will only take three minutes."

He sighed, dropped his hand to his side, and stepped off the elevator.

Bright lights blinded him as the woman slipped an arm under his, and brought a microphone up to her lips.

"Mr. Dandy, we have witnesses who saw you with the body of Moondance Wolf this morning. They say you put something into your pocket. Would you care to comment on that?"

He stared at a man with a television camera mounted on his shoulder.

Sonofabitch.

The woman shoved the microphone into his face. "Mr. Dandy?"

"It was a handkerchief. I'd run down from the Adams Mark and wiped my face with it."

"It wasn't a notebook?"

"No. The police already asked me about that. I told them it was my handkerchief."

"So you don't know anything about a notebook?"

"No, I don't—"

"But you knew the shaman. And you knew she was involved in preserving Native American artifacts."

He pulled his arm free. "No, I didn't—"

"What do you suppose is in the notebook?"

"How would I know?" He jumped back into the elevator. "Dirty pictures?"

"What do you think happened to the notebook?"

He mashed the second-floor button. "I just told you I don't know anything about it."

She made no attempt to follow, but held out the microphone to pick up his voice. "Does this have anything to do with Colorado State University?"

He mashed the button again. "How would I know?"

"You are taking a trip sponsored by the university?"

But the doors finally shut on the pretty face and the bright light blasting him from the television camera.

Sonofabitch.

Now everybody would know about him and the shaman woman, not only those on the Elderhostel, but the whole damn world.

Eight

Jim marched out of the elevator and down the hall, slipped his key into the lock to their room, and shoved open the door.

Dodee jerked around to him, a rolled-up paper in her hand. "Where were you—"

"Giving a television interview. Is that the painting?"

"Yes." She stretched a rubber band around it and handed it to him. "Where were you?"

"I just told you."

"Damnit, Jim—"

"A woman reporter caught me in the lobby." He told her about it as he fit the painting in the long flower box and closed the lid.

"Why did they think you knew about a notebook?"

He set the box on the dresser and gave her a wide-armed shrug.

"What's in the notebook?"

"Dodee, think about it." He grabbed the television remote and plopped on the bed. "If I never saw the notebook, how would I know what's in it?" He started surfing through the channels. "Let's see if they have anything on the news."

She sat next to him on the bed. "So you don't have any idea what's in the notebook?"

He pressed his lips together and glared into her big blues.

"Okay." She held up her hand. "No more." She picked up her nightgown. "While you're looking I think I'll use the bathroom. Let me know when something comes on."

He glanced at his watch. "Probably nothing for half an hour," he called after her.

He continued surfing and found a national news channel, but—surprise—they weren't discussing the death of a non-famous woman in downtown Denver.

Now if the shaman had jumped off the top of the White House, it would be on every channel.

And how did she get on the roof of the White House? That's what America wants to know. We have invited two experts to share their opinions with us, one from the Republican side and, to rebut it, a Democrat. Afterward we'll tell you what the latest poll says about permitting people who want to jump off high places to have access to the White House roof.

The door opened and Dodee came out in a nightgown printed with a teddy bear and the words I'M HUGGABLE. She came to him as he sat on the bed, opened his legs and, with her back to him, sat down between them, lowering her head.

"What are you telling me?"

"You could massage my neck while we're waiting."

"Oh, I could?"

"And then later on I could massage you in a different place."

He massaged her neck, gently working his fingers into

52

the tight muscles as he breathed in the aroma of her peach perfume, mixed with something else now, like vanilla, and enhanced by a lavender scent of soap.

She groaned. "I could kill for this." He laughed and she turned to him. "What?"

He shook his head. "Nothing."

"There must be something—"

"You say that every time I massage your neck."

The local news came on and a woman with blond hair and earnest eyes stared into the camera.

"Good evening everyone, I'm Maureen Blount. We have more on the woman who fell to her death in downtown Denver today. We go to Tom Mack on the scene."

A black man with gray sprinkled through his curly hair stood in front of an arched doorway, the same doorway Handlebar Mustache had charged out of. And now that he thought about it, he had never mentioned Handlebar to the police. Should he call and tell them?

"A woman fell to her death here today," Tom Mack said, "here on the street by the landmark Duffy's Restaurant. As tragic as that may seem, we are now fitting the details together in what may be more than a simple accident."

The camera zoomed-in to the newscaster's face.

"Moondance Wolf, a Native American, plunged to her death early this afternoon, dressed in the clothes of a shaman or medicine woman. Questions have arisen as to whether she fell, jumped, or was pushed. For instance, if she fell, what was she doing on the roof in the first place? We have learned that eyewitnesses saw her on the roof sunning herself, but possibly hiding from someone, just before she went over the side, almost hitting a bicycle messenger when she landed."

The scene shifted to earlier in the day. Tom Mack stood next to a man with a helmet, straddling a bike.

"A few seconds earlier and I'da been creamed," the messenger said. "I had to brake and swerve to keep from hitting her. I ran over to see if I could help her, but I could see right off she croaked. I shouted for someone to call the police and stayed by her side until the ambulance came."

"That's bullshit," Jim said, wrapping his arms around Dodee's waist and pulling her close to him.

"How do you know?"

"Because I was the first one to reach the woman. Everyone else stood thirty feet away."

"And did you notice anything about her?" the announcer asked.

"Yes, I noticed she was dressed in Native American garb, and I said to myself, this is an Indian shaman woman."

Jim rolled his eyes. "Yeah, right."

"Shh, let them finish."

The scene shifted back to Tom Mack in real time. "We have since found out that Raymond Wolf, the woman's brother, has rented storage space in the building and was suppose to meet Moondance Wolf here earlier in the day. He was held up paying a traffic fine and he got here just in time to identify the body. Mr. Wolf wouldn't talk to us, but we have it from the police that Moondance Wolf had called him early in the morning to tell him someone was stalking her, and that she was afraid for her life. There is speculation that Ms. Wolf, still in native dress, came into town early this morning straight from a Native American ceremony of some kind."

Tom Mack started walking toward the curb.

"We have learned one more piece of information,

54

Maureen. A small notebook Moondance Wolf always carried on her person is missing. Witnesses say a Good Samaritan, an emergency medical technician from Maryland, was first on the scene and was observed putting something in his pocket, but after a check with the police it is believed to have only been the man's handkerchief."

"Sonofabitch." Jim held his hand out to the set. "That's all it was."

"Rumor has it the notebook contained information on the whereabouts of a Native American artifact. What is actually in there, or if it was in her possession when she plunged off the roof, no one knows. But what we can say, when the police arrived on the scene to find Moondance Wolf's body right at this very spot"—he stamped his foot—"they found nothing to indicate that an artifact or a notebook existed. That brings us up to date, Maureen, back to you."

The scene shifted back to the blond Maureen Blount.

"We are still trying to obtain the identity of the Good Samaritan who came to Moondance Wolf's aid. However, we did talk to Tiffany Jewels, a mystery author who was an eyewitness to Moondance Wolf's plunge over the side."

The screen filled with chubby face of the fortyish author from the hospitality room at the Adams Mark.

"I'm the author of *Pick Your Friends, But Not Their Noses*, and I saw it all from this very window. It reminded me from a scene out of my book, *Pick Your Friends, But Not Their Noses*, but the police have asked me not to speak about it. They say it might mess up solving their case, just like in my book, *Pick Your Friends, But Not Their Noses*, and so I have nothing to say."

"When we come back," Maureen Blount announced, "we'll have the weather."

Jim rubbed Dodee's stomach, covered by only her linen nightgown. "Tiffany Jewels had no problems speaking to me." He ran his hands up to feel her ribcage. "Just the damn opposite." He slipped his arms under hers. "I couldn't shut her the hell up." And cupped his hands over her breasts.

She craned her neck to him, big blues staring into his. "What?"

"If you're still watching television, sweetheart, playing with those dials will not get you a channel change."

"No, but it might dial me into something else."

She twisted around in his arms and gave him a long kiss. "You have to ask yourself, punk," she said through clenched teeth, "do you feel lucky?"

"Yes, I do, and Lucky does, too."

"Then if it's playtime, there're two more questions, punk."

"And what might they be?"

"Are you going to turn off the television, punk?"

He picked up the remote and snapped it off. "You're really getting into this, aren't you?"

"And are you going to make it in and out of the bathroom before I fall asleep, punk?"

He blinked at her, then bounced her onto the bed and raced for the bathroom. Should he shave? He gazed into the mirror and felt his cheek.

Screw it.

He gave his teeth a cursory brush, slapped on some PS For Men cologne by Paul Sebastian, and stripped down before he realized he had left his pajamas in the other room.

56

Screw that, too.

He turned off the light and slipped back into a darkened bedroom, only a soft glow coming through a crack in the drapes from a lone car racing down the two-lane highway. He felt his way to the bed and climbed naked under the covers where the equally well-dressed Dodee awaited him. And they played together, like children, more like teenagers, exploring hidden places, garden spots they hadn't visited for awhile, rambling together, between kisses and caresses, until a primordial urge gripped them both and their breathing turned into a primitive growl that welled up from somewhere deep inside, and spilled over into cries that shattered the stillness, again, and again, to finally fall back into gasps and whimpers, heavy breathing slowly ebbing into the stillness of night, interrupted by a whisper.

"Thank you, sweetheart."

"My pleasure, lady."

NINE

Jim slipped out of bed, eased open the drapes and stared into the sun just peeking above the horizon. A square vehicle rolled out of it on the single ribbon of road.

The return of the television truck?

No, an airport van.

It disappeared around the side of the motel as a lone, lanky figure emerged from the same spot and strode into the morning, arms pumping in an orange jacket, yellow cap on his head, breath condensing in the morning air—Max Solnim out for his huff and puffs.

Too bad. Jim had missed his chance to accompany the old man. And with a little luck, he'd miss it for the rest of the trip.

He crossed the room, clicked on the television, immediately muted it, and watched the national news in silence. When the program switched from national to local news, he ratcheted the sound down to a whisper and clicked off the remote. They played a repeat of the Moondance Wolf story from the night before, with one notable exception. This time a beautiful Chinese-American asked some rapid-fire questions of a wide-eyed

58

gray-haired man, and in spite of him denying he knew anything about a notebook, damned if she didn't make it sound like he did.

Sonofabitch.

He turned off the set and stared at the blank screen.

The good thing was it hadn't played the night before, so, with a little more luck, and if he kept his mouth shut, and they got the hell out of town, perhaps no one would catch it this morning.

He washed up, dressed in a light-weight, long-sleeved shirt, jeans and loafers, and started out of the room when Dodee stirred in the bed.

"What time do we have to be down for the bus?"

"Bags packed and outside by eight forty-five. Breakfast is from seven to eight-thirty." Her big blues stared back at him, mind processing what he had just said, but not computing. "I said breakfast is—"

"I need to figure out if I'm hungry or tired." She lay her head back on the pillow. "Will you come back for me at seven-thirty?"

"No problem."

He shut the door and took the stairs, peering around corners for television crews, but all he found were some of the early rising Elderhostelers.

"Morning, Jim," John Walsh said, sitting at a table with the frizzy redhead Erynn Sunflower, and almond-eyed Claire Renquist. "Good night's sleep?"

"Like the world had come to an end. I need coffee." He filled a Styrofoam cup from an urn on the counter.

"After our talk about the shaman last night," John Walsh said, a smile spreading on his Irish face, "we all went back and watched it on the news."

"Watched it myself." He added three tubs of half-and-half and pulled up a chair between Erynn and Claire.

The thing was, had anyone seen it that morning?

Erynn Sunflower peered at him through her glasses. "What do you think?" She wore her multicolored peasant dress with a large crystal dangling between wine-jug breasts. "Did someone push her off?"

"I don't know." He glanced at Clair, her long black hair piled high on her head now, and back at Erynn again. "Fortunately, it's not my problem."

"Didn't someone mention that Dodee had painted a medicine woman?"

"Just a coincidence."

Claire's soft-brown eyes took him in. "I do hope I can see Dodee's painting somewhere along the way." A small smile complemented her oriental features. "I'm always looking for fresh artists for my studio."

Three young women in dark blue uniforms burst out of the elevator and into the lobby, overnighters trailing behind on wheels.

"Airline hostesses," Erynn Sunflower said.

An airport van pulled up and the women hurried out through the double doors as Max Solnim trundled in from his walk, unzipping his orange jacket and pulling a yellow cap off his hairless head.

"Well," he said in his squeaky voice, "I see some of you have finally made it out of bed." He strode up to the table and nodded to Jim. "Looked for you this morning before I headed out."

"I didn't make it."

Max's lips turned down, rearranging the crevasses of his face. "No biggy. Catch you tomorrow. Better carry a coffee up to the room if I want a shower. Any decaf?"

"The one on the right," John Walsh said.

"Getting back to Dodee's painting," Claire said, running a delicate finger along the small scar on her jawbone, "what's the chance she'll let me see it?"

"Yes." Erynn swung around in her chair, a small tinkling sound accompanying the movement. "Like to see it, myself."

He shrugged. "You'll have to ask Dodee about it. Speaking of which, I better go make sure she's awake."

He refilled his coffee cup.

What were the chances of them seeing Dodee's painting?

He made a second cup with Equal and cream.

About the same as finding a goose with constipation.

He turned at a tinkling sound as Erynn Sunflower swayed her wide-track hips up beside him, bells hidden somewhere about her body.

"Think I'll have a second coffee this morning," she said, exposing a small butterfly tattoo on her inside wrist as she poured. "Hope it doesn't have any adverse reactions on the bus."

He trudged back to the room and entered to the sound of water running in the shower. He cracked the bathroom door.

"I brought you some coffee," he said, above the splashing. "I'll leave it on the sink."

"Thank you, sweetheart. I'll be out in a few minutes. Decided to get up for breakfast after all."

He packed his suitcase, zipping it up as she came out in a bathrobe, her cup held in both hands.

"Good morning." She wore a fresh face with bright eyes and smelled of lavender soap mixed with an herbal

61

perfume. "Thank you for the coffee. I'm amazed you remembered how I like it."

"I remember how you like a lot of things."

She smiled. "So you showed me last night."

He glanced at the ceiling and shook his head. "I wasn't talking about that. I mean a lot of little things. I guess it's called love."

She put an arm around his neck and gave him an innocent kiss. "Love you, too." And kissed him again, not nearly so innocently.

"We don't have time. Not if we want to have breakfast."

"Your call, sweetheart."

"If I was eighteen, I would have attacked you in the shower. At sixty-plus, I better try for All-Bran."

He printed her name on the flower box containing the horse painting while she dressed in blouse and slacks. "Good thing we're leaving this behind," he said. "People have already been asking me about it." He looked up to see her stick two pen-sized flashlights in her carry-on. "You still packing those?"

"Never know." She zipped up her bag. "We found them handy on our other Elderhostels."

Oh, yeah, just handy enough to get them into trouble.

He carried the flower box down to breakfast, making sure the girl at the front desk taped it shut before he left it with her. Dodee waved to him from a table with Claire Renquist and the hairless Max Solnim. He picked up two sweet rolls along with two patties of butter and a glass of juice, and wound through the buzzing Elderhostelers to the seat Dodee had saved for him.

Claire rubbed her almond-shaped eyes. "I think

the heat in the motel is drying up all the mucus in my nose."

"Dry climate," Max said and nodded. "Yep, big difference between here and the water-laden air in Florida. Can take three or four months to get completely used to it. Same with the altitude."

Jim spread butter on his sweet roll. "I figured out about the altitude yesterday when I ran down the block from the Adams Mark. It damned near killed me. Back home in Maryland . . . well, it would have damned near killed me."

"What were you doing running down the street?" Claire asked.

He took a bite of sweet roll.

Yeah, right, what was he doing, aside from getting into the Indian shaman business?

"I left my bag in a taxi and had to chase it down before a red light changed," he answered.

Dodee's eyebrows rose and a smile drifted across her lips.

John Walsh placed juice and a croissant on the table. "Looks like we're all up and about."

"A lot healthier out here, though," Max said to Claire, "once you get used to it. Don't feel the cold or heat as much as when there's a heavy load of humidity. But you better keep your water bottle handy. You can get dehydrated pretty fast."

"You say it takes four months to get acclimated?"

"Is what I hear."

"In fact, some never do." John Walsh closed his eyes for a moment, then made the Catholic sign of the cross. "It's worse up in Golden—that's a town west of Denver, just at the foot of the mountains—and in Santa Fe, New Mexico," he said, sipping his orange juice. "Altitude sickness can strike you after about five days, leaving you light-headed and nauseous. Best cure for altitude sickness is to get back down on the flatlands."

Jim grunted. "Sounds like an old W.C. Fields joke. Best cure for insomnia? Get plenty of sleep."

"Good morning, folks." Ace Rudavsky's voice rose over the buzz of conversation. "Good morning. Everybody have a good night's sleep?" Nods around the room. "Today we're heading south. We'll tour the Pueblo Museum in, surprise, Pueblo, Colorado, and eat a box lunch there. Then we're off to the Holiday Inn Express in La Junta, which is about sixty miles southeast. Should get there around four and we'll have a wine and cheese party."

"Awright," Max shouted out and laughter spread around the room.

Ace's ruddy face broke out in a smile. "How come whenever I mention wine and cheese to a group of Elderhostelers I get their immediate attention?" A few more giggles. "After dinner we'll have a lecture on the trail from yours truly." He looked at his watch. "It's eight-ten now. We have another twenty minutes for breakfast, but we need to check out of our rooms and have our bags ready and outside by eight forty-five to load up when the bus comes. Let's see," he paused, shaking his finger, "there was something else."

"Don't forget your name tags," Martin J. Martin called out.

"That's not it," he said, still shaking his finger, "but right, don't forget your name tags. They will be your entrance fee to all the places we'll be visiting."

"Make sure you have your water bottles filled," Max said.

"No, there was something else, but listen to that,

everybody. Make sure you have your water bottles. Keep them filled. Drink from them often—oh"—he pointed at them—"I know what I was going to say. The bus has a bathroom, but it's strictly for emergencies. Since there aren't many dump sites, the bus would get pretty ripe by the end of the day. We'll try to provide pit stops along the way, but a word to the wise: Take care of what you can take care of before we load up in the mornings. If that's not a mixed metaphor. So, we depart at nine sharp. As my kids say, be there or be square."

Jim bit into second sweet roll as a general exodus erupted around him. Elderhostelers, good at taking suggestions, finished up their coffee, croissants, and sweet rolls, gathered fresh ones in napkins for snacks along the way—determined to meet all contingencies—and set off to take care of the things they had to take care of.

Dodee stood and picked up her coffee. "Think I'll head up."

"I'll join you," Max said, then cackled. "Well, not join you, but walk with you."

Jim turned to John Walsh and motioned after Max. "How's your roommate working out?"

"Oh, fine. He's interesting to talk to. Knows a wealth of history."

"Lived a wealth of history, too."

"Like the rest of us, I suppose."

"No, about thirty more history years."

John turned to Jim. "How old is he?"

"He told us ninety-three."

"Max's ninety-three?" Claire asked. "He doesn't look it."

John shrugged. "Healthy living and exercise. I've known priests like that."

Jim finished his coffee. "I guess I better get upstairs." He dumped his trash and took the elevator. When the doors opened he saw the Martins standing there, suitcases in hand, and smiled. "How you doing today, Martin Martin?"

He smiled back. "Just Jim Dandy."

One thing more about Elderhostelers, as opposed to the young. Tell them to have their bags ready for loading at eight forty-five and they'll be there at seven. No one wants to be left behind. Or get jammed up in a crowd.

He entered the room and followed Ace's admonition. He waited while Dodee applied lipstick, then they put on light jackets and headed downstairs, Jim toting both bags and Dodee following behind with her sketchbook case and combination pocketbook and carry-on. She took the keys to the counter and he carried everything outside into the cool morning air. He smelled cigarette smoke and turned to see a squat man with a square head, black hair and eyes, name of Narcisco Ramos on his Elderhostel name tag.

"I figure I better get my fix in before I get on the bus."

Jim nodded. "The world has gotten a lot tougher on smokers."

"Not the world, just the United States." He put his hand up, as if testing the air. "I wonder how cold it will get."

"Supposed to be warm today," John Walsh said, coming across the grass, holding a small yellow flower.

"What have you got there?" Jim asked.

"A dandelion. Found it growing in a damp spot of shade."

The sound of a big diesel engine broke in upon them as a Greyhound-type bus rounded the corner, big yellow stripes on the sides below darkened windows, and lettering that spelled out COLORADO STATE UNIVERSITY.

Their covered wagon had arrived.

Ten

As soon as the bus pulled to a stop, the lobby doors opened and, like floodwaters, Elderhostelers poured out with their suitcases, anxious not to be left behind, anxious to make sure their bags got packed away, anxious to claim a seat.

A young woman skipped down the bus's steps, mid-twenties, five-foot-four and well shaped, slightly on the chunky side as if built for the long haul. "Don't get too close to the bus, please," she called out. "I need room to open the panels."

She cranked open a storage door, swinging it up until it caught on a catch, revealing a cavernous space in the belly of the beast. Everyone surged forward to offer their suitcases like sacrificial lambs, but stepped back when she moved on to crank open a second panel, and again surged and pulled back as she cranked open yet a third door. She took two of the proffered pieces of luggage and half crawled in the cave to place them as far back as she could reach, then climbed out for two more.

Jim snaked through to the front and grabbed bags from the curb and fed them to her as she struggled to maximize bags to space. When she filled the near side of the compartments, she moved to the driver's side and Jim helped carry bags around, joined by Ace now, and filled that side as well. That left the front compartment which they loaded with ice water, ice chests, and box lunches.

When they finished she gave Jim a contagious smile, lighting up her round face, pretty except for a ring in her nose. "Thanks for the help."

"No problem."

He climbed on board and found Dodee halfway down next to a big window. "Where's your sketchbook?"

She showed him how it slipped in a space between her seat and the side of the bus. A sputtering noise crackled over a public address system and he turned to see Ace Rudavsky blowing into a mike, his short, round frame silhouetted in the middle of the aisle.

"Okay, folks, let me have your attention for a moment. Our driver is Harriet Callahan, and everyone calls her Harry. You can say 'Dirty Harry' if you wanna get slapped upside your head. Everyone say good morning to Harry."

"Good morning, Harry," rang out in the bus like kids in grade school.

Harry gave them the contagious smile and a wave as she swung her twenty-five-year-old body into the driver's seat.

"I'd be happier if she was a little older and a man," Max said to Jim from the seat across the aisle.

"And didn't have a nose ring," Jim added.

"She has a nose—"

Ace's voice boomed out of the PA system again. "Harry has been driving for Colorado State University for the past five years. And in case you're wondering, she got her driver's

69

license the day she turned sixteen—which was the same day she won the junior drag-strip championship—then went into stock car racing where she collected more trophies than you can shake a stick at. While we'll be traveling at a more sedate pace this week, she still manages to go and tear them up in six or eight races a year. If that's not enough, she also placed second two years in a row in a statewide driving contest, maneuvering a bus through pylons. So you're in good hands with Harry Callahan."

Max leaned across the aisle. "Maybe she'll do after all."

"At least we're covered if we have to make a fast getaway," John Walsh said from the seat behind Max.

Jim turned to him. "I can see it now, 'Elderhostelers Rob Bank and Make Getaway in Greyhound Bus.'"

Martin Martin leaned forward from behind Jim's seat. "Make that 'Hostel Elders Rob Bank.'"

Jim smiled. "We ought to paint that on the side of the bus. 'Hostel Elders Aboard. Don't Do Anything To Piss Us Off.'"

"And everything pisses us off," Max said, giving his hairless head an emphatic nod and cackling. "Yes, indeed."

Harry revved up the bus and moved them out, swinging around the airport hotel square with the Moonlight Diner in the middle and onto the two-lane road toward the teepee-like airport perched on the horizon. They took a right when they reached Peña Boulevard, followed it to an exit to E470, and turned south, back into the wilds. The plains stretched out forever on their left, with an occasional deer or white-faced pronghorn passing by the blurring fence posts. On the right, green mountains with patches of last year's snow scraped the sky free of clouds.

70

Dodee turned to him from the window. "I keep thinking what this place must have looked like one or two hundred years ago. There were buffalo out here, weren't there?"

"One account said the ground was black with them, from horizon to horizon."

"And look now. When was the last time you saw a buffalo?"

"Yesterday."

She squared her shoulder to him. "You saw a buffalo yesterday?"

"So did you."

Her eyebrows arched. "All right, I'll bite. Where did I see a buffalo?"

"Between your buns."

"If this is going to be crude—"

"At the Moonlight Diner. Your buffalo burger." She looked down her nose at him and he leaned closer. "See, it's in the eye of the beholder. Dirty mind, dirty thoughts."

"It's also in the mind of the beholder to think looking at chopped meat is the same as the animal on the hoof. Dumb mind, dumb thoughts."

"Not dumb, just technically precise."

She turned back to the window.

Ace's voice boomed over the PA system about an hour and several miles later. "If you look off to the left you'll see a rock formation on top of a small hill that looks like a castle, which gave the town its name, Castle Rock, Colorado."

Later on his voice boomed out again. "We're making pretty good time here, ahead of schedule, so if you like we can stop off at the Air Force Academy Visitor's Center in Colorado Springs. Let me see the hands of those who would like to stop off."

Jim looked at Dodee, who had her hand up.

"Raise your hand," she said. "We want to stop."

He raised his hand.

"Okay, fasten your seatbelts, folks, and we'll get Harry to kick it up another notch." A minute went by before he came back again. "Just kidding about Harry."

They approached over a knoll to see an athletics field down below and, at the edge of the mountains, a building with bright A-framed gables reaching for the sky.

"This is an unscheduled stop, folks," Ace said, "so please let's keep it to twenty-five minutes. We still have a lot of ground to cover." He bent down and looked out of the window. "Notice the high roof of the chapel sticking out against the mountain? The saying here is that there are fifteen of those spires, or gables, whatever you call them, one for each of the apostles and the Joint Chiefs of Staff."

They parked in a spot reserved for buses and walked up a long concrete path to the Barry Goldwater Air Force Academy Visitor's Center.

A polished aluminum ceiling looked like the curved edge of an airplane wing, with a yellow sailplane hanging from its center. Dodee headed for the gift shop, but Jim wound around a gentle ramp, studying panels on the discovery of flight, the development of the Academy, and a mock-up of a cadet's room: bunk along one side, night table and lamp beside it, chest-high shelving, and a desk with bookshelves above. Small, neat, utilitarian.

By the time he got back to the gift shop, Dodee had five children's Air Force Academy T-shirts over her arm. "For the grandchildren," she said.

He blinked at her. "I thought you only had one, what's-his-name."

"Corby, and you have Joseph, Courtney, Wendy, and Morgan."

"How do you remember that?"

"How do you remember how I like my coffee?"

"Here, I'll pay for them."

"No, I'll pay for them."

"But you only have one—"

"I want them to be my gift." Then her big blues turned up to him. "Or have you even told your children about me?"

"Yes, I told them about you. Don't you remember the cooking Elderhostel in Baltimore? I wanted us all to get together for dinner, but you had to rush back because your daughter was expecting. Your daughter . . . what's-her-name?"

She smiled and shook her head. "And my name again is?"

"Sally? Sam? George?"

He bought a *Denver Post* and did a quick search for his name in the Indian shaman story on the front page, then breathed a small sigh of relief at not finding it. Apparently the paper had gone to bed before the Chinese woman had shown up.

"You know," he said, carrying the bags of T-shirts, "these things are going to clutter up the trip."

"Just until we get to the first post office."

"And where do we find the stuff to pack them in?"

She batted her eyelashes at him. "Padded envelopes bought at the same post office."

They strolled down to the bus with the Martins, the last ones aboard, it turned out. Jim laid the paper on his seat and opened the overhead compartment.

"Where did you get the paper?" John Walsh asked.

"In the Visitor's Center."

"You did? I couldn't find any."

Jim stowed the T-shirts in the overhead and handed Walsh the *Post*. "Be my guest."

"I don't want to take your paper before you've had a chance to read it."

"No problem. I'm thinking of shutting my eyes anyway."

"Next stop is Pueblo, Colorado, folks," Ace's voice rang out. "If you forgot to visit the restrooms inside you'll have to clench your teeth 'til we get there. Okay, Harry, take us to warp drive."

Harry Callahan slipped her five-foot-four body into the driver's seat and they wound through the Academy's well-kept grounds and buildings. Even the clear blue sky, dotted with paragliders and hang gliders, looked like it had been bought and paid for to go along with the setting. It reminded Jim of the quote attributed to George S. Koffman when he viewed bulldozers rearranging the landscape of Moss Hart's new farm to put in ponds and creeks:

"What God could have done if He only had money."

ELEVEN

They pulled off the highway at Pueblo, drove past some new fast food places, wound though an older section of town with some of the buildings dating to the early nineteen hundreds, and finally pulled up outside the Pueblo Museum, a state historical site. Ace and Harry passed out box lunches and sodas and split the group in two, half to tour the museum while half ate lunch.

Jim and Dodee got in the lunch-first group, entered the building through the gift shop, passed by the restrooms, and into a canteen. He sat at the first of six round tables, Dodee next to him, and opened the box lunch to find a croissant ham sandwich, lettuce and tomato salad with dressing, a small noodle salad, a fruit cup, a can of papaya juice, an apple, napkin, plastic utensils in a wrapper, and something called a fruit candy bar.

"All right, looks like we won't starve."

Max took the chair next to Dodee, checked the contents of his box, then turned to her. "Want my ham, little girl?"

She blinked at him. "What?"

"I don't eat meat."

She grinned. "I didn't know what you were talking about. No, but I'm sure Jim will," she said, turning to him. "He'll eat anything."

"Thanks a lot. You make me sound like—"

"Do you want Max's ham or not?" she asked.

He stared into her big blues for a moment. "Well, rather than throw it away."

"I rest my case."

The ham was duly transferred from Max's croissant onto Jim's, making it look like a hero sandwich.

John Walsh took the seat next to Max, bowed his head for a moment, then made the sign of the cross. "How you doing, Roomie?" he asked Max, then looked across to Jim. "See where they ransacked that building in the paper?"

"What building?" Dodee asked, taking a bite of her sandwich.

"You mean my paper?" Jim asked. "The one I haven't seen yet?"

John smiled, spreading the freckles on his face. "Yep, the very one."

"What building?" Dodee asked again.

"The one the woman shaman fell off of."

"What about it?" Jim asked, sipping on his root beer.

"It was ransacked last night. The shaman's brother said it happened sometime between six and midnight."

"What were they looking for?"

Jim shook his head. "We don't want to know—"

"An artifact of some sort, apparently." John opened a can of papaya juice. "Or a notebook police speculate might lead to the artifact."

Dodee chewed on her sandwich. "What do you think?"

Max shook his head. "Always hearin' about Indian artifacts and antiquities out here. Don't pay any attention to them, myself."

After lunch, he and Dodee wandered through the museum's exhibits of life in the Old West.

Dodee took his arm. "It must have been an adventure living in those days."

"Oh, yeah. Just staying alive was an adventure."

"Enjoying the simple things. Tilling the garden and enjoying fresh vegetables."

"Washin' with crik water, hangin' out clothes, cookin' over buffalo-chip fires."

"No television or radio."

"No time for television and radio, which only left building big families."

"Clean air and healthful occupations and natural life."

"Diphtheria and cholera and small pox."

She slapped him on the arm. "You. No romanticism." She motioned toward the way they came in. "I'm going to get my sketchbook from the bus. Be right back."

He nodded and stopped to read about James P. Beckworth, who was born in 1800 and lived in the wilds for sixty-six years. Dubbed the "mountain man's mountain man," he rode with Kit Carson, helped establish El Pueblo, blazed the Beckworth pass, was a Crow Indian war leader, and took part in the conquest of New Mexico and California. The amazing thing was that he'd been born a Virginia slave and freed by his white father at the age of twenty-four.

The next plaque described another mountain man's mountain man: Richens Lacy Wootton, who'd traveled with Beckworth, trapped beaver on the Yellowstone, fought Indians, and saved an Arapaho woman from being killed by the Utes. "Uncle Dick," as he was known to new pioneers, was a teller of tall tales and thrived on adventure, was feared as an enemy and valued as a friend. Later on he took to ranching, domesticated buffalo, managed a saloon and danced the fandango in Santa Fe. He lived from 1816 to 1893.

Seventy-seven years old. And Beckworth lived to be sixty-six, a feat for those days.

Maybe Dodee was on to something about a more healthy life.

He looked around to make sure he was alone, then twisted on one foot and kicked out the other.

And they danced the fandango in Santa Fe.

The thing was, he had never heard of either one before. How many others made the trip out from Kansas City, or up from Mexico, ordinary unsung people who died along the trails, were killed in the continuing wars and Indian raids, or died of hunger and thirst in lean times?

Ace's ruddy face appeared around a corner. "About time to get on the bus."

"Okay." He scanned the room. "Have you seen Dodee?"

"She's out front, sketching a little boy on a bench." He ran a hand through his sandy hair. "Doing a good job of it, from what I could see."

Jim found her sitting cross-legged in the middle of the sidewalk, sketchbook across her knees, Elderhostelers standing in a semicircle behind, as she stroked the paper with a pencil, face-time divided between it and the subject a few feet away.

A boy of four or five sat at one end of a wooden bench,

his dark eyes shifting from the woman at the other end—obviously his mother—to Dodee, to the candy bar held in his lap. Black hair grew down behind his neck to the collar of a plaid shirt. A belt held his jeans about the waist tight enough to stop his blood flow. A smile played on his cherubic face whenever he glanced down at the candy bar.

"Okay." Dodee nodded at the boy. "You can eat it now."

She didn't have to tell him twice. He ripped off one end of the paper and bit into the candy with all the gusto of one too young to hide his pleasure.

Dodee's big blues focused on Jim and she reached up her hand. He took hold and helped her to her feet. She stepped across to the boy's mother and showed her the sketch.

A grin broke out on her face and pride welled up in her eyes. "Or, yes, nice. Yes, yes nice."

Dodee turned over the sketchbook to the hard backing and handed the woman her pencil. "I want to paint this, but if you'll give me your name and address, I'll send you the sketch when I'm finished. Okay?"

The woman nodded that it was very okay, and as Jim watched her write her name and address, he recalled the names on the placards he had seen inside, and a chill of loneliness slipped over him, an awareness of how this age stacked up against Beckworth and Wootton's, when lone men found company in the wonders of the wilderness, and today found isolation in the middle of crowds. Dodee packed the sketchbook back in the black case and smiled up at him, and as they waited to board the bus, he felt privileged to put an arm around her waist and hug her to him.

"So," she said, "what about the ransacking of that building back in Denver?"

Welcome back to the twenty-first century.

"It's not our business, lady."

"I was just asking."

He helped the nose-ringed Harry Callahan load the water cooler into the bus's hold, and when he made his way down the aisle, he found Dodee already reading his newspaper, devouring the details of the Indian shaman's death.

"Somebody ransacked the storage area rented by Raymond Wolf," she whispered as he plopped down onto the seat beside her. "Sometime between six and ten o'clock last night."

"That's what John said." He put on his reading glasses. "Give me the paper."

"I'm not finished. Why would anyone ransack it?"

"Maybe the brother did it himself. Give me the paper."

"I'm not finished, sweetheart." She shuffled through the paper, apparently looking for the rest of the article.

"Okay, folks," Ace's voice crackled out of the PA system, "wasn't that an awesome box lunch?"

"Listen," Dodee said as the rest of the bus agreed with Ace, "Moondance's brother Raymond had been assisting the police at the time of the break-in—"

"Probably means they were holding him for suspicion. Give me the paper."

"We'll be having box lunches most of the trip," Ace said, "since we'll be underway all the time, but I should tell you the box lunch today was like the Cadillac of box lunches."

"Then what are the others going to be like?" Martin Martin called out.

Dodee nudged him. "When the police returned with Raymond Wolf to inspect the storage area, they found it had been ransacked. How could he do it himself if he was with the police?"

"Probably hired someone to do it."

"Compared to today," Ace said, "the rest of the lunches are like a mid-sized Taurus. Remember to keep sucking from your water bottles."

Dodee closed the paper, holding her place with her fingers, and turned to him. "The police speculate that the intruder-slash-intruders were searching for a religious artifact, or a notebook the shaman always carried that describes the artifact and its location."

"Next stop is La Junta, where we'll have our wine and cheese party after we check in."

Dodee blinked. "Sure there wasn't a notebook by the shaman's body?" He stared into her big blues. She patted his hand. "Sorry, sweetheart, but what could they be looking for?"

"Okay, Harry, move 'em out."

"If you give me the paper—"

"In a minute," she said as she burrowed into it again.

He took off his reading glasses and pocketed them. The bus started to move and he glanced past her out the window. Across the street a short, thin man folded his arms and leaned his butt against an old, dusty, green Chevrolet. A large cowboy hat shielded his facial features except for a pair of dark aviator glasses, which tracked them as they moved. Then he slipped from view as the bus picked up momentum.

Dodee read aloud from the paper. "'Raymond Wolf said his sister, the medicine woman, had called earlier in the day to say someone had been stalking her. He also said he believed it had something to do with an artifact. Meanwhile the police have learned she had been working with the Bureau of Indian Affairs.'" She closed the paper and turned to him. "If it had to do with Bureau of Indian Affairs, the artifact must be Native American. Right?"

"Don't know, don't care."

He eased his seat back and stared out the window as the big bus barreled down the highway, heading east away from the mountains and foothills, out into the plains to a lower elevation, all reflected in the air conditioning popping into overdrive. He had just slipped into a light snooze when the bus bounced off the smooth highway and groaned to a stop in a rutted parking lot.

"Are we in La Junta?" someone called out.

"Be right back, folks," Ace said.

He jumped off the bus and ran across the lot as fast as his short legs and paunchy stomach would allow, disappearing into the Rocky Ford Popcorn Factory.

Harry swung around in the driver's seat. "It's cool," she said. "La Junta's only ten or fifteen miles down the road."

A few minutes later Ace emerged with a two-foot burlap bag under his arm. He pumped his short legs back to the bus and climbed aboard as Harry shut the door and moved out.

"Sorry for that little personal stop. I had to pick up my winter's supply of popcorn. This is the best in the world, with almost no unpopped kernels, and the biggest popcorn you ever saw."

"Oh, well, thanks for telling us," John Walsh called out. "Not like we might want to buy some."

"And you are going to share with us?" Erynn Sunflower asked, the large crystal swinging from her neck.

"Ah, no," Ace said, dropping the bag on his seat. "My wife would kill me if we got snowed in and we ran out of popcorn because I'd given it away."

John Walsh tapped Jim on the arm. "Whaddaya say we hide it?" His eyebrows flicked. "Let him sweat it out for a day."

Jim grinned. "When we get off the bus. You keep him busy and I'll sneak it away."

"Where will we put it?"

Dodee shook her head. "You guys are like a couple of kids." She pointed to the overhead compartment. "Stick it up here."

John shook his head. "No, he'll find it." He rubbed his big nose, then nodded. "Yeah, why not. It's just to give him some fun."

Ten minutes later the bus pulled to a stop in front of the Holiday Inn Express in La Junta, Colorado.

After everyone climbed off, Jim grabbed the ten-pound bag of Rabbit Brand popcorn and tucked it in the overhead compartment above his seat.

Only problem was, it was John Walsh's idea, but who was going to be implicated when the popcorn was found?

He yanked it out and tucked it in above John Walsh's seat.

TWELVE

He helped Harry pull the bags out of the hold as La Junta's afternoon sun turned the black tarmac into an open-pit oven. He followed the others into the motel, squeezing into the air-conditioned lobby. He skirted the crowd milling around Ace at the front desk, crossed a hallway to a gray-tweed couch in the lobby, dropped the bags, and sat down. Dodee eased in beside him, resting the sketchbook case between her knees. Two easy chairs, four-person tables, soda machines and a coffeepot made up the rest of the room, along with a door and window opening onto a street at the back of the motel.

Claire Renquist turned toward them, an eyebrow lifted above one almond-shaped eye, then she sauntered over and sat in an easy chair.

"You two have the right idea. We're not getting a room any faster by standing."

Jim yawned. "Seems like the older we are the more anxious we get to find our rooms, get a seat on the bus, or in line at the airport."

"And perhaps go to the bathroom," Dodee said.

He yawned again. "Or take a nap."

Claire pointed a delicate finger to the sketchbook case. "Do you think I could have a look at your painting?"

"We don't have it," Jim said. "We left it at the motel in Denver for safekeeping."

"How about the sketch of the boy on the bench? Maybe you could paint it?"

Dodee shrugged. "It wouldn't be finished—"

"I know, but it will give me an idea of your work, and if it's the type of thing we sell." Claire palmed-up a hand and let it drop. "Listen to me go on. I told you I'm the manager of Maggie's Gallery in Palm Beach? I've only been at it six months and I guess I'm overanxious to make good, more to prove her trust in me than the fact that I own a part of the business."

"That must have been expensive," Dodee said. "If it's as famous—"

"Oh, no. Maggie's my best friend." Claire ran her finger over the small scar at her jaw line. "When her no-good husband cleaned out their bank accounts and took off with an exotic dancer, she was about to go bankrupt, financially and emotionally. I'm married to a very successful lawyer so I loaned her some money and bought a small part of the gallery to show I had confidence in her." She smiled. "That was fifteen years ago. Since then Maggie's built up an international reputation. How about your gallery?"

Dodee folded her hands in her lap. "My husband was an alcoholic who beat me up a few times; when I saw signs that he'd also abuse the children, I moved out and started the gallery with my aunt's help. It was touch and go for a long time, but it's kept us alive and now we have three employees, including my daughter, who manages it. But she had a lot of experience before I turned it over to her."

"Oh, I did too. After the kids were grown and gone, I was looking for something to do and Maggie offered me a job. That was about five years ago. She slowly gave me more responsibility, like buying artifacts and sculpture."

"Yes, Alison has added sculpture to our gallery."

"So now I'm running the whole show. Tell me about your painting with the horses and medicine woman."

"What kind of artifacts do you carry?" Jim asked, trying to head off the medicine-woman stuff.

Claire shrugged. "Original works, nothing cheap."

Dodee sat forward. "Native American artifacts?"

"Yes, while I'm out here I want to see what I can pick up."

"Claire Renquist and Betty Baskins," Ace called out from the front desk.

"Oops, that's me," Claire said, popping up.

"Maybe I can rough-out the sketch in watercolor this afternoon. It won't be finished—"

"That's fine. Bring it down to the wine and cheese party and we'll see how everyone reacts."

Jim watched her go. "Saved by the bell."

"What do you mean?"

"I just don't want you—don't want us to get involved in that shaman business."

"What makes you think—"

"I saw you perk up when you asked Claire about the Indian artifacts."

"Me? You brought up the subject."

"I was trying to steer us away from your painting."

The crowd had cleared out by the time Ace called Jim's name. "For you and Dodee," he said, handing over plastic keys.

"The wine and cheese party, where?"

Ace waved to a hospitality room next to where they were sitting. "At four-fifteen." He swung back to Jim. "Be there or be—" His jaw dropped as he stared out the lobby doors. "What's he doing here?"

Jim followed his gaze to see Harry talking to a tall, lanky man in his mid-thirties, yellow hair and goatee, looking a bit like old pictures of General Custer, except for wearing a blue sports jacket, gray slacks and a yellow tie.

"Who's he?"

"Huh?" Ace's ruddy face came back to him. "Ward Longtree, my boss. I better go see want he wants."

Jim and Dodee took the elevator to the second floor and down four doors to their room, typical of most motels, bathroom on the left, two double beds, television on the dresser opposite. He opened the drapes to let in the light and stared down at the yellow-striped Colorado State University bus with Harry Callahan and Ace standing beside it, talking to the tall, lanky man in the sports coat.

Dodee came up to put her arms around him. "You having a good time?"

"Are you here or not?"

"What does that—"

"If you're here I'm having a good time."

"Well, that's sweet."

"I'm a sweet guy."

"And humble."

"And humble."

"What are you looking at?"

"Ace's boss. Ward Longtree." He turned and kissed her on the forehead, and when she raised her face to him he repeated it on the lips, warm and innocent. "Wine and cheese's at four-fifteen. What do you want to do?"

"I'd like to paint the sketch of the boy. Would you mind?"

"What you're telling me is you want some concentration time." He sat on the edge of the bed and pulled off his shoes. "I just happen to have an activity in mind that will allow you that."

She unhooked the portable easel from her sketchbook case and smiled at him. "Napping is not an activity."

"Depends on how hard you play at it."

He lay back on the bed and crossed his hands under his head and watched her set up the easel at an angle to the window. She unzipped the black case, pulled out her sketchbook and cut the sketch from the pad with a razor knife. Then she unzipped the back pocket of the case, slipped out one of the square plastic laminates, taped the sketch to it, and held it up for him to see.

She had captured the likeness of the boy, cute with his black hair and that slight hint of a smile when he looked down at the candy bar.

"Of course, it's not finished yet," she said.

"Looks finished to me. Thought you were going to send it to the boy's mother."

She mounted it on the easel and broke out her paints. "I'll send her the painting instead."

He watched her quickly rough-in a light-blue background, her slim body silhouetted in the light from the window. Then he yawned and closed his eyes to afford her the promised silence to complete her work.

"Sweetheart," she said, "you want to go to the wine and cheese party?"

He popped open his eyes and glanced over to the sketch on the easel, covered now with a blank piece of paper clipped top and bottom to the laminate backing. He glanced at his watch to find he had been out for forty minutes. "I ought to get a reward for giving you some quiet time."

She smiled and shook her head.

"What's that supposed to mean?"

"You were snoring like a steam engine in heat."

"I was?" He put on his shoes. "I don't usually snore."

"How would you know?"

He entered the bathroom and washed his face, coming to the door as he dried off. "Besides, a steam engine is always in heat, that's why it's called a steam engine."

She picked up the covered sketch. "Would you bring the easel?"

He folded it up and followed her out.

They found the party in the hospitality room, cheese on platters, wine in boxes. Dodee glanced around at the beige-colored walls, then crossed to a big window at the rear of the room and turned to face him, spread her arms and slammed her feet together.

"You're saying you want me to put the easel right there?"

She smiled and batted her big blues.

"What have you got there, Dodee?" Ace asked, the paunchy coordinator coming over with a plastic wine glass in one hand, a floppy-big piece of yellow cheese in the other.

"It's the drawing she did of the little boy," Jim said.

She mounted it on the easel. "Claire wanted to see it painted, so I did a quick water color of it."

"You gonna uncover it?"

"In a few minutes."

"I haven't seen it, either," Jim said.

"Patience, sweetheart. I want to wait until Claire gets here. Create a little more drama."

"What have we got here?" Helen Martin asked, coming over with her husband.

Jim smiled at them. "How you doing, Martin Martin?"

"Just Jim Dandy. This the painting of the horses that we've heard about?"

"No, it's a painting of the little boy she sketched this afternoon. We're going to have the grand unveiling soon."

Jim poured himself a glass of red box-wine and cut a slice of Brie. Life is sweet. Yeah, buddy.

Ace's lanky boss entered, yellow hair and goatee, cool blue eyes in a tanned face.

"Can I pour you some wine?" Jim asked him.

"What do we have?" he asked, rubbing the palms of his hands together.

"We have red," Jim said, patting one box, then the other, "and we have white."

"Ah yes, box wine. The white, I suppose."

Jim poured him a glass.

"Thanks." He motioned with the glass to the painting. "What is this?"

"It's my girlfriend's painting. We're waiting for the grand unveiling. Are you with Elderhostel?"

A smile spread the blond goatee. "I'm Dr. Ward Longtree, the head of the Elderhostel Program for Colorado State University. I'll be giving a lecture tonight about the Santa Fe Trail."

"You're a historian?"

"Professor of Native American History."

"We have a professor of anthropology with us."

"Really? The lines between them gets blurred here in the Southwest. My primary research of late has been the relationship between the Mayans and the Plains Indians."

"I didn't know there was a relationship."

"Many learned people would agree with you. It's theoretical of course, but strong facts lead to the conclusion that commerce did exist between them."

Max Solnim walked up, a grin splitting his crevassed face. "Ah, Jim, mind if I get at those rectangular wine jugs?"

Jim moved out of the old man's way. "Max Solnim, Dr. Ward Longtree. Max's our anthropology professor."

"Semi-retired, yep," he said, filling his glass.

"Ward is a professor of Native American History."

"Yes, I'm Dr. Longtree," Dr. Ward Longtree said, "I'm glad to meet you."

"Yep, I'm Dr. Maxwell Solnim," he said, with flick of his eyebrows and a slight smile. "Are you the one I hear came in from Colorado State?"

"Yes, I'll be delivering a lecture on the Santa Fe Trail this evening."

A new man, curly back hair with emerald green eyes, stole into the room like a gatecrasher, except he wore an Elderhostel name tag, Hank Adamo. He hadn't been on the bus, yet Jim was sure he had seen him before.

Where?

Or maybe someone who only looked like him?

Dodee, standing with Ace, motioned him over.

"What can I do you, schweethart," he said with a mouthful of spit, imitating Humphrey Bogart.

"I think it's time to take off the cover."

Ace nodded. "Have to make it fast. We need to load up for dinner."

"Will you take it off?" she asked.

"Me? It's your painting."

Her eyebrows arched. "I didn't want a grand production. I thought Claire would be here by—oh, here she is."

He turned to see Claire Renquist walk in with the frizzy-haired Erynn Sunflower at her side, the squat redhead looking like a hippie in her red, blue, and earth-toned peasant dress, with bells tinkling in the hem, compared to Claire's elegant figure in a straight-lined aqua gown.

"Is this it?" Claire asked.

Dodee folded her arms and nodded.

"Going to unveil it?"

She gave Jim a small smile. "Will you do it, sweetheart?"

He nodded, surprised to see her suddenly so shy, and realized that she was concerned about Claire's opinion.

"Okay, everybody," Ace raised his voice. "We have to load up for dinner soon, so gather around for our own one-minute, one-woman, one-painting show."

"It's not a big thing," Dodee said, turning to Claire. "I only had a hour."

Jim held the cover sheet in place while he slipped off the clips, then stepped to one side and whisked it away with a grand flourish. "Tadaaa!"

Dodee's jaw dropped and her big blues popped wide.

"There she is!" Betty Baskins pointed at the picture.

Jim snapped around to the painting.

The black-haired little boy sat on the bench with a little smile playing on his face, but behind him, impressionist-style against the roughed-in background, stood the same medicine woman who had sat on one of

Dodee's Adams Mark horses.

Betty Baskins parked her plump little five-foot body right in front of it. "Yep, that's the same shaman woman who jumped off the building in Denver."

THIRTEEN

"Okay, folks," Ace said, his voice commanding attention, "the one-minute, one-woman, one-painting show is over. Time to load 'em up and move 'em out if you want to hit the chow wagon."

Claire turned to Dodee as everyone started for the door. "I like your work, except for the woman."

"But I didn't put her there."

"You didn't?"

"It wasn't there when I put on the cover sheet."

Claire studied the painting. "Yes, I can see that. Completely different style."

"Then who did?" Jim asked.

Dodee's lips stretched thin. "I don't know."

Claire turned back. "You know," she said, fingertip tracing the small scar on her face, "this could be a big seller in spite of everything. People will pay high dollar for a painting with a little a mystery to go with the fine art."

Jim shook his head. "We better get on the bus."

They headed for the exit, but he grabbed Dodee's hand and held her back. "You're sure," he whispered, "that is, there's no way, like even in a trance—"

Dodee lips thinned out again. "I was not in a damn trance," she whispered back. "I didn't paint the shaman, not today, and not on the horses yesterday."

"Then how—"

"I. Don't. Know." She turned to the easel. "Should we take it up to the room?"

He threw out his arms in a shrug. "Doesn't make any difference now. Everyone has already seen it."

He followed her out to the lobby, but stopped at the sight of those waiting to board the bus. "Second thought, I will run it up. Don't let them leave without me."

He rushed back, collapsed the easel, and carried it all up to the room. He dropped the easel on the floor, unzipped the inside back pocket of the sketchbook case, and tucked in the laminate with the sketch still attached. He closed the inside zipper, shoved the sketchbook into the front compartment, zipped that, and hustled the works under the bed for safekeeping.

Maybe everyone had seen it, maybe not, but they weren't seeing it again.

He tore out of the room and down to the bus.

Dr. Ward Longtree stood with a foot on the lower step talking to Ace Rudavsky. "Who is the new man?"

"Ah." Ace shook his finger. "Glad you brought that up. I'll introduce him now rather than tonight. You did say you were going to do the lecture?"

Dr. Ward Longtree nodded. "The new man. How did that come about?"

Ace pulled in his chin and widened his eyes. "It came from the office. I assumed you knew."

"I've been absent for the last two days." The cool blue eyes shot a look at Jim, then Dr. Longtree grabbed the

95

handrail and climbed onboard. "I'll communicate with them in the morning."

Ace motioned for Jim to board.

"Unusual for someone to join the group this late, isn't it?" he asked, climbing the steps.

"Never happened before," Ace said. "He drove his own car down here to catch up."

Jim trundled down the aisle and slipped in beside Dodee.

"Before we start," Ace said on the PA system, "I want to introduce a new member to our Elderhostel group: Hank Adamo." He motioned to the black-haired man sitting near the back of the bus, a stray black curl hanging over his forehead. "Hank missed his connections and had to drive down to meet us. Welcome, Hank, I'm glad you could make it."

Hank Adamo waved. "Good to be here."

"We are also privileged to have Dr. Ward Longtree aboard with us for the night. Be nice to him, he's my boss. Dr. Longtree will be giving us a lecture on the Santa Fe Trail after dinner."

Jim put his head up close to Dodee's. "I hid the painting under the bed."

She smiled. "I'm sure no one will ever think of looking for it there."

"Well, not just that, I hid it in the back compartment of the case." He looked into her big blues. "No idea how the shaman got there?"

"I wish I did."

"When we get to dinner," Ace continued, "you'll find good, solid food, but it's not fancy. It's one of the ways we keep down the cost of this Elderhostel."

A short time later Harry pulled up to the Student Center of the Otero Junior College and the Elderhostelers exploded through the cafeteria doors. Some students jerked around and stared wide-eyed at the invasion of the geriatric cohort as they bunched up at the sodas, drinks, and tray rack on the right.

Jim saw a second group of trays farther down and bypassed the crowd, scooping up napkins and utensils, and marched straight on to the hot tables. A student worker gave him a plate of spaghetti and meat sauce with a side of string beans. He moved across the room and picked up a couple of slices of pizza at the sandwich counter, considered, then passed on a hamburger, and carried his booty into the dining room, and took a chair at one of the tables. John Walsh came right behind and sat opposite him.

"I could see you were a man on a mission," he said, smile lighting up his freckled face, "so I followed along. I'm going to get some iced tea. Want some?"

"Sounds good."

Jim spread a napkin on his lap and chomped down on a piece of pizza. The food might be typical of school cafeterias, but it was hard to screw up pizza and spaghetti.

John returned, with Dodee tagging along behind him.

"You got through fast, sweetheart," she said, setting her tray of mashed potatoes, green beans, and meatloaf beside his.

"When there's food, I don't mess around." He took the glass of iced tea from John. "Thanks."

"No problem." John sat, blessed himself, and bowed his head.

"Can you share that with us?"

97

The light-blue eyes came up to take them both in. "Sure. Lord, bless all our Elderhostelers here, thank You for the camaraderie and for the safe trip thus far, bless this food which we receive as a gift of Your love, bless all who prepared it, and remember those less fortunate this evening. Amen."

"Amen," Jim said, and picked up his fork. "That was a good prayer."

John shrugged. "I'm a good prayerer," he said, and half a slice of pizza disappeared into his month.

Dodee scooped up a forkful of potatoes. "I heard Claire call you Father John."

He shrugged again and a small smile spread on his Irish face.

"You're obviously not her father?"

"I'm a retired priest."

"Retired?" Jim spun spaghetti around his fork. "That mean you can now go out and start running around with wild women?"

The small smile spread into a wide grin. "I don't budget for Viagra, if that's what you're asking."

"I always wondered about the wild women business anyway."

Dodee's big blues turned to him. "Wondered what about wild women?"

He glanced at her and back to John. "So what happens when you retire?"

"It means I no longer have parish duties. Free to come and go, but I usually help out on Sundays and when someone goes on vacation."

"You didn't answer me," Dodee said, touching Jim's arm.

"It was just an academic question."

"Uh-huh."

He gave her a phony grin. "I was just wondering about sowing what you reap. So if I sowed booze, wild women, and song, would I reap more booze, wild women, and song?"

"First, sweetheart, you have to be able to sow wild women."

"May we join you?" Harry Callahan asked, the mid-twenties driver accompanied by the ancient Max Solnim, effectively book-ending the age of the Elderhostel group.

Jim nodded. "Of course, glad to have you."

Max set down his tray containing two small plates of green beans, one of buttered mashed potatoes, and a large salad. "So, Jim," he said, folding his lanky body into a chair, "we goin' for huff and puffs in the morning?"

Jim looked at the hairless man. "I guess we can."

"You forget your meat, Roomie?" John asked.

"No, indeed. I'm a vegetarian."

"Really? Were you always one?"

"No, I got into eating wild berries and roots and grains while I hiked through the mountains about thirty years ago." He popped a cherry tomato into his mouth. "Found out I didn't miss meat and felt much better without it."

Harry took a big bite out of her hamburger. "I thought about doing that," she said. "I have friends who don't eat meat."

Jim took in her young face, just this side of beautiful, but he couldn't yank his eyes away from her nose ring.

"It's supposed to be healthful," Dodee said.

"Yep." Max nodded. "I attribute it and exercise to the

fact I'm still kicking. I also think it makes me less aggressive. I think vegetarians are more peaceful."

Jim looked into the watery blue eyes magnified by the man's thick glasses. "Did you know Adolph Hitler was a vegetarian?"

"Well, so much for that theory."

"How old are you?" Harry asked, starting on a new burger. "Or isn't it cool to ask—"

"At my age it's braggin' rights. I'm ninety-three."

"Oh, wow. You could be my grandfather."

"Missy, I could be your great-grandfather," he said and cackled.

Jim finished off his spaghetti and stared across at Harry. "Ace said you won your first race at sixteen?"

"Um." She shifted hamburger into her cheek. "My dad was into racing and, like, I really dug it. He started teaching me on the track when I was thirteen, with him crammed into the cockpit with me. So I was primed the day I got my license and entered a junior class for novices. Here are all these big ol' guys and here I am this little woman and, man, I swept the field. It was so cool it was awesome."

"Driving the bus with this group must be boring," Dodee said.

"No, it's cool."

"With all us old folk?" Max asked.

"That's cool. Everyone's quiet and polite. Better than a bunch of basketball players who think they're gods."

Jim stood up. "Excuse me, I need a dessert fix. Can I bring some back for anyone?"

Dodee looked up to him. "See what they have, sweetheart."

He found the desserts at the end of the salad bar. He picked up two vanilla puddings and turned at the ringing of little shoe bells, realizing they must be sown into the hem of Erynn Sunflower's peasant dress.

"Jim, I want to speak to you about Dodee's painting." She kept her voice low as she scanned the room. "She said she didn't paint the shaman?"

He shrugged. "It's what she said."

She sucked her lips between her teeth. "And no one could have played a trick?"

The new man with the black curly hair passed by on his way to the sandwich counter.

"Who is that guy?" Jim asked.

Erynn shrugged. "No one could have played a trick?"

"It was never out of our sight."

She nodded and laid a hand on his arm. "Let's talk later, you and Dodee and me." She nodded. "I have some ideas on this."

He watched her stroll back into the dining room, bells ringing to the sway of her wide-track hips.

Oh yeah, that had to be good.

He returned to the table with one dish of pudding for himself, and one to share, but since no one wanted vanilla, he was forced to eat them both himself.

*F*OURTEEN

Jim and Dodee sat in the Holiday Inn Express's hospitality room. Chairs had been set up facing a long table by the back window. Ace rested his rear end on the front of the table; his yellow-goateed boss sat erect in a chair behind it, hands folded on top of it.

"Okay," Ace called out. "Okay, folks. I want to introduce our lecturer for tonight, an all around swell guy"—he grinned—"who just happens to be my boss."

Polite laugher rippled through the room.

"He's the head of Elderhostel programming at Colorado State University as well as a professor of Native American History. He has written four books on the subject." Ace read from a paper. "*The Impact of Spain upon the Pecos Pueblos; Trade Routes in Pre-Colombian Americas; The Mayan Connection;* and, *Tracing Relationships of the Peoples of Central and Continental Americas Through the Use of Native Artifacts.* He has also published many many papers and articles on Native Americans and has lectured all over the world." Ace lowered his paper. "We are honored to have him with us tonight to give us an overview of the Santa Fe Trail, my friend and boss, Dr. Ward Longtree."

Dr. Longtree stood, tall and resplendent in a cool, blue sports jacket which matched the color of his eyes, and a yellow tie, which matched the color of his hair. He rubbed the palms of his hands together.

"Thank you, Ace, your employment is safe for another week."

Another ripple of polite laughter.

"Unlike any of the other trails that brought people west, settlers and pioneers and the forty-niners seeking gold, the Santa Fe Trail was established as a trading route. A man by the name of William Becknell led a party of twenty-five or thirty men out of Missouri in the autumn of eighteen twenty-one. It was many years before Horace Greeley said, 'Go west, young man, go west,' but they set out with loaded pack mules to seek their fortune trading with the Indians for horses and ponies and the pelts of beaver and buffalo."

Jim looked over to curly-haired Hank Adamo, one row forward down at the end, and leaned in close to Dodee. "Doesn't he look familiar to you?"

She pursed her lips. "You mean like pictures of General Custer?"

"Huh? No, I mean Hank Adamo," he said, nodding in the man's direction.

Dodee turned down her lips and shook her head.

Dr. Longtree rubbed the palms of his hands together again. "They traveled west, encountering few natives and little commerce, and eventually blundered into a troop of Mexican soldiers."

"I know I've seen him somewhere."

"It's hard for us today to remember that this land was a part of the territory of Mexico—which in turn was a colony of Spain—in the early eighteen-hundreds. Ten years before the Pilgrims landed on Plymouth Rock, Spain had already established the El Camino Real trade route between Mexico City and Santa Fe, which they'd established in sixteen-ten."

"Could be he looks like someone else you know?" Dodee asked.

"During their rule, Spain maintained an iron grip on all outside commerce, a fact adventurer Robert McKnight learned when he set out to make his fortune in eighteen-twelve. McKnight, with a load of trade goods, traversed west, following the Arkansas River to what is now Pueblo, Colorado, where you all had lunch today—"

"At the museum," the plump Betty Baskins called out, "where Dodee painted the medicine woman and the boy on the bench."

Longtree smoothed his goatee and looked around. "Yes. What happened to that painting?"

"I took it back to our room," Jim said. He leaned in close to Dodee's ear. "Damn woman won't let the shaman thing die."

Longtree rubbed the palms of his hands together. "As I said, Robert McKnight continued west out of Pueblo on an old Indian trail, up the Sangre de Cristo Mountains, down the Rio Grande, and lo and behold, stumbled upon Santa Fe, where, although the residents profoundly desired the manufactured items McKnight carried, and he profoundly desired to trade for them, the Spanish-appointed governor promptly incarcerated him for trespassing on Spanish soil. So much for McKnight's fortune."

"Why are you worried about it?" Dodee asked him.

"The Spanish had prohibited their citizens, not only

in Santa Fe but throughout the Mexican territory, from trading for manufactured goods and anything made out of steel because, first, they wanted to protect their own industries in Spain, and second, because of the fear the settlers would follow the American example and seek independence. This fear was subsequently justified because Mexico was declared independent of Spain in eighteen twenty-one, after some three hundred years of Spanish rule. So it was that only nine years after McKnight's trip, the soldiers of newly independent Mexico greeted William Becknell's party and encouraged them to take their trade goods to Santa Fe."

"What am I worried about? What if the police find out about your paintings?"

"Becknell did just that, arriving on November sixteenth, eighteen twenty-one. Unlike McKnight, Becknell's party traded all their goods and hightailed it back to Missouri with beaver pelts on their pack animals and silver pesos jingling in their pockets, arriving home in the opening days of eighteen twenty-two."

He put his arm around Dodee's shoulder. "Think about it. If you painted her, obviously you had to know her. And guess who found the body? Just your little old boyfriend. Don't you think that's going to arouse suspicion? Especially with a missing notebook?"

"As the news spread that trade was now welcome in Mexico, Becknell quickly organized another expedition and embarked on what was to rival for a time the riches of the Old Silk Road in Asia"—Longtree stretched out an arm and pointed west—"the Santa Fe Trail."

"Worse yet, suppose the television people get hold of it and want to come back for another interview?"

"With the demand for manufactured goods in Santa Fe, and the need for raw materials in the East, profits continued to soar so that at its zenith, when a worker could be employed for eight dollars a month, this trade amounted to over a million dollars a year."

Jim glanced back to the black-haired Hank Adamo. "I think I've seen him since I came to Denver."

She raised her eyebrows at him.

"Adamo. I'm sure I've seen him since I've been in Denver."

"These were the days of the famous 'Westward ho' wagon train leaders like Kit Carson, Thomas 'White Head' Fitzpatrick, and Charles Bent. You'll be hearing more of these men as we go along. In fact, we'll visit Charles Bent's fort tomorrow."

Dodee shook her head. "If you saw him, it wasn't with me."

"When wasn't I with you?"

"During this time, however, the Plains Indians started raiding the wagon trains in an effort to hold back the white man's westward migration. To combat that, the traders banded together in large caravans and carried along artillery pieces. Later they prevailed upon Congress to have the army accompany them. When war broke out between the United States and Mexico, the trail became the main route for sending troops to fight in the west, and forts were established for its protection—Fort Riley, Fort Wise, Fort Union, Fort Mann near Cimarron, and Fort Leavenworth back in Kansas—and in eighteen forty-six, by right of might, Santa Fe became part of the US."

Jim turned back to Hank Adamo again. "And does he

look like he's fifty-five to you? You have to be fifty-five to go on an Elderhostel."

"Finally, the death knell sounded when the railroads started inching west, carrying goods and people faster and cheaper than the old Conestoga wagons. By eighteen-eighty, when the railhead reached Santa Fe, the trail, which for a time rivaled the Old Silk Road in Asia, became only a memory."

Longtree rubbed the palms of his hands together yet one more time.

"May I suggest in the days ahead, to achieve the full flavor of this Elderhostel, envision the trail as the first traders did when they embarked into the clear fresh air where endless grass plains met endless azure skies at Forever's border. Think of them sitting in four-wheeled vehicles pulled by six or eight oxen, rather than four-wheel-drive vehicles powered by two hundred horses compacted under the hood, on hard buckboards with only a canvas cover to protect them from the stifling heat, rather than plush leather seats cooled by air conditioning. And instead of spending nights in the isolation of sterile motels, think of them camping under a vault of stars amid the company of others making the westward trek, swapping stories, singing songs, sharing hardship and hospitality. Try to see it the same way those who left the security of friends and family and the civilization of St. Louis or Kansas City, and struck out to seek their fortune, moving west, along the Santa Fe Trail."

*F*IFTEEN

Jim caught Hank Adamo as the crowd broke up. "Hi. Hank, isn't it? I'm James Dandy. Haven't we met before?"

Hank's lips turned down and he shook his head. "Your face looks familiar to me, too, but I don't think so."

"On a plane maybe, coming into Denver?"

"I live in Denver." He brushed a stray black curl off his forehead. "Maybe I just look like someone you know."

Jim nodded.

No way was he fifty-five.

"Hey, Jim."

He turned at the sound of Max's squeaky voice.

"Huff and puffs in the morning?"

Screw his damn huff and puffs, except, staring into Max's watery blue eyes magnified by his thick glasses, was there a plea lurking in there? At ninety-three Max had to be concerned about tottering along the streets alone.

"Okay, give a knock on my door five minute before you're ready to start and we'll huff and puff together."

A smile stretched the crevasses on his face. "You got it."

Jim turned back to Hank Adamo, but the man had left.

He searched for Dodee and found her with Erynn Sunflower and Claire Renquist. "What are you ladies talking about?"

"Erynn was just asking me about the painting."

"I'd like to see it again," Erynn said.

"I put it away. I'm not taking it out," Jim replied.

"Sweetheart—"

"It's created enough furor already, Dodee."

Claire's oriental eyes took him in. "What concerns me is that the shaman was only marginally part of the composition. Thinking back on it, the style is completely different."

Erynn turned to Jim. "This is the woman who was pushed off the roof?"

He held out his hands and shrugged.

"You said it was, sweetheart."

"Well, yeah, it resembles her, sort of. Like an impressionist painting."

"Well, I better get along," Claire said, giving them a little wave. "I don't want to keep my roommate awake."

He touched Dodee's arm. "We should probably go up."

"You know, I'm a student of psychic phenomena," Erynn said. "Been studying it for twenty years. Some of the things everyone is referring to as 'New Age' now, but it's a lot more than that. Some people possess a psychic energy that can make things happen. I'm thinking the shaman who was pushed off the roof—"

"Or fell."

"—must have possessed that energy."

Jim rolled his eyes. "You think the shaman got onto the painting through some kind of voodoo stuff? Like Dodee went into some sort of a trance—"

"No, I didn't," Dodee said, shaking her head.

Erynn held out the hand with the butterfly tattoo. "How would you know?"

"Because I was with her the whole time," Jim said.

"When I covered that picture only the boy was on the paper. The same when I painted the horses in the Adams Mark lobby."

"I was with her then, too, sort of, on my way through to see if the shaman was dead."

Erynn fingered the large crystal hanging between her wine-jug breasts and stared across the room so long Jim turned to see what she was looking at. "So Dodee was painting at the same time the shaman was killed?"

He shrugged.

"It all begins to make sense." Erynn went back into her long stare. "Follow this," she whispered. "Suppose someone pushed the shaman off the roof—"

"Or she fell."

"—and when she hit the pavement, her spirit was released—"

"No doubt about that."

"So what does she do?"

"Goes to the Happy Hunting Ground—"

"Sweetheart," Dodee said, a sharp edge to her voice.

"Suppose her spirit won't, or can't move on until her killer is brought to justice? The first thing she has to do is to make sure someone knows she is still around."

"So she slaps her picture on Dodee's painting?"

Erynn held out two chubby hands. "The shaman's psychic energy reached for something to grab onto, and found Dodee doing her painting."

"Why Dodee? Why not me? I was right there."

"Because she was in a creative state, receptive to endless

possibilities. She could also be a natural receptor, open to the shaman's transmitter." She fixed her hazel-colored eyes on Dodee. "Have you ever had the feeling of a strange spirit trying to tell you something?"

"I don't know. Maybe."

Jim rolled his eyes again. "I knew this was going to get weird."

Erynn reached under her glasses and rubbed her eyes. "I think the shaman is trying to communicate with you." She let the thick glasses plop into place and went back into her long stare. "Didn't the papers say her death might have had something to do with a missing artifact?"

"What artifact?" Jim asked.

Dodee shook her head. "I don't know. I wasn't there."

"Then possibly the shaman is trying to reach Jim through you."

He shook his head. "There is no artifact."

"Are you sure, sweetheart? What about the notebook?"

"There is no notebook."

"There's something," Erynn said. "What we need to do is find out what the shaman is trying to tell us."

Dodee's brow wrinkled at that. "Maybe we should tell the police?"

Erynn shrugged. "Could be that it's sacred to the shaman, in which case she wouldn't want it to fall into the wrong hands."

"There is no artifact. There is no notebook. This is all hooey."

The big blues turned on him. "Then how do you explain the shaman appearing in the painting?"

See, that was the one thing that stumped him.

If he could explain that, maybe he'd be on his way to solving the riddle of the universe.

He hadn't come any closer to the solution by the time he brushed his teeth, slapped on a splash of sexy PS For Men cologne, and got into his pajamas.

Screw it.

Let the police handle it.

As to the shaman popping up in Dodee's paintings, he had a simple answer to that as well: Don't paint them anymore.

Passing headlights of highway traffic sent shadows skittering about the ceiling of their darkened room as he felt his way to bed and slipped under the covers.

"Are you asleep?" he whispered.

"Be quiet. I'm communicating with the spirits."

"See, I told you this stuff was going to be weird. Yeah, buddy. Erynn's a New Age junkie."

Dodee slipped into his arms, warm body against his. "You have to admit it's the only explanation we have so far."

"That doesn't mean it's worth a damn."

"I don't want to hear about it."

"Psychic energy, oh, yeah."

"Sweetheart, I don't want to hear about it."

"Can you believe that—"

"Sweetheart." She kissed him, long and wicked. "I mean I *really* don't want to hear about it."

"Oh, right, you mean you really *really* don't want to hear about it."

He returned her kiss, feeling her tongue gently entwine with his, and he ran his hand down the small of her back, caressing the muscular cheeks of her bottom and pulling her closer to him.

Dodee broke off the kiss. "Maybe we shouldn't be so quick to dismiss Erynn's spirit theory. I'm feeling something trying to get through to me right now."

"That's because you're such a good receptor."

And they set off on a spirit trip of their own, gliding across surreal treetops in the soft light of night, plunging down into darkened arroyos and up the other side, together, receptor and sender, swooping up to the mountain tops and hanging there, levitating, weightless, waiting, then crashing down in a massive free fall to land against the bed covers and pillows amid gasps and groans and whimpers. Hard breathing ebbed into a cadenced rhythm.

She gave him a feather kiss on the ear. "Thank you, sweetheart."

"The pleasure was all mine."

"That's what you think."

He snuggled her against his chest, holding her softly and caressing her shoulder, as more shadows skittered across the ceiling like spirits visiting their room.

He closed his eyes.

He had heard enough about spirits for one day.

If the shaman wanted to contact somebody, let her contact Erynn. Use the big crystal hanging from her neck and show her the missing notebooks and artifacts.

He popped open his eyes as another shadow slipped silently across the ceiling.

What artifact? Did she know something he didn't? Like she knew what it was, just not where it was?

"Do you think Erynn was trying to pump us for information?" he asked softly.

But Dodee's even breathing told him her spirit had departed for the night.

He bit the side of his lip and studied the ceiling some more.

But if Erynn knew about the artifact, how did she find out? Something on television? Something he had missed when he found the shaman's body?

He searched back through his memory to the scene on the sidewalk. If something had been there, he hadn't seen it. And the only other ones around were the two policemen. And the ambulance woman. And the guy who ran from the building with the black curly hair and—

"Sonofabitch. Hank Adamo is Handlebar."

Dodee stirred at his side.

The man had shaved his upper lip, or maybe the mustache had been a phony, but Hank Adamo was Handlebar.

Awright, at least one mystery solved.

He closed his eyes.

But if one mystery had been solved, three more had slipped in to take its place.

What had Hank Adamo been doing in that building?

More importantly, what was Hank Adamo doing tagging along on the Elderhostel?

And, finally, if he had recognized Hank Adamo even without his mustache, why had Hank Adamo not recognized him?

Sixteen

A soft knock pulled him out of a deep sleep and he swung out of bed.

What the hell?

Oh, great.

Sonofabitch. Max. Ready for huff and puffs.

He glanced back to his deserted spot, soft and warm beside Dodee, and across to the door as the knocking resumed.

Just what he wanted, to snail along the street at the crack of dawn with old sonofabitch Max.

Great, really great.

Another knock.

He slipped across and cracked the door. "Give me five."

"You got it," came Max's squeaky voice. "Don't forget your water bottle."

Jim rushed through his morning ablutions, bladder emptied, face washed, gray hair combed. He grabbed his water bottle and hurried down to the lobby dressed in shorts, T-shirt, and walking shoes.

Max beamed. "Awright," he said, slapping a yellow cap on his head, "glad for the company."

Oh, yeah. Miss sleeping-in and early coffee so they can wander about like a couple of old turtles with the gout. Just what he wanted.

He followed Max outside and joined the lanky old man in some stretching exercises. The day promised higher temperatures on La Junta's plains than back in Denver, but for now the morning was cool and the early birds sang out joyously to one another.

Shut up, you damn fools.

Jim took a pull from his water bottle and they started up the hill in the direction of the college, leaving behind the highway and railroad tracks, and marched through a neighborhood of single-story homes.

Only, what happened to the turtle pace?

Max charged out like they were in the Monte Carlo Grand Prix. He should have slapped a number on his back so the spectator crowd of lizards, cats, dogs, and bugs would know who he was.

"You're okay with this pace?" Jim asked between labored breaths.

"You bet. Like to keep a sprightly step." Max turned to him. "Or do you want to take it up a notch?"

"No, no," Jim said, puffing as they passed under a cottonwood, "I don't want to take you out of your routine."

"Figured we'd take it easy, considering we're supposed to be doing a bit of walking later on."

A bit of walking?

What the hell were they doing now?

Well, not walking. Marching, maybe. Hiking, tramping, trotting, sprinting, whatever word fell just short of flat-out racing.

What was wrong with snailing? Meandering? Strolling, promenading, moseying? Mosey was good.

And all the time the damn birds cheered them on.

Why was he puffing so much?

He should be able to keep up. Hell, Max was ninety-three. Well, he was keeping up. Barely.

Unless it was the altitude.

"Wonder what our elevation is here?" he asked, gulping from his water bottle as they turned a corner.

"Reckon it's around four thousand."

The altitude. That had to be it. Probably Max was used to it—

"Where you from, Max?"

"New England."

Sonofabitch. New England.

Just absolutely great.

They rounded another corner, bearing downhill toward the motel, and his spirit lifted like the old proverbial horse heading for the barn.

Max's pace never faltered.

No problem. Jim could make it now. With the knowledge of how many more blocks were left to go, he reached down deep to keep on keeping on. Then the motel came into sight and he started counting off the paces, counting off the feet, counting off—

"How about we cut left here," Max said, "and see what's up this way?"

How about ripping out the old man's jugular?

"Can't do it. I don't get Dodee her morning coffee, I'll never hear the end of it."

They took a couple of snail-pace laps around the parking lot to cool off while the squat, square-headed

Narcisco Ramos stood beside the entrance, smoking a cigarette.

"Saw ya on the tube this morning."

Jim paused with his hands on his hips. "What do you mean?"

"Yeah, talking to that lady about taking a notebook from that medicine woman before comin' on the Elderhostel."

Jim shook his head and followed Max inside.

Now everyone would be asking him about it.

Max raised his fist in the air as they passed the front desk. "We did it, Jim. Got out all the cobwebs." He turned and strode down the hall. "Ready to take on the day."

Right, he'd like to tell him where to shove his day, and his huff and puffs to go with it.

John Walsh slouched in one of the hospitality room's chairs, dressed in faded Levis and short-sleeved shirt, face buried in a newspaper.

"What's new in the world, John?" Jim asked as he crossed to the coffee counter.

"Saw you on television last night. Something about the Native American shaman and something to do with a notebook?"

"There was no notebook." Jim shook his head. "This thing is getting blown out of proportion."

"Oh, one thing that might interest you." John flipped through a few pages, scanning them, then his lips turned down on his freckled face. "Anyway, the new theory is the notebook had information or research about a Mayan artifact. A gold prairie falcon with diamond eyes. The theory is it was a sacred symbol to the shaman, and rather than reveal its hiding place, she took the plunge."

"To preserve a sacred symbol? Why not take it to the police? And if it's a Mayan artifact, what's its connection with Denver?"

"Didn't say, except they think the notebook will reveal its whereabouts." John's light-blue eyes focused on Jim. "You know anything about that?"

"No, I don't." He took a sip of coffee and shrugged. "I better hit the shower before Dodee wakes up and grabs it."

He opted for the elevator rather than the stairs, and leaned against the wall as the doors slid shut.

Did it make more sense for the shaman to have jumped off the roof?

He scrolled back to the vision from the Adams Mark window, trying to remember if someone else had been on the roof, but it had only been a flash across his eye-screen.

The elevator doors opened and he started down the hall.

But if it was the Mayan falcon, what was it doing in Denver? More importantly, where was the notebook? He didn't want another television camera jammed in his face.

He eased open the door, glanced across at Dodee snuggled under the covers, and peeled off his clothes. He put them in an empty drawer at the bottom of the dresser and hopped into the shower, letting the hot water splash over him.

The Mayan Falcon.

Sounded like an old movie from the thirties or forties with Humphrey Bogart and Peter Lorre.

And Sidney Greenstreet, the fat man.

He lowered his voice to a guttural base.

"For the story of the falcon, made of solid gold and

encrusted with precious stones, we have to go back to the Knights of Malta."

He dried off, shaved, slapped on some PS For Men aftershave, something they used to call Paul Sebastian. So why did they change the name? He pulled on fresh underwear and jeans, checked the time as he strapped on his watch, then crossed barefooted to the bed. "Dodee?"

She sat bolt upright and stared at him through half-lidded eyes.

"Time to get up if you want breakfast before we get on the bus."

"Coffee?"

"I've got some news about the shaman woman." He briefly told her the new theory.

She blinked at him a couple of times.

He shook his head. Nothing was getting through those half-mast blues. "Hop in the shower and I'll get you some coffee."

He went back down to the hospitality room, meeting some Elderhostelers already at breakfast, some calling out they had seen him on television—just really great—and picked up a couple of coffees. He ran into Betty Baskins on the way up, Miss Little-five-foot-big-mouth.

"Morning, Jim. Saw you on television last night."

"Yeah, thanks."

"Coffee for Dodee?"

"Takes her a little longer to wake up in the mornings."

"I'd love to see Dodee's paintings again. Does she sell them?"

"She has a studio in Kansas City, but you'd have to talk to her."

"I think I will."

"I don't think they're cheap."

"I wouldn't want them if they were." She shook a plastic prescription bottle at him. "I better get some breakfast so I can take my pills."

He continued up to the room and kicked on the door. It cracked and Dodee peeked out before letting him in.

"Thank you, sweetheart."

She held a hairbrush in one hand, and was dressed in blue blouse, shorts, socks and walking shoes. She stepped into the bathroom, leaving the door ajar. "Did you say something this morning about the shaman jumping off the building?"

"Didn't think it got through to you."

"I was awake."

He retold John Walsh's tale about the Mayan connection.

"The Mayan connection?"

"I just made that up."

"Doesn't Ward Longtree have a book called *The Mayan Connection*?"

He turned down his lips. "Don't know."

"Maybe we should ask him."

"The thing is, the artifact is a Mayan statue of a bird, made of solid gold with two diamond eyes. The Mayan Falcon. I made that up too, like the movie, *The Maltese Falcon*."

She came out of the bathroom and batted her eyelashes at him. "I wouldn't know, sweetheart; they made it before I was born."

He let it slide. "There's something else. It came to me last night where I'd seen Hank Adamo before. When I was bending over the shaman woman, trying to see if I could help her, a man with a handlebar mustache came running out of the building—"

"That was Hank Adamo?"

"Same face minus the mustache." He stared into her unblinking blues and could see the wheels spinning inside. "Now before you go off in all directions—"

"How come he said he didn't recognize you?"

"My thoughts exactly. Unless he was traumatized by the sight of the shaman lying in a pool of blood."

"Then why shave off his mustache?"

He blinked at her.

Right, and why follow along on the Elderhostel?

SEVENTEEN

Jim sat on the buckboard of his mind, back a hundred and fifty years ago, as he drove oxen over the curve of the earth to see Bent's Fort sticking out of the tabletop plain in the middle of Nowheresville. It resembled something from a western movie. Brown, stucco-covered thick adobe fortifications, flat sides, flat ramparts, flat roofs. Only two round bastions broke the square mold, sticking out of the northeast and southwest corners to provide fire power along the walls. But his covered wagon approached it at sixty miles an hour rather than sixty miles a day, and the flag over the fort's entrance carried fifty stars.

A woman met them in Native American dress, buckskin with leather streamers hanging from the arms, and rattles hanging from her hem that clacked as she walked, an old-time version of Erynn Sunflower's New Age dress. She wore her black hair in braids, but blue eyes looked out from olive skin.

Ace introduced her as Morning Cloud Campbell, two-thirds Cheyenne, one of three women who did tours of the fort.

Morning Cloud beckoned for them to follow and she

led them past the entrance into the shade of one wall, shelter from the already hot September sun. She motioned with flat hands paralleling the ground for everyone to gather about her as the smell of the prairie sage mingled with Narcisco Ramos's cigarette smoke.

"This fort is a restoration of the original, based on old diagrams, historical reports, and the original foundation. After making a few overland trading trips along the Santa Fe Trail, the Bent brothers, William and Charles, and their friend and partner, Ceran St. Vrain, decided to build this fort as a place to trade with the French, who came into the area fur trapping, and the Mexicans from Taos and Santa Fe, and the Cheyenne and the Arapaho—who had moved into the plains from up north—and the Anglos from Missouri. Any and all could come here and trade their goods. This was a strategic location, being past the halfway point along the Santa Fe Trail, a place where those weary after long weeks of following oxen would find a place to relax, repair their wagons, get fresh water, and trade for fresh animals."

Morning Cloud turned and, with a waist-high motion, moved her flat hand over the earth.

"And out here were the teepees of my people. The Cheyenne and the Arapahos."

She stretched out her arm at the shoulder and swept the horizon with a flat hand.

"And out there on the plains, as far as the eye could see, were the buffalo. When the men went out to hunt, the land would become black with them and the air filled with the thunder of their stampeding hooves. When the men killed the buffalo, the women would go out, skin the hide, flesh it out, bring it home."

"Oh, yes," Betty Baskins said, nodding, "the women do all the hard work."

Morning Cloud's lips turned down and she nodded. "It was hard, yes, but life was hard in those days. Men did not do women's work; people who came out here thought the men were lazy. The women fleshed the hides, brought in the wood, cooked the food, and built the teepees. But the teepee was the woman's home, and the man was a guest in her home. The men could divorce their wives, but the women could divorce the men as well, by just taking all their clothes and setting them outside the teepee. The man's job was to bring home the food and protect the family. If the man was fleshing hides or gathering fuel and an enemy popped up over the horizon, and he had to go search for his weapons, how was he going to protect the family? So the men had their jobs, and the women had their jobs."

"You said the Cheyenne and the who?" Betty Baskins asked. "What other tribe?"

"On this side of the river were the Cheyenne and the Arapaho." She turned and motioned with a straight arm and hand. "On the other side of the river, which belonged to Mexico, were the Apache, Kiowa, and Comanche territories. Often our men would go across the river and steal horses from them, and then they would come over to this side and steal their horses back and some of ours as well. It was a good way to get a wife or two."

She cleared her throat, glanced down at the ground for a moment before looking up.

"On one of these raids, one of our chiefs, Yellow Wolf, came upon two white men named Bent camping along the river. Through sign language, the Bents told Yellow Wolf they were trying to decide where to build a fort, and Yellow

Wolf told them if they would build the fort here, he would bring his people in to trade with them. So that was the incentive." She motioned toward the entrance. "Let's go inside the fort now."

Jim took Dodee's hand. "I think we should take this Indian way of life as an example for us."

Her big blues turned up to him. "Meaning?"

"You will do the woman things, like cleaning up, washing the dishes, taking out the garbage, cooking—"

"And pre-chewing the meat if it's too tough?"

"I would not overburden you, but rubbing my feet would be nice."

"And kissing them, I suppose."

"And I would learn the ways of protecting the family by watching the Washington Redskins fight the Dallas Cowboys."

"You also have to go out and get the food."

"I can do that. Point me in the direction of the nearest Kentucky Fried."

"And when you come back, sweetheart, you'll find your clothes outside the door."

They entered a large, square courtyard or plaza, with what looked like a wine press out in the middle. Rooms, two floors high, made up the inside of the walls with outside walkways on the second floor making shaded verandas for the rooms on the first level.

Morning Cloud motioned them into a half circle around her. "All the walls you see here were originally made of adobe. The Bents brought in Mexicans, who were earning a dollar and fifty cents a month in Taos and Santa Fe, and gave them six dollars a month to build this fort. They took mud and added a binder to it, straw or wool,

126

whatever would give it strength, mashed it with their feet to the proper consistency, then they set the mud in brick molds and put them in the sun to dry. Once hardened, the bricks were laid out crosswise, layer after layer, making strong, thick walls. The adobe not only provided stability, but also insulation from the heat and wind and cold. These walls here are adobe, but now they are made with modern technology, and covered with cement. Back in those days the women made a sort of stucco and plastered it over the adobe bricks with their hands, requiring a constant renewal to maintain it against weathering. It was said that the women had quarter-inch calluses on their hands."

Dodee leaned in close to him. "I suppose you want to hire me out for that as well?"

He turned his lips down. "Six bucks a month is six bucks a month."

"You realize these are dangerous words."

"You know me, live life on the edge."

Morning Cloud then took her strange assortment of over-the-hill tourists, varying in dress from white shorts showing knobby knees to Erynn Sunflower's long, multicolored dress, out of the bright sun and into the deep shade of the council room where all the trading took place.

"Everyone sat on buffalo pelts on the floor, which was the Indian custom, to maintain close contact with Mother Earth, and they spoke in the only common form of communication they had: sign language. The Indian men would sit in a circle and do all the trading, but the Bents soon learned that the Indian women sitting behind the men were making sure the men traded for what the women wanted and made a good trade. They might start with offering one pot for one buffalo skin, and the man would signal 'bad trade,' and so on until they'd end up with a pot, some tobacco for the man, a knife, and some colored beads the women could sew onto their dresses."

Morning Cloud lifted the hem of her dress, which gave out a hollow rattle. "These are porcupine quills here, which give off a sound as I walk, but now these woman could get brass rings, bracelets, bells, ribbons and beads of any color they wanted."

"Where did they get the beads?" Helen Martin asked.

"They came from Italy, part of the international commerce that's the mainstay of our world today."

"Who did they trade with?" Narciso Ramos asked. "The Bents on one side, but on the other, the Cheyenne or—"

"Everyone. Cheyenne, Arapaho, Apache, Kiowa, and the Comanche, also the Mexicans, and the French who came here to trap beaver, maybe the mountain men with bear pelts, and the Anglos coming in hot and dusty on the long, two-month trip from Missouri."

Claire Renquist raised a hand. "I thought the tribes fought one another."

"Yes, but they all traded here, so they didn't fight here. Bent called them in and told them if they didn't make peace here he would stop trading with them all. And so they did. This fort was a place where all could come and trade fairly and in peace. At first it was beaver pelts that were the big demand, which was why the Bents originally established the fort. Why beaver?" Morning Cloud asked.

"For fur coats?" Dodee asked.

"No, for beaver hats. Back in the east all men wanted a beaver hat. It sat tall upon their heads and made them look important. Then one day someone made a top hat out of silk, then everyone wanted their hats made out of silk and the beaver trade collapsed. So the Bents started looking around for something else to take their place, and guess what the found?"

"Buffalo?" John Walsh asked.

"Buffalo." Morning Cloud nodded. "Buffalo hides came into great demand because, among other things, the industrial revolution was starting about this time and machine belts made out of buffalo hide lasted longer than any other kind. The Bents could buy them for fifty cents here and sell them in Missouri for six dollars. Oh yes, the Bents were rich and lived well here, and in peace, up until the time the army came during the Mexican-American war and declared all the land that Mexico claimed, and all the land the Native Americans claimed, was now part of the United States. What had been a peaceful trading station now became a military fort and the Indian wars began."

Morning Cloud led the way through the rest of the ground floor, showing them Bent's private quarters, the carpentry shop and the blacksmith's stall, where anything could be made or repaired, and the cistern and well rooms, the storehouses and powder room. They examined the rotary press out in the middle of the courtyard where skins of every kind had been pressed into compact, ninety-pound bales for shipping east. Up on the ramparts on the second floor they visited a poolroom complete with pool table, an amazing luxury for that time—it had taken two months for the pool table to be brought in by covered wagon from St. Louis—and they ended up on the round bastion where a cannon used to announce the arrival of wagon trains.

Jim squinted out at the empty plains baking in the

high overhead sun, and tried to see the teepees that once surrounded the fort, and buffaloes roaming in the distance. He heard the clang of the blacksmith's hammer and the braying of horses and mules, and the daily commerce of men preparing for the long trip back to Missouri, or on to Santa Fe. He breathed in the smell of wood smoke within the walls, dung fires without, the frying of meat, the curing of hides, the ripening of latrines commingling with fresh barnyard droppings.

Dodee's arm slipped into his. "Wouldn't it have been an adventure to live back in those times? Living close to the land."

"Oh, yeah. No showers, no ice cream, no dentists." She poked him in the side. "Ow. Of course, had I been with you, sweetie, with a loaf of bread and a jug of wine—"

"Tell me you weren't looking out over the countryside and thinking about what it was like back then."

"You're partly right. I was looking over the countryside and thinking, get me back on that air-conditioned bus."

He gazed out over the plain again, but stopped short when he saw an old, dusty, green Chevrolet down in the parking lot. Where had he seen it before? Then it popped out of his memory banks: across the street from the museum in Pueblo when the bus pulled away, the same car or one like it, with a short man in cowboy hat and aviator glasses watching them leave.

He turned and scanned the courtyard below.

The Elderhostelers mingled with other tourists now, the fort crowding up, but he could see no one—then he picked him out.

A short, thin man stood in the shade by the council room, a cowboy hat shielding his face from view.

Was he following them?

He hurried down the stairs and across the plaza, but when he got there he found only the lanky Dr. Ward Longtree sitting on a bench in the shade, looking a bit like General Custer with his yellow hair and goatee.

Eighteen

They left Bent's Fort and headed for Las Animas with the bus's air conditioner turned up high, but in the full blast of the midday sun it was only holding its own.

"Ace," Martin Martin called out, "you didn't tell us how your popcorn turned out."

"It's disappeared. You didn't happen to take it, did you?"

"Not me."

"Maybe you should have shared it with us," John Walsh added.

"Or at least let us buy some of our own," called out someone from the back of the bus.

They stopped at a covered picnic area with benches and concrete restrooms.

"Okay, folks," Ace's voice boomed out of the bus's PA system, "we'll stop here for lunch and a pit stop. Make sure you continue to suck on your water bottles."

John Walsh paused at Jim's seat as everyone started off the bus. "Should we give him back his popcorn?" he whispered.

Jim nodded. "Go ahead. I'll take care of it."

He let Dodee out and hung back until the bus was empty, then he retrieved the burlap bag of Rabbit Brand popcorn and dropped it on Ace's seat as he got off.

Harry and Ace had lined up sodas, juices, and water jugs on a bench, while Dr. Ward Longtree passed out a box lunch to Hank Adamo and handed another one to Ace.

"Ever call the office about him?" Ace asked, nodding after the retreating Hank Adamo.

Longtree's lips thinned. "A special case. We'll discuss it."

Jim picked up a cold Mug Root Beer. "I hope you saved one of those box lunches for me."

Ace spun around to him. "Oh, I thought there was someone missing. Here," he said and held his box out to Jim.

"No, that one's yours," Longtree said, and shoved another box into Jim's hands.

"What's the difference?" Ace asked.

Dr. Longtree smiled. "I put in some extra cookies for you."

Jim looked into Dr. Longtree's cool blue eyes. "I didn't know you were coming with us."

"Just for the day. I have to give a lecture at Colorado State tomorrow."

Jim ambled over to a shady picnic table where Dodee sat across from John Walsh. "You going to say grace?" he asked the retired priest.

"Sure." John said a short prayer and blessed the food, then opened his box. "This is like a little surprise package, never knowing what you'll find inside."

What they found was a ham and cheese sandwich, a bag of chips, an apple, a napkin, and two cookies.

"What about the popcorn?" Dodee asked.

"I dropped it in Ace's seat." He pointed to an extra box lunch on the table beside John. "Whose is that?"

"Erynn's. She went to the restroom."

As if on cue, the frizzy-haired redhead struggled her wide hips over the bench seat, ringing the little bells in her dress, and plopped down opposite Dodee. She opened her sandwich, stared at it a moment, then her glasses came up to Jim. "Want my ham?"

"Sure." He added it to his sandwich. "You don't eat ham, or—"

"I don't eat meat," she said.

"Wait a minute. Didn't you sign my paper the other night for eating Rocky Mountain oysters?"

She nodded. "I used to eat meat before I knew better. Fact, I liked mountain oysters cut thin and served with a hot sauce. But now it's against my beliefs."

"Really?" John turned to her. "What beliefs are they?"

"I believe we're all here for a purpose." Erynn took a bite out of what was now a cheese sandwich. "I was just at a Cosmic Energy Symposium before I came here. I try to go to at least one a year ever since I learned so much from Lily Dale."

"Who?" Dodee asked.

Erynn smiled. "Not who, Dodee, where. Lily Dale, New York. I spent a couple of seasons there. Thousands of spiritualists visit every summer. A non-profit religious corporation, the Lily Dale Assembly owns all the town land and works hard to keep out the charlatans, tea-leaf readers, and crystal-ballers. It's the spiritualist capital of the world. But that's different from the symposium, which was held this time in Denver." She took another bite of her sandwich.

"We know there is cosmic energy all around us and in us and in every living thing. Which is why I don't eat flesh, because I would be altering my energy with the animal's energy."

"Interesting," John said. "And you're a spiritualist? You certainly have the name for it."

"Erynn Sunflower is my spiritual name. My birth name was Irma Stoval, but I changed it legally to conform with my spirituality." She took a sip from her soda. "The spirits are all around us; some are always trying to communicate with us. We can let them, if we know how."

"Max Solnim is also a vegetarian," Jim said, trying to steer her off the New Age stuff. "If I could get both of you to sit with me, I could have a really thick ham sandwich."

Dodee passed her chips to him. "Max does it for health reasons."

Erynn nodded. "Me too, along with my beliefs. We really don't need to have animal fat clogging up our arteries. Our system is cleaner without it and we are less aggressive."

Jim took another bite of his sandwich, toyed with the idea of telling her about Hitler, then let it pass.

"So you've been here awhile?" John asked. "I mean, in Denver?"

"Since last Sunday, which is one of the reasons I chose to come on this Elderhostel. Kill two birds with one stone." She gathered up her box lunch. "Only I wouldn't actually kill a bird, one stone or two." And picked up her soft drink. "I think I'll go ask Ace if we can have some vegetarian lunches tomorrow. You don't mind if I desert you?"

John waved his hand. "Not at all."

"We'll muddle through," Jim said as she departed.

Dodee took a bite out of her apple and turned to John Walsh. "Do you think there's anything to what she said, John, Father—what do I call you?"

A small smile lit up his Irish face. "John seems to be working pretty well so far." Then he flicked his eyebrows. "Unless you want me to hear your confession."

"No, I don't—well, it's a sort of confessional. Weird, is what it is."

Jim turned to her. "Some dark secret out of your past?"

She glanced at him and back to John. "It's about my paintings and what Erynn said last night."

Jim glanced toward the sky. "OooOOOooo."

"Well, it won't hurt to ask John. He's a priest. He's studied these things."

John rubbed his large nose. "You might want to talk this over between—"

"You saw my painting last night. At the wine and cheese party?"

"The boy on the bench and the Indian lady? I thought you did a good job."

"On the boy, maybe, for the amount of time I had."

Jim leaned his elbows on the table. "Dodee didn't paint the shaman. The Indian woman. At least not that we're aware—"

"Damnit, I did not paint the Indian woman." She looked across to John. "He thinks I went into a trance—"

"I'm just saying it's one possibility."

"When I put the cover sheet over the painting, there was only the boy on the paper. We carried it downstairs and unveiled it"—her eyebrows rose and fell—"and there she was."

John's light blue eyes shifted to Jim. "I can see what you mean by 'oooOOOooo.'"

"You haven't heard it all." He glanced around. "Can we tell you this in confidence?" When John nodded, Jim told him about Dodee painting a picture of the Adams Mark horses at the same time the shaman plunged off the building.

John nodded. "You're saying it was the same woman? In both the paintings?"

"A little fuzzy, like an impressionist style, but clear enough to know it's the shaman."

Dodee folded her hands. "So what do you think?"

"I think this is really, really oooOOOooo."

"Erynn thinks—"

"Erynn's a New Age hippie," Jim said.

"Erynn thinks the shaman is trying to contact me. Trying to tell me something."

"You mean like a spirit?"

She nodded. "What do you think?"

The priest turned his lips down and shrugged. "I don't know. At one time we used to think the soul of the dead hung around for a few hours after death while the body got cold. Now we don't. But who's to really tell?"

Jim ripped open Dodee's bag of chips. "Well, I wish the shaman's spirit would beat it. Anything you can do about that?"

"You mean like an exorcism?" He crossed his index fingers and held them up to Dodee. "Begone, evil spirits, begone, begone, begone."

"Wow," Jim said, dropping his potato chips, "that's it? That's all you—"

"I'm kidding, I'm kidding. That's as effective as saying

137

'rain, rain, go away, come back on mother's washing day.' Before I could do an exorcism I'd have to get permission from the local bishop, they'd have to do an investigation, find out if the person was actually possessed or just a fruitcake. The Church doesn't take this thing lightly."

"But it is possible?" Dodee asked.

He shrugged again. "Anything is possible. Death is one of the big mysteries in life, the separation of spirit and body. The fact that she was a shaman adds to it, a holy woman, supposedly able to see things you and I don't."

"And that's possible?"

He held up his hands and let them drop. "We all have gifts. Whose to say what gifts God gave to the shaman? Prophesy, healing touch, who knows? And if He did, I'm certainly not going to argue with Him about it." He rummaged through his cardboard lunch box, pulled out an apple, and stared at it a moment. "The thing is, the papers said she jumped rather than reveal the location of a sacred artifact. If they're right, what does that say about her faith?"

Jim popped some chips in his mouth. "It could also be an act of insanity."

John studied his apple again, turning it over. "There's a fine line between faith and superstition. If all one does is go to church once a week and nothing else, is that faith or superstition?" He tossed the apple in the air and caught it. "I better go to the restroom while I have the chance."

He swung his legs over the seat, then turned his shoulders back to them. "You know"—he pressed his lips together for a moment—"sometimes I've seen the way a sick person clings to life way beyond reason. We say 'What a fighter.' But why? Fear? It happens even in people with

138

an iron faith and a desire for heaven. If the shaman truly communicated with spirits, she'd have no fear of the jump or her own death." He polished the apple against his shirt. "I don't think it's the person's spirit that's clinging to life, but the body clinging to the spirit. It knows that once the spirit is gone, only a decaying shell remains." He stood up and flicked his eyebrows. "Just my opinion."

Jim watched him go. "Interesting, but it doesn't help our problem."

"Maybe we need to ask Erynn what the spirit is telling us."

"Forget Erynn. Stop painting."

"One thing John said that absolutely, definitely, positively made sense."

He turned to her.

She batted her eyebrows at him. "I'm going to the restroom while I have the chance."

He looked up at her as she stood. "And leave me here all alone?"

"You're a big boy."

"You figured that out last night?"

She bent down and placed her lips so close to his ear he could feel her breath. "Don't be crude, sweetheart." Then she licked his ear lobe and sent a shock wave through him.

He turned, but she was already heading off toward the restroom. He swung his gaze to the water, and yanked it back in a double-take as it registered that Hank Handlebar-Mustache Adamo was staring at him, but by the time he locked onto the man's now-shaven face, Adamo appeared to be studying a flock of sparrows flying overhead.

Longtree said he was "a special case."

What did that mean?

NINETEEN

"This is Bent's New Fort," Ace said on the loudspeaker when Harry pulled to a stop on a dirt road in the middle of the boonies. "When the army came in, sometime in the eighteen-forties, the Bents deserted their original fort. William Bent was married to the daughter of the highest member of the Cheyenne tribe, the Keeper of the Arrow, and the Cheyenne were free to come and go in the fort. But when the army came, planning on driving the Indians away, the Bents sold out, moved up here and established Bent's New Fort. Unlike the reconstructed fort we visited this morning, there is nothing left here except the site and some low walls. It's a bit of a walk here, about two hundred yards, all uphill. The temperature's in the upper nineties and there is no shade, so if you want to stay on the bus, I'll understand."

"You going?" Martin Martin asked his wife.

"Yes," Helen answered, "why not?"

"I didn't know if you wanted to walk that far."

Betty Baskins stopped in the aisle beside them. "They told us there would be walking on this Elderhostel," she said in a voice made to carry. "If we can't make the walk,

140

we shouldn't have signed up."

Jim turned to Dodee. "We going?"

"After Betty's comment?"

He helped her down from the bus and fell in beside Ace as they started up the rocky hill. "How long were the Bents here?"

Ace wiped sweat from his forehead. "Not long. The railroad came in around that time and changed everything."

They trudged on, but Ace stopped three-quarters of the way up, his ruddy face flushed, breathing labored, and again wiped sweat from his brow.

"You okay?" Jim asked.

"Don't I look okay?"

"Frankly, no. You could be coming down with the flu."

"You a doctor?"

"No, but I'm a semi-retired physical therapist and an EMT."

Ace waved Jim's diagnosis off and lumbered on.

They found a concrete-and-stone monument with a seat built into its base at the top of the hill; a plaque declared it the site of Bent's New Fort.

"Well, that makes it official," Jim said. Ace blinked at him. "Hell, you could have stopped in any old field and we'd have believed you."

He smiled and turned to those gathering around. "The Bents established a new fort here in eighteen fifty-three, close to the Arkansas river you can see along there." He pointed to a green ribbon snaking through the dry prairie, with glimpses of water and a bridge in the distance. "The new trading post never flourished as well as their first, and

141

so, when the army came along in eighteen fifty-nine and wanted to buy it, the Bents sold it to them. The name was changed to Fort Wise, and then changed again a year later to Fort Lyon."

Jim scanned a flat horizon underlining a cloudless sky. Only a few yucca plants, some sage, and tufts of prairie grass grew on the hill, but over the rim treetops testified to the river's presence. He started walking toward them.

"Take ten or fifteen minutes," Ace called out, "look around, but if you find any artifacts, leave them behind unless you want to get arrested. And don't go too far in the direction of the river. There're some cliffs and you could get hurt."

Dodee caught up with him. "Where are you going?"

"I want to take a look at the river."

"Didn't you hear what Ace said?"

John Walsh caught up with them. "Checking out the river?"

"Yep. Wondering how wide it is."

Dodee stopped. "Didn't you two hear what Ace said? You could get hurt."

Jim held out his hand. "I like to live on the edge."

"Suppose you fall off the edge?"

John grinned. "I'm just following Jim."

Jim jumped down a few rocky shelves and gazed down from the top of a cliff at the water, viewing the transition from brown prairie plants stuck in rock crevasses, to green grasses and cottonwoods springing up from the bottomland no more than fifty feet wide.

"Hey, look." John pointed to some bright yellow flowers. "Dandelions. Out here. How about that?"

Dodee slipped her hand around Jim's arm and he

turned to her. "I thought you didn't want to come down here."

She nodded to the river. "Why didn't they just build the fort down there?"

"Because it's easier to defend the high ground," John said.

"And because of flash floods." Jim spread his free arm to take in the countryside toward the distant bridge. "Everything must drain through here like a funnel. Get a major thunderstorm across the plain and this trickle of water could change into a raging torrent in minutes."

They retraced their steps up the hill.

"Ace mention anything about the popcorn?" John asked.

"Not to me," Jim said.

"I watched. He just pushed it aside and flopped onto his seat."

Dodee motioned to the bus path, changing direction to skirt the hill and catch up with the others on their way down, but Jim saw Ace was still sitting on the concrete seat built into the base of the monument, bent over, elbows on his thighs, head almost between his knees.

"You go ahead. I'll catch up."

Ace lifted a flushed face as Jim approached. "Check out the river?"

"Yep." He cocked his head. "You sure you're feeling okay?"

The Elderhostel coordinator glanced around, as if making sure they were alone. "To tell you the truth, no. I was fine this morning, but this afternoon I'm feeling worse as the minutes slip by."

"Are we going back to the motel?"

"I wish. No, we're heading down to Boggsville first."

"We don't have to, you know."

"I'll make it." Ace lumbered to his feet. "Maybe I'll feel better back on the bus."

They walked down and Jim followed him on board, watching him sink onto his seat.

So much for kidding him about the popcorn.

When Harry pulled into the parking lot in Boggsville, the temperature had crept over the one hundred mark. Ten Elderhostelers elected to stay on board, although the bus's air conditioner was struggling to keep it cool.

Ace led them down a two-rut driveway in full sun toward an old house a hundred feet away.

"The Santa Fe Trail came right along here," he said, motioning to the edge of the lawn to his right, "about ten feet into the field. If you look closely you'll be able to see where the wagons, one following the other, compacted the earth so it's still visible today."

"What did these guys make," Jim asked, "a hundred miles a day?"

Ace turned a flushed face to him. "These were Conestoga wagons, heavy all by themselves. They required six or eight oxen to pull them fully loaded, and when they came to river banks they had to tie ropes to the back of each wagon, maybe take oxen from another team, everybody working to ease each wagon down one at a time. Then they might hitch two teams of oxen together to pull them across and up the other bank, that's if the river didn't flood and topple it. Then they had to go back and do it all over again for the next wagon. They also had to stop at night and during the heat of the day to rest their animals."

"I'm talking average. Fifty miles a day?"

"More like fifteen to eighteen miles on a good day."

Sonofabitch. Eighteen miles a day? That was twenty minutes in his Lincoln. A minute and a half on a jet plane.

They walked around to the front of the old house into the shade of two large cottonwood trees. Ace pointed to where their two-rut driveway continued straight on. "Not far over there is the Purgatory River where Kit Carson had a house during the final years of his life."

A mid-fifties man came out of the house and told them how they were restoring the village as grant money became available, and then invited them inside.

Jim stopped Dodee. "I'm historied-out for one day. You go ahead and I'll meet you back on the bus."

He got directions to the restroom and crossed a two-board bridge—twenty-two inches wide—over a five-foot irrigation ditch, to a small trailer-sized building. He climbed a porch and tried the door marked Restroom. Locked.

"Be right out," a woman's voice called to him, and a few seconds later Erynn Sunflower emerged. "Next."

When Jim came out, Erynn still stood there, one hand on the railing, the other gripping her large crystal, head bent, wide-hipped body blocking the way to the two-board bridge.

"You all right?" he asked.

She brushed back her frizzy red hair and turned her hazel eyes to him, blinking behind her glasses. "It happened right here," she said, voice dropping to bass, as if talking from the basement of her being.

Oh shit, what now?

"It happened right here," she said again in the bass voice, as if she were possessed.

145

He didn't want to know what happened right there.

She swayed back and forth, bells tinkling in the hem of her dress. "Right here."

And if she were waiting for him to ask what, she'd wait until hell froze—

"An Indian shot right here. Before these houses were built. A member of a raiding party, yes he was, and had stolen an Indian maiden, yes he did, and was trying to get back to his tribe when they caught him, yes they caught him."

She closed her eyes.

"I see two arrows ripping into his chest. Breathing hard now, blood bubbling from his mouth, yes it is. One of the pursuing braves holds up a knife. Steel knife. It is glittering in the sunlight. The fallen Indian holds up his hands, yes he does, but the brave slices through and plunges the knife into the fallen man's chest. Then the brave stands, holds the knife in the air. Blood drips onto the ground. He starts shuffling in the dust and chanting, asking forgiveness for spilling blood on Mother Earth."

Erynn opened her eyes and shook herself.

"Ugh, grisly, grisly," she said in her normal voice, then smiled. "Well, better get back."

He watched her cross the two-board bridge and head toward the house.

What the hell was that?

This was all getting too weird.

First the shaman turns up on Dodee's paintings and now Erynn falls into a trance and witnesses an Indian being massacred before her very eyeballs, give or take a couple of hundred years.

Oh, yeah.

What new surprises awaited them by the end of this trip?

He crossed the bridge and cut behind the house to the bus, giving Erynn a wide berth. He stopped at the edge of the parking lot to check out the dirt ruts, but he had only Ace's word that they were from wagon train wheels traveling the Santa Fe Trail. Of course, if Erynn was here with her magic crystal, she could probably tell him the name of the woman buckboard driver and how many pimples she had on her butt.

He turned toward the grumble of the diesel engine. Harry leaned against the bus's yellow side in what little shade it provided, partially obscuring the letter T of the Colorado State University painted on the side.

"Air conditioner working?"

She flopped her hand back and forth. "If we knew it was going to be this hot, we'd have brought the other bus. It's brand new and has more power."

Jim waved toward the door. "Think I'll grab it anyway."

He climbed onboard and strolled down the aisle, passing a short lady stretched out on two seats. He couldn't remember her name; what else was new? The same for a couple leaning against one another a seat behind her.

Nap time.

Not a bad idea.

He dropped into his seat, leaned his head back, and closed his eyes. Let the world go on without him. He started at the roar of a broken muffler and opened his eyes in time to catch sight of a dirty green Chevrolet rumbling by, its smoking exhaust mixing with a cloud of kicked-up dust.

TWENTY

When they got back to the hotel, Jim helped Dr. Ward Longtree get a doubled-over Ace off the bus. John Walsh held the door as they walked him into the lobby.

"I think you better get him to a doctor," Walsh said.

"No, I'll be all right," Ace said, gasping. "Just need some rest and some Gaviscon."

Jim looked into Dr. Longtree's cool blue eyes and shook his head.

The professor nodded. "We will engage a doctor just to be prudent and allow him to decide. I will take over the Elderhostel while you're incapacitated."

"Got a wine and cheese party to set up. Let me take care of that—"

"No, I shall take charge for tonight."

Dr. Longtree asked the clerk about a doctor. Fortunately they had one they could not only call, but one who agreed to come around. Jim waited until the doctor arrived, a petite, dark-haired woman who walked in and took over like Napoleon. He left when she told the clerk to call an ambulance.

"Ace's sick?" Dodee asked when he entered their room.

"As a dog."

"Is he going to be all right?"

"I hope so." He wrapped his arms around her. "Big-time cramps in his stomach. If I were to hazard a guess, I'd say he has a flu virus."

"I hope it doesn't run through the group."

"We'll ask John to lay hands."

"That's not funny."

He looked into her big blues. "It was just a . . . what's wrong?"

She shrugged, then wrapped her arms around his neck, head on his chest. "I'm spooked about all the spirit things that are happening. Erynn telling me the shaman woman is trying to communicate with me."

"Fagedaboudid, as Barry Rhodenbarr used to say. Remember him from canoeing in South Carolina?" He felt her head nod against his chest. "Well, fagedaboudid."

She pulled back. "How can I when every time I paint something the Indian woman shows up? Erynn says—"

"Fagedaboudid. You know what she told me at Boggsville? I came out of the restroom and she's acting like she's in a trance. Says an Indian was killed in that exact spot a couple of hundred yeas ago."

"She told me."

"She did? And you don't think that's weird?"

The phone rang and they both jumped. He picked it up on the second ring. "Hello?"

"Jim, this is Dr. Ward Longtree. Could I prevail upon you to orchestrate the wine and cheese party this evening? We are transporting Ace to a hospital and I want to be sure he is admitted without difficulty."

Jim grimaced. "I guess. Where's all the stuff—"

"In Ace's room. I'll arrange for a key with the front desk."

He hung up and turned to Dodee. "They're taking Ace to the hospital and Longtree asked if you would set up for the wine and cheese party."

She arched her brows and stared at him.

He held up his hands. "Okay, us, he asked us to set up—okay, he asked me, but you're going to help me, right?"

They found Ace's open suitcase on one bed in his room, stuffed to overflowing with clothes. A smaller suitcase, stuffed with books, sat on the dresser, along with four wine boxes. Assorted packages of crackers—Wheat Thins, Harvest Crisps, Triscuit Originals—cluttered up the small desk.

"Here're the blocks of cheese," Dodee said, holding open the top of a cooler. "We have to cut it up."

They carried the wine and cheese down to the hospitality room and set everything up, finishing as the short and plump Betty Baskins walked in.

"Did I see an ambulance pull away a little while ago?" she asked. "One of us, I wonder?"

Jim opened his mouth to answer, but Erynn Sunflower cut him off.

"Ace Rudavsky just left in an ambulance, didn't he?" she asked, marching into the room, small bells tinkling in her blue, red, and earth-toned dress. "I saw it this afternoon when we were on the hill at Bent's New Fort." She tapped her head. "An ambulance with Ace in it."

Dodee turned to him and he shook his head.

All he needed was for Dodee to believe the woman talked to spirits. Hell, anyone with a eye could see Ace was sick and it didn't take a whole lot to figure who the ambulance was for.

"Is it serious?" Betty asked.

Erynn fingered her crystal. "Um, no. But we shall not see him for a few days. And, let's see . . ." She turned to look at Jim. "Dr. Longtree will take over for him."

He glanced into Dodee's cornflower-blue eyes, shook his head again, and poured himself a big glass of red wine.

"And did you lock your room, Jim?" Erynn asked.

He blinked at her, then smiled. "The door locks automatically."

Now she blinked. "Yes," she said, putting a hand to her cheek, "that's right."

"Where's the wine?" Max Solnim asked as he came through the door. "Where's the cheese?" He grinned, rearranging the crevasses in his ninety-three-year-old face. "Am I in the right place? And would someone please tell me my name? I've met so many strangers lately."

"Your name is Harry Truman and you're in the right place," Betty said, hurrying over to pick up a plastic glass. "But you have to get in line behind me."

Jim picked up four cheese cubes and moved over to the window, popping one in his mouth and a sip of wine to go with it. John Walsh came in, followed by curly-haired Hank Adamo, the ever-present stray lock hanging down over his forehead.

If Erynn wasn't weird enough, there was Hank Adamo.

Okay, he could accept the traumatized theory, that the sight of the dead shaman kept Hank from recognizing him, except why had he shaved off the handlebar? And why had he been in the building? And just what the hell was he doing here on the Elderhostel?

Dodee eased up to him. "So what do you think?"

"What do I think about what?"

"What Erynn said about knowing Ace would go to the hospital."

"It's all bullshit. Why do you listen to her?"

"And what was that business about locking our door?"

He took a breath and let it out. "Who knows? The woman is weird."

"Ah, Dodee, there you are." Claire Renguist's soft brown, oriental eyes took them in. "I've been meaning to talk to you about hanging some of your paintings in my gallery, if you don't think it would compete with your own business."

Dodee shook her head. "No, I'd like that. Spread my horizons."

"You're from Palm Beach?" Jim asked.

"Yes—well . . ." She spread a white-toothed smile across her olive face. "I was born on the island of Trinidad in the West Indies. My father was British and my mother Chinese."

"But you don't sound—"

"My parents emigrated to south Florida when I was two. Now you know everything about me." She refocused her almond-shaped eyes on Dodee. "Back to the paintings. How about one of those with the Indian shaman?"

Dodee grimaced. "If I'm going to send you something, it's going to be something serious."

"But these will sell. Think of the publicity. 'Strange Spirit Appears Unbidden in Artist's Painting.' There's already the business of Jim on television and now here's the shaman herself mysteriously in the picture. In fact, why not get the police involved to authenticate it? Know how much money that will bring in?"

"That's Barnum and Bailey. My art is more than money. It's my life, the way I feel about what I'm representing, things that lurk unknown in my memory, it's all there on the canvas. I can't cheapen that. It would be like selling my . . ." She pressed her lips together for a moment. "Sometimes, when I get it right, when all the things come together, it's like being touched by God. And you want me to make a circus of that?"

"But the Indian shaman . . ." Claire closed her eyes, raised her head, accenting her already straight posture, and smiled at Dodee. "You're right, of course. My eyes just got full of dollar signs." She ran a fingertip across the scar on her jawbone. "You know, why don't you deliberately paint a whole canvas of the medicine woman? Maybe that's what she wants."

"Oh, boy." Jim shook his head. "You've been talking to Erynn."

She turned to him. "About what?"

"All that stuff about the medicine woman and the spirits trying to communicate with us."

Claire took a sip of wine and sniffed. "No I haven't, but maybe I should. And don't be so sure they're not." She turned and walked away.

"Don't make her too mad, sweetheart. I really would like to sell some of my work through her gallery."

He nodded and sighed. "Okay. I still have another five days to make nice to her."

Dodee put her hand into his. "And perhaps the shaman is trying to tell us something. As John says, who really knows what happens when our spirit slips out of its shell? And if Erynn wants to help us find out—"

"That's bullshit, Dodee."

"And what do I do when the shaman keeps showing up—"

"Stop painting."

"That's like not breathing."

"There's gotta be a logical explanation for it."

She reached up and straightened his collar. "And that would be?"

He frowned. "I wish I knew."

She took his glass. "I'll get you some more wine while you're figuring it out."

He gazed out the window at the scene behind the motel: the sinking sun created long shadows from buildings and cars and a few strollers. He brought his head against the pane and searched up and down the street for the dusty green Chevrolet with the smoking exhaust, but if it was there, it had morphed into a red Toyota pickup.

Which would go right along with Erynn's spirit bullshit.

If he could figure out how the shaman kept popping up in the paintings he could stop all of that. Any simple explanation would do.

Instead, his world had suddenly turned into too much oooOOOooo to suit him.

Yeah, buddy.

Twenty-One

Dodee insisted on bringing her sketchbook along when Harry drove them to Otero Junior College for dinner, as if to refute his suggestion that she stop painting.

Dr. Longtree showed up as they finished the meal and gathered them into a classroom down the hall from the cafeteria. While they piled into chairs he stood in a doorway at the front of the room and talked to someone on the other side. On top of an Indian blanket placed over a table was a musket, lead balls, hatchet, knife, and various hide packs. Longtree nodded at the someone outside, stepped back in the room and stood there rubbing the palms of his hands together until everyone quieted down.

"Allow me to reintroduce myself. I'm Dr. Ward Longtree, head of the Elderhostel Program at Colorado State University, as well as a professor of Native American history. I shall be coordinating this Elderhostel for Federico Rudavsky—"

"Who?" one of the older Elderhostelers asked.

"Ace," Max called out in his squeaky voice.

"Oh," the Elderhosteler said. "Why didn't he just say Ace?"

Dr. Ward Longtree loudly cleared his throat. "As I was saying, Federico Rudavsky, or Ace, has been taken to a hospital. It is not life-threatening. The doctor's prognosis is a mild case of food poisoning. We assume, since these symptoms appear to be singular, he ate a contaminated snack somewhere during the day."

Dodee turned to Jim. "So what do you think now?"

Jim shrugged. "Ace's in the hospital."

"Since he will be incapacitated for a few days, I shall carry on in his absence," Longtree announced.

Jim shrugged again. "Not only that, he'll be there a few days."

She frowned. "No, I mean about what Erynn said."

"As I said, I have a Ph.D. in Native American History with four books on the subject, and I coordinated this program before I delegated its management to Ace, so we shall not miss a beat as we study the Santa Fe trail."

"Let's not get back into Erynn."

"She said Ace would be laid up a few days and it would not be life-threatening and Dr. Longtree would take over."

Longtree rubbed the palms of his hands together again. "I believe Harry has a get-well card circulating the room. If you sign it, we will make sure Ace gets it. Now. We have a special treat for you tonight, a visit from Kit Carson. Are you ready, Kit?"

"I reckon I'm just about there," came a soft voice from the hall.

A man about five foot six entered with a long rifle in the crook of his arm, dressed in a buckskin coat with fringes of leather hanging down the back of the arms and across the chest. He wore a wide-brimmed hat, homemade moccasins, and buckskin pants with more fringes at the sides. He smiled, spreading a blond mustache in a thin face that looked remarkably like pictures Jim remembered of Kit Carson.

"Evenin' everybody. I just stopped by on my way to Santa Fe. Promised friends of mine, Jim Beckworth and Uncle Dick Wootton, I'd visit with 'em. They're having a fiesta and we'll probably all have a glass or two of mountain liquid and end up dancing the fandango all night."

He lay the long rifle on the table, and started pacing, as if he were nervous talking to a crowd.

"I left Missouri when I was fourteen or sixteen, no way a knowin' fer sure, we didn't have birth certificates in those days, and even if I had one, I wouldn'ta been able to read it. Never did learn to read, all my life. I hooked up with a wagon train and set out to make my fortune. Later on I even ended up as a trail captain or wagon master a time or two. I met some of the mountain men, like the friends I mentioned, Jim Beckworth and Uncle Dick Wootton, who were trapping beaver, and I thought I'd try that for awhile and headed up into the hills."

Dodee opened her sketchbook and started drawing in bold black lines.

Jim leaned in close to her ear. "What are you doing?"

"I'm dancing the fandango."

He shook his head.

Ask a stupid question, get a stupid answer. "I meant, you're not going to paint him?"

She shrugged as she continued to sketch. "I want to get some photos afterward."

The man kept pacing as he told them of his adventures as Kit Carson, how he killed deer and elk and cured the skin to make his clothes, sewing together the jacket, pants, and moccasins he wore, about marrying an Indian woman, trying out ranching, and when the Civil War broke out, how he led a group of volunteers for the Union, continued to serve in the army during the Indian wars and rose to the rank of general.

Someone asked about his buckskin coat.

"This is a replica of the coat actually worn by Kit Carson. You can see it in the museum in Trinidad. They were good enough to let me measure and photograph it and so it is very close to the original. I made it myself, just like they did in the time of Kit Carson, and wore out my hands pushing needles through the buckskin. It weighs about twenty pounds and in the summer is hot as the devil. You all are welcome to come up and look at it."

When they got back to their room, Jim pulled the black case from under the bed and slipped her sketchbook inside.

"You want the bathroom first?" Dodee asked.

"No, you go ahead." He sat on the edge of the bed, picked up the remote, and snapped on the television as she rummaged through her things. He changed channels, searching for the news, then switched his attention to the big blues staring down at him. "What?"

"Someone's gone through my drawers."

He grinned. "I thought that was my job."

"This is not funny, Jim. Someone's been in here since we went to dinner."

"Sure you're not imagining it?"

Her mouth stretched into a thin line.

He nodded and hopped off the bed. "Okay, show me."

She pointed to a yellow nightgown on top of a pile

of clothes. "I was saving that for later in the week." He nodded. "Well, sweetheart, it's on top."

"Uh-huh."

She let out a breath and put one hand on her hip. "I wasn't wearing it until the end of the week so I put it on the bottom. Someone's turned the pile upside down. Is all your stuff the way you left it?"

He checked his bag and the dresser drawers. "Exactly." Except. He opened the top drawer again. Except he had put his huff and puffs clothes in the bottom drawer and now they were in the top.

He bent down and looked under the bed.

"What are you doing?"

He eased past her, checked out the bathroom, then slipped the night chain on the door and crossed over to the telephone.

"What are you doing?"

"I'm calling the police."

"So you believe me. Don't call the police."

He wrinkled his brow. "Why—"

"Let's see if anything is missing first."

He hung up and they went through their suitcases and clothes pockets. Nothing was missing. And nothing had been added, like a stash of drugs slipped in for safekeeping.

"Okay," he said, picking up the phone, "so now we call the police."

"If nothing's missing why call them? Maybe it was the maid."

"Oh, now it's the maid? Before you were ready to call out the army."

"Nothing's been taken. The police will only keep us up half the night."

He gave up, flopped back down on the bed, and went silently back to switching channels. He took over the bathroom when she was finished, and by the time he came out the lights were off.

How did she know he didn't want to watch television?

Maybe he should turn it on just for spite.

He shook his head. That would be stupid.

He crawled into bed and she came to him, cuddling up to his chest.

"I'm sorry I upset you, sweetheart."

"No big deal. I got upset for nothing."

He hugged her and stared up at the ceiling for a moment. "One thing. You said someone had been in here since dinner. If that's so, how could the maid have done it? They clean up in the morning and afternoon."

"It wasn't the maid."

"Then why didn't you want me to call the police?"

"Who else has been doing strange things to us? Like popping up in my paintings?"

He let out a long, deep breath. "You're telling me the shaman was here rearranging our stuff? Come on, Dodee. The woman is dead. But even then, why would she do it?"

"Because, like Erynn said, she's trying to contact one of us to track down her killer."

He stared at the ceiling and let it go.

Only thing is, why else would someone search their stuff? Unless someone thought he had the Mayan Falcon. Or the notebook that told where it was. One problem with that theory. If it were fact, they'd be back.

He slipped out of bed and rechecked the night chain. Latched and sturdy.

"What was that about?" she asked when he cuddled back up to her.

"I'm just making sure that if we're visited during the night, it's by someone who can walk through closed doors."

Twenty-Two

He awoke at the sound of a soft rap, pried open his eyes, glanced at a sliver of gray light coming through the curtains, then over to the door.

"Oh, shit."

"Huh." Dodee stirred beside him. "What?"

"Go back to sleep, sweetie." He kissed her on the cheek and swung out of bed.

"Jim," came a squeaky voice from out in the hall, "you awake?"

"Meet you in the lobby in five minutes."

"You got it."

He went to the bathroom and looked at himself in the mirror.

Why was he doing this?

Screw Max. Let him go huff and puff by himself. With any luck he would croak. Fall down, shiver and quake, then expire on the spot. Ha.

He washed his face, climbed into his walking clothes from the day before—T-shirt, shorts, shoes—started for the door, then went back to grab his plastic key and water bottle.

He found Max just outside the lobby door, yellow cap on his bald head, flexing hairless legs. He joined the old man in limbering up.

"All right?" Max's magnified blue eyes fixed on him from behind his thick glasses. "Let's hit it." And he charged up the street like he was a greyhound and the dawn a rabbit.

Jim charged after him, catching up, keeping up, over the same route as the day before; his breath wheezed in and out while Max breezed along.

Great, just great.

A dawn zephyr chilled his skin, bringing with it a whiff of desert sage, as sparrows chided him from the trees. They turned a corner and a zillion miles away the sun peeked over the horizon, sending a shaft of light straight down the street. It brought back an early morning memory of something his father always said while driving him to school.

"God's love is like the sun coming up in the morning and dispersing the shadows of night."

Too bad Max wasn't a shadow.

The hairless one led him around another corner. "Like to keep a sprightly step, don't you?"

"Right," Jim said between gasps, "sprightly."

He staggered into the motel parking lot, puffing like Dodee's steam engine in heat, while Max looked hardly winded.

Why was that?

He quick-walked two miles a day at home with ease. Now he felt like mainlining oxygen. Could be the altitude. Except why, sonofabitch, hadn't it affected Max?

He took a cool-off lap around the parking lot and came

upon the squat, square-headed Narcisco Ramos sucking a deep drag from his cigarette.

"Morning, Nico."

"Mornin'," he answered and nodded. "See ya been out walking."

Jim placed his hands on his hips. "Yeah, if that's what you want to call it."

"'S good for ya." He took another drag. "I gotta join ya one a these days."

"Like to have you."

He picked up a coffee in the lobby, nodded to some early rising Elderhostelers, and carried it up to the room. He eased the door open and studied the lump on the bed.

Her wheat-colored hair contrasted softly with the pillow. Her nose flared under even breathing. Her soft lips pursed in repose.

Temptation bid him to kiss the lips, caution told him to forget it.

He slipped out of his clothes and into the shower. When he came out she stood like a zombie in the doorway. He smiled at her. "Hello, sunshine."

Half-mast blues squinted up at him. "Coffee?"

"Let me get some clothes on and I'll fetch you some. Unless you want me to streak down the hall in the buff?"

She shook her head. "Don't want the old ladies to die laughing."

"Thanks a lot." He put his arms around her, feeling her warm body under her nightgown, and kissed her, running his hands down to her muscular rear, and feeling himself come alive.

"My bladder's about to burst. Besides, we have a bus to catch." But she put her arms around his neck and gave him a long, wicked kiss. "That's coming attractions for tonight, if I can get some coffee to keep me alive until then."

"I'm on my way."

He pulled on a pair of jeans, a light-yellow short-sleeved shirt, and barefooted it down to the lobby. He felt alive. And slightly horny. Strenuous exercise did that to him. The feeling alive part. It gave him a sense of accomplishment— did it again, yes!—and relieved the stress of the day. The horny part came from the proximity of Dodee's body.

Yeah, buddy.

He found John Walsh studying a newspaper at the front desk.

"Morning, John. Any more on the shaman-jumping-off-the-roof thing?"

Lips turned down in the freckled face. "Don't see anything about it on the front page." He picked up the paper and started going through it. "Let you know. How's Dodee?"

"Starved for coffee. I have my marching orders."

He skirted some suitcases, already brought down to the lobby, like the bus was going to leave them behind, and poured two cups from the coffee machine. He stuck a sweet roll between his teeth, a coffee in each hand, and headed back up, nodding to Martin Martin on the way.

"What'sa matter, Jim, sweet roll got your tongue?"

He raised one finger above his cup and kept walking. He set a cup on the floor long enough to get in the room and heard the shower running. It stopped as he opened the bathroom door and set her coffee on the sink. "Coffee's here," he said, after taking the sweet roll out of his mouth.

"Thank you, sweetheart." Her head popped out from around the curtain. "I see you've already started breakfast."

"Want a bite?" he asked, taking one himself.

"I'll wait." Her forehead wrinkled. "When you pack, see if anything is different from last night. Just in case."

"You think the ghost came back to visit us again?"

She frowned and shrugged.

He closed the door and studied the room.

Flesh and blood had moved things around, not spirit. The big question was, why? The obvious answer? Someone thought they had the Mayan Falcon. Or the notebook that told where it was.

He pulled the sketchbook case from under the bed and unzipped the inside pocket to see the bottom of the painting still taped to the plastic backing. He zipped it up and set it by the door. Then he packed his suitcase as Dodee came out of the bathroom, bright-eyed, bushy-tailed, and whatever other cliché you could use to show she was fully awake and ready to take on the world.

They gathered up their things and started down the hall.

"How did your walk go this morning?"

"Don't ask."

She glanced at him. "Remember, sweetheart, he's ninety-three. I wouldn't go too fast—"

"Too fast? For him? I'm running ragged and he acts like he's strolling through the park."

They joined the milling Elderhostelers at the breakfast bar, Dodee collecting a bagel and OJ while Jim picked up another sweet roll, and sat down at a table with Max.

The old man smiled at him, rearranging all his wrinkles. "Tell Dodee about our early morning huff and puffs?" He turned to her. "You should come with us. Wake you right up."

She grimaced. "All the same to you, Max, I'd just as soon ease out of sleep."

Max nodded. "Got children like that. Even so, a good brisk walk gets the blood flowing, all the muscles limbered up, everything functioning. Makes you mentally alert, although this morning I'm wondering if I'm starting to lose it."

Jim took a bite of sweet roll. "What makes you say that?"

"Stuff in my room. Notebooks and research papers I brought along. I must have gone through them because they're out of order, but damned if I can remember doing it."

"You mean like someone searched your room?"

"Either that or I'm losing it."

Dodee leaned forward. "I thought that too, like a spirit moved my things around—"

"Spirit?" Max cackled. "Not here, Dodee. Maybe up at the St. James Hotel when we get to Cimarron. Supposed to have the ghosts of Wyatt Earp and Billy the Kid walking the halls up there."

Jim took another bite of his sweet roll. "You're telling us someone searched yours?"

Max adjusted his glasses. "Well, that's what I thought at first." He ran a hand over his hairless head. "But then I got to thinking that that was crazy. They didn't take anything. Didn't take my laptop. So, what could they be after?" He came back to Jim. "What could they be after?"

He shrugged. "You're researching Native Americans, right? How about artifacts? You ever hear of a gold falcon or eagle with diamond eyes—"

"The Mayan Falcon?"

"You know of it?"

"Yep." He cackled again. "It's one of the many legends that circulate around the Southwest, like the Lost Dutchman Gold Mine." He sat back and crossed his legs. "S'posedly one of the early conquistadors in Mayan territory found a solid gold falcon with diamonds for eyes."

"You mean like in a diamond ring?"

He shook his head. "They wouldn't have the tools for that. Probably means precious stones rather than diamonds. Anyway, treasures like this were s'posed to be sent back to Spain, but the man who ultimately ended up with it, Don de la Hara Guzmon, was killed before he could ship it off and the falcon disappeared."

"In Mexico?" Dodee asked.

"So the story goes. S'posed to be cursed because the next time the Mayan Falcon came to light someone had carried it up the old El Camino Real to Santa Fe, s'posedly to move it on to St. Louis, Mo. But it never leaves Santa Fe because the man is killed. So the legend makes it accursed."

Jim let the silence stretch out, but Max had apparently finished. "That's it?"

"Far as I know, off the top of my head. Don't pay much attention to these things. I could maybe hook up my laptop and do a search for you when we get to our next stop."

"That would be good."

"All right." The bald head gave a nod. "I will." He uncrossed his legs and leaned forward, lowering his squeaky voice. "You tellin' me someone searched my room because they think I know where the Mayan Falcon is?"

Jim told him about the dead shaman and the missing notebook. "Since you're an expert on Native Americans, maybe they figured I passed the notebook on to you."

Dodge pointed at Max with her thumb and forefinger. "What's this you mentioned about the hotel in Cimarron?"

"The St. James?" He grinned. "It's famous. Been on television lotsa times. S'posed to be ghosts roaming the place, old cowboys who had scores to settle, gunfights in the middle of the night, card games in the lobby, everyone standing around playing roulette. People have seen them, so they say, raising the hair on their skin, but by morning they're gone without a trace."

Jim grit his teeth and shook his head.

That's all he needed, more weird spirit shit.

Twenty-Three

Dr. Ward Longtree had taken over Ace's front seat on the bus when Jim dropped in beside Dodee, only two seats back now.

"We're moving up in the bus," he said, "if not in the world."

"Two seats at a time, but tomorrow we'll be on the other side and heading backward."

"Easy come, easy go."

Longtree stood in the aisle dressed in a red sport jacket and blue tie, the mike to his mouth. "I communicated with the hospital this morning, and Ace, Federico Rudavsky, is recovering and hopes to catch up with us in a day or so."

That brought a round of applause.

"We're on our way to Trinidad where we shall visit some houses along the trail and spend the night. Tomorrow we'll drive into Santa Fe over Raton Pass."

Harry moved them out and as they reached the higher elevations they started seeing deer again, the odd pronghorn, and cattle in herds. Prairie falcons sat on fence posts or soared through the high desert air.

"If this was two hundred years ago," Dodee said.

"Buffalo would be roaming all over the place and life would move at a slower pace."

"Oh, yeah. Like eighteen miles a day rather than the sixty to seventy miles an hour we're making now."

"The freedom to set off in whatever direction you pleased."

"Or drought and famine forced you."

"Living off the land."

"Or dying of hunger."

She shook her head. "You have no romance."

"I have romance. I have a lot of romance. I just like my romance in an air-conditioned motel on a soft bed rather than on hard ground with rattlesnakes all around."

"That's not romance, sweetheart, that's sex."

They slowed as they drove into Trinidad on East Main Street, past three-story commercial buildings with storefront shops, a bank with a couple of faces sitting atop sturdy granite columns, then took a right on Animas Street and hopped over a small river. Harry appeared to be heading for a building anchoring a spot where three streets formed a triangle, but off to the left Jim spotted a sight that gave a lift to his heart.

"See what's over there?" he asked, nodding toward the window. "Dairy Queen."

Dodee raised her eyebrows. "You want ice cream at this hour?"

"You haven't ever had a Blizzard?" She shook her head. "Blizzards are God's foretaste of what the food in heaven is like. They are made of ice cream and crunchies of different kinds of candy bars and nuts and fruit and things, all beaten up into something so thick you can turn it upside down and it sticks to the cup."

"It's almost lunch time."

"If they let me off this bus, come with me or not, I am having a Blizzard. My only salvation is that they don't have a Dairy Queen in Prince Frederick, Maryland, or I'd be called Butterball."

They pulled off the road into a parking lot across from the building in the triangle.

"Ladies and gentlemen," Dr. Longtree said on the PA system, "we are at the Visitor's Center here in Trinidad, Colorado. We shall remain here for thirty minutes to give you a chance to use the restrooms. They also have study brochures of the area. When we leave here, we will travel a short distance to a park up the hill where we shall have our box lunch. You need to be back on the bus in thirty minutes. If you are tardy, you hold up your fellow Elderhostelers."

"You coming?" Jim asked when they got off the bus.

"I'll walk up with you, but I'm not having any ice cream."

He took her hand and started toward the Dairy Queen two blocks away.

"Maybe I'll have a taste of yours."

He stopped and pulled her around. "No. I'll buy you one if you—"

"I can't eat a whole one."

"—and I'll eat what you can't finish of yours, but you are not getting a taste of mine. I love you, lady, but you are not getting my Blizzard, not half, not a quarter, not a spoonful."

They started off again, cut left to follow the angle of the street, passed a service station and entered the Dairy Queen. He looked up at the Blizzard menu board.

"May I help you, sir?" asked the woman behind the counter.

"I'm deciding, I'm deciding," he said, studying the list, then narrowed the choice to three, praline pecan, Heath, and Butterfinger.

"Sweetheart, the lady is wait—"

"All right, all right, I'm deciding. I'll have a large Heath Bar."

"And you, ma'am?"

"I'll have a small Snickers," Dodee said, then clamped a hand over her mouth and hunched her shoulders. "You're a bad influence on me."

He grinned. "Oh, yeah."

She smiled back, batted her eyelashes, then turned to the woman. "Make that a medium."

A few minutes later, after the whir of mechanical beaters and the exchange of wampum, he walked out into the sunshine with Dodee at his side, gazed down to where the old trail led to Santa Fe, and spooned a rich mixture of ice cream and Heath Bar into his already watering mouth, letting it linger there, tasting its cool delight, and let it slip slowly down his throat.

"Great, huh?"

"Umm."

"Umm?"

"Umm."

"I like that. I buy you a Blizzard and all you say is—"

"'Thank you, sweetheart, thank you for this magnificent treat. It's great, wonderful, superb, fantastic, fabulous, sumptuous and divine."

"You're not gilding the lily there, baby."

He took another spoonful and all was right in this the best of all possible worlds.

Twenty-Four

After another lunch, Harry drove them to a museum on Trinidad's East Main Street where Dr. Longtree, because of the size of the group, split the Elderhostelers in two, half to tour the museum and the other half free to wander about town. "But," Longtree said, "I shall expect you back in precisely one hour to begin your tour."

Jim and Dodee made the first group and walked up a steep hill to a courtyard entrance separating a two-story brownish-red house from a squat museum building where they found the Kit Carson coat in a glass case.

"What do think?" Dodee asked.

"Looks the same as the one from last night."

They found some old photos of Trinidad, a downtown section called "El Corazon de Trinidad" with rutty dirt roads and men on horseback, and a crude "Exchange" sign pointing to either a place or a street.

John Walsh tapped his finger on the placard under the picture, TRINIDAD AT THE END OF THE LAST CENTURY. "They're going to have to change their signs. The end of the last century is only a couple years ago, not the late eighteen-hundreds."

"That's right," Dodee said. "They'll have to do that in a lot of places."

A museum guide led the first tour past an unrestored stage coach to the front of the three-story Bloom Mansion, named for the Yankee merchant banker who built the red brick Victorian home in 1882. Bloom went on to become a cattle baron, and the owner of a coal mine just in time for the arrival of the new railroad.

By contrast, the brownish-red Bacca House next door, constructed only twelve years before, was Territorial in style and built of adobe, and because its eighteen-inch walls could hold heat inside in the summer as well as the winter, all the warm-weather cooking was done outside in a Spanish orno, an outside oven. It was named for Filippe Bacca who bought it for twenty-five thousand pounds of wool.

When the tour was over, Jim and Dodee stepped out onto the Santa Fe Trail, now called East Main Street, and stood in the warm, lazy afternoon.

"Had enough history?" he asked.

"It's interesting," Dodee said.

"We have over an hour. Take a turn through town?"

She took his hand and they strolled up the sleepy street, past gift shops and commercial buildings, all closed, and ran into Betty Baskins and frizzy-headed Erynn Sunflower heading back for their museum tour.

"Don't bother," Betty said, turning her lips down on her plump face as she motioned in the direction Jim and Dodee were headed. "Everything's closed."

Jim motioned to Hank Adamo walking with Narcisco Ramos on the other side of the street. "Know anything about him?"

"Smokes too much," Betty said.

"No, Hank Adamo."

"I see a black cloud over him," Erynn said.

"Doesn't he look too young to be on an Elderhostel?"

Betty shrugged again. "Dodee looks too young to be on an Elderhostel."

"I am." Dodee grinned. "I'm only twenty-nine, but they let me come because my roommate is a crusty old man."

"Oh, yeah, right."

Erynn raised her glasses and rubbed her eyes. "Well, twenty-nine might be pushing it, but"—she let the glasses drop back down as she stared at Jim—"you're lucky to have her. Don't let her travel off with someone else." She looked from one to the other and lowered her voice a notch. "Any more mysterious things from our friend on the other side?"

Jim frowned. "What?"

"The spirit friend who keeps appearing in Dodee's paintings."

"No. Maybe the spirits take Sundays off."

He took Dodee's hand and they continued along the sleepy town until they came to a memorial statue of three coal miners, crossed the street and headed back. They passed a corner saloon where patrons shouted at a televised football game, and came to A. R. Mitchell Museum of Western Art. Jim opened the door and saw a small group of well-dressed people standing around drinking cocktails. A man hurried up and asked if they were part of the reception. Jim started to tell them Dodee was an artist, but she pulled him away.

"You just don't go barging into a reception and say I'm an artist."

"We might have gotten a free drink."

"These people are probably patrons and in a small town like this they all know one another. We would've stuck out."

"Maybe so, but we'd be sticking out with free drinks."

"I'll buy you a drink."

They found John Walsh leaning against a brick wall when they got back to the bus. "Not much going on in town?"

"To put it mildly." Jim glanced down toward the river, then looked at his watch. "We still have thirty minutes. Whaddaya say, Pardner"—he motioned down Chestnut Street to a sign proclaiming Ju Jo's Pub—"shall we mosey on down to the saloon and git us some firewater?"

"I could use a beer," the retired priest said.

"Good." He led the way across Main Street. "Dodee's buying."

"Oh, am I?"

"Didn't you just say you were going to buy me a drink?"

She shrugged. "I guess I did."

Halfway down the block John veered over to a shady spot next to a commercial building and bent down.

"What are you looking at?" Jim asked.

"There's a dandelion here," he said, clearing some debris away from a bright yellow flower growing in a crack of the sidewalk. "Must be some moisture here. I think the dry air would get them otherwise."

Ju Jo's Pub turned out to be a sports bar. They entered through a door angled from the street, the bar to the left with a television on top. Another television rested on top of a cooler by a popcorn machine, and still another, a big screen jobby, hung on the wall above a catty-corner stage opposite the entrance, all showing the same thing, Cleveland playing Denver with the Broncos in possession of the football. Only two people in cowboy hats watched the game while two couples clicked balls around on a pool table.

Jim led the way to a table by a window and a pretty woman followed him with a bowl of popcorn and a dimpled smile.

"What can I get you folks?"

"You have Fat Tire?" John asked.

"You know, I think we do have a few."

"What's a Fat Tire?" Dodee asked.

"A Colorado beer," John said. "Try it."

Dodee nodded at the waitress and Jim held up three fingers. He popped a handful of popcorn into his mouth and stared out at an open deck with more tables, a road beyond that, and the river down below the road. "I bet they do a lot of business here." He turned and nodded toward the television. "Now if that was the Washington Redskins playing, it'd be a different story. They're playing tomorrow night."

"I didn't know you watched football," Dodee said.

"Watch them when I can, but I'm not obsessed with it." He turned and looked into John's light-blue eyes. "Speaking of obsession, you seem to be fixated on dandelions."

He smiled and shrugged. "Just surprised to see them here."

The waitress arrived with their Fat Tires and Jim took a long gulp. "Not bad. Especially," he said, grinning at Dodee, "since it's free."

"Nothing is free, sweetheart. I'll take it out in trade later on."

"Nice thing to say in front of a retired priest."

"I meant as a therapist. I mean for a massage. I mean for my neck—oh, I give up. I'm not going to win this one."

They laughed.

Jim turned to John Walsh again. "Get back to the dandelions. You've mentioned them three or four times on this trip."

Walsh took a pull on his beer and wrinkled his brow. "It's a bit of a story."

Jim motioned toward the television. "The Bronco's are plastering Cleveland by twenty points in the only other show in town."

John smiled and took another gulp of Fat Tire.

"One year, while I was still thinking about becoming a priest, I was the head of a study group for people thinking about joining the Church. I had a day of reflection planned and I was looking for a priest to lead it, but I couldn't find anybody. And as the day got close, I realized I was going to have to do it myself, and I had nothing to say. I mean nothing. No matter how much I prayed, nothing came. Have you ever prayed and wondered if anyone up there was listening?"

Jim nodded. "Big time. When my wife was dying."

"Well, I'd reached the point where I was wondering not if anyone was listening, but if anyone was even up there. In the midst of this funk, completely drained, I came out of the building where I worked at the time, turned a corner"—he held his arms wide—"and saw this field of dandelions. A zillion of them. Bright yellow faces laughing in the sunlight. Immediately I thought how much like Christians they were. Everything on a dandelion plant can be eaten and they're rich in vitamin A. They even unite the old and the young, old Italian men making dandelion wine, and"—he blew and wiggled his fingers as he moved his hand through the air—"and young children send these magical parachutes flying on the wind. Sort of like the alpha and the omega. So here were these little guys ready to feed the world, and what does the world do? In the quest for the perfect lawn, we mow them down, gouge them out, and glop them with poison. Yet, like the followers of Christ, their yellow flowers keep popping up to give glory to God."

John took another sip of his beer.

"Now I had my story to start the day, and everything else fell into place. The lesson was: While I thought my prayers weren't being heard, the Lord was actually preparing me for this great gift. If I hadn't been emptied of all ideas and emotionally drained when I came around that corner, all I would have seen was field and flowers, trees and sky. Instead"—John bit his lip as the Irish face struggled to gain control—"instead, I saw the face of God."

John swirled the beer in his glass, then looked up and smiled at them.

"After that, I could no longer deny that I was called to enter the priesthood. If for no other reason than to tell you this story."

"It's true?" Dodee asked.

"It's true."

"So if you hadn't seen the dandelions?" Jim asked.

John shrugged. "Who knows. But that gift is still with me. Whenever I see a yellow face or a fluffy seedpod, I recognize it as a whisper of His love for me, and I know I'm not alone."

Jim palmed-up a hand. "But they're all over the place." He watched John grin, then he nodded. "Oh. Yeah. Right."

"Dandelions have become part of the signs and symbols of my life. It is my gift. Given to me." His light-blue eyes stared at Dodee for a moment, then to Jim. "And now I give this gift to you. So someday when you are walking in your own personal desert, or alone at some far corner of the earth, and you look down and see one of those bright yellow flowers, or watch a child send a seedpod full of magical parachutes sailing through the air, you, too, may hear the whisper of God's love, and know you are not alone."

Jim stared down into his beer.

Would he had known that in the days after Penny's death. He could have used a dandelion then. He could have used a zillion of them.

He took a sip and stared out the window, but instead of bright yellow flowers, he saw the back of a tall man climbing into the passenger seat of an old, dusty, green Chevrolet.

Twenty-Five

Jim shot out of the chair and scrambled across the room. "Be right back," he shouted as he bolted through the door.

He raced down the hill, but by the time he got there, puffing and panting, the dusty green Chevrolet sped off, black smoke pouring from its exhaust, muffler banging away, and turned left, heading up to East Main.

He swung around to charge back up the hill and stopped.

Oh, yeah. He could run fast enough to follow a car. Right.

He trudged back into Ju Jo's Pub.

"What was that all about?" Dodee asked.

"You see that car—that green Chevrolet?" He turned from one to the other, getting no response. "It's been following us."

"Us?" Dodee's brow wrinkled. "You mean you and me?"

He sat down. "You, me, everyone on the bus. I first saw it in Pueblo outside the museum. I saw it again at Bent's Fort. I was trying to get the license plates."

"You're sure it's the same car?" John asked.

"I'd know if I had gotten a look at the driver."

Dodee placed her hand on his. "Why would he be following us?"

"If I knew that I wouldn't have raced down the street and risked a heart attack."

"Maybe they're studying the Santa Fe Trail like we are and keep crossing our path."

"I also saw it at Boggsville."

"Well, that's part of the Santa Fe Trail."

John looked at his watch. "Speaking of following, if we don't get back to the bus, we'll be following it on foot."

They drank up and hurried back, the last ones on board.

"We were wondering where you were," Helen Martin said.

"Thought we were going to have to send out a posse," her husband added.

"How's it going, Martin Martin?"

"Just Jim Dandy."

Harry swung the bus down the street past Ju Jo's Pub and took a left, then angled off toward the river and got onto I-25. They followed up a long hill and swung into a Best Western, rooms lined up along the right side of the parking lot, a pool, hot tub, and office on the left. Dr. Ward Longtree headed into the office for room keys while Jim helped Harry unload the bags.

"You haven't noticed anyone following us?"

She paused as her eyebrows shot up.

"A car that keeps turning up everywhere we go—an old, dusty, green Chevrolet with a smoking exhaust. You haven't seen it?"

Harry yanked two more bags out of the hold. "No, I

can't say that I have." She grabbed two more and handed them to Jim. "You think it's following us?"

"I don't know." He set the bags off to the side and reached for two more. "Maybe I'm imagining it. No one else seems to have noticed."

She hefted out the last two bags to him. "A green Chevrolet with a smoking exhaust. I'll keep my eyes open and let you know." Then she climbed onto the first step of the bus. "Everybody," she called, "hello, everybody, I have to go gas up. If you all step back and give me room, I'd appreciate it."

Everyone stepped back and Harry swung the big bus around and headed out of the lot.

"Sweetheart." Dodee stood near the pool with her camera and pointed to where the highway sloped down into the valley of Trinidad with a mountain looming up on the other side. "I want to get a picture of you, okay?"

"It'll cost you a kiss."

She wrapped one arm around his neck and gave him a passionate kiss.

"Hey," Martin Martin called, "none of that stuff out here."

"It's not that kind of motel," called Betty Baskins.

Max Solnim turned to her. "It ain't? Think I got hooked up with the wrong crowd."

Jim looked into the big blues. "More previews of coming attractions?"

She smirked and pointed. "Stand there."

He stood there, and smiled, and crossed his eyes.

She clicked off a few shots from different angles.

"You want a picture of me or the hill?"

"You and the hill. I need you for perspective."

"Oh, great, glad I could help."

She closed up the camera. "I want to sketch this while I have the light."

"While you're doing that, I might study the inside of my eyelids."

Dr. Longtree emerged from the office with a handful of keys. "May I have your attention, ladies and gentlemen. We shall have a wine and cheese party in my room. I'll require some time to wash up and lay everything out, so, say in forty-five minutes."

Dodee picked up their key and Jim carried the bags to room 121, two beds with a night table in between, dresser with mirror opposite, two sinks with another big mirror against the back wall, with the bathroom to the right, just what he was looking for.

When he came out Dodee already had her sketchbook and pencils and collapsible easel in her hands. "Okay. I'll be outside if you need me."

"No problem."

He opened the drapes on a picture window, and watched her cross the parking lot and set up on a grassy knoll. He turned to the black sketchbook case she left on the chair.

How come the shaman appeared in the paintings, but not the penciled drawings?

He lay down on the bed and stared at the ceiling.

Was he missing something here?

Maybe there was something in the paint the shaman needed to pop up in the picture? Which made no sense. How could a shaman, spirit or not, just paint herself onto the canvas?

He folded his hands behind his head as the clatter of a car passed by the window.

Maybe it took the extra concentration Dodee put into thinking and executing colors, like maybe guiding Dodee's hand without her realizing it.

But if the shaman could do that, why not letters?

If the spirit wanted to tell Dodee something, as Erynn said, why not just spell it out?

Hey, shitbird, John Doe killed me.

Simple, swift, unmistakable. Why go into all the hocus-pocus of putting an out-of-focus likeness of herself in the painting?

He closed his eyes and let it go, feeling himself drifting off.

The loud car returned, stopping outside his window, muffler popping away. He heard a door slam, then the trunk slammed, all the while the muffler continued to pop, pop—

Sonofabitch.

He charged off the bed and raced to the door, yanking it open to see the old, dusty, green Chevrolet.

The sun back lighted a short man in a large cowboy hat and dark aviator glasses.

"Wait a minute!" Jim yelled.

But the man spun around and hopped into the car.

"Hey, wait!"

The loud muffler exploded as the driver roared across the parking lot and cut over a corner of the grass to keep from smashing into the big yellow bus as it came up the drive, Harry leaning on the horn.

"Dodee," he yelled, pointing, "there's the car. Dodee!"

Only she wasn't there.

He blinked, like he was missing something, easel tipped over on its side, sketchbook on the grass, like if he just looked harder, thought about it a little more, he would be able to see her—

He whirled around to the green car speeding for the highway, and listened in his mind again to the pop-pop of the muffler outside the motel door, to the slamming of the car's trunk, and a sick feeling welled up from the pit of his stomach.

He charged out in front of the bus, waving his arms as the air brakes hissed and the tires screeched, and ran around to the door.

"That guy in the green car just kidnapped Dodee!"

Harry blinked at him, then grabbed hold of the wheel. "Hop on and hang on."

She jammed the pedal to the floor and swung the bus around, almost throwing Jim out the door. "There's a cell phone in my bag. Grab it and dial nine-one-one."

He flew across the bus as she swung around the opposite corner and hurtled down the street for I-25. He dug into the bag and came out with the cell phone, then banged into the side wall as Harry careened around another corner onto the highway ramp.

He clutched the cell phone with one hand, grabbed the front railing with the other, stood in the stairwell, and slapped both eyeballs on the massive windshield.

Way up ahead, like a zillion miles and gaining ground, he could see the black exhaust and the dusty green of the old Chevrolet.

Twenty-Six

"He's getting away, he's getting away!"

"No, he's not. Dial nine-one-one."

Jim braced himself against the rail and punched in 911 on the cell phone. He got the police, but then had to go through another switchboard before he was connected to Trinidad.

"We're chasing a car down I-25 toward town."

"I beg your pardon?"

"He kidnapped my girlfriend! He's got her in the trunk of the car! We're chasing him down I-25."

"Okay, calm down. You heading north or south?"

He turned to Harry. "We heading north or—north. We're heading north."

"And what make is the car?"

"He's turning off," Harry said.

"He's turning off," Jim said into the phone. "He's heading into town."

"What exit?"

"Shit, I don't know."

"Careful, sir, you're going out live to our police cars."

"I don't know, I don't know. When we get up here I'll tell—fifteen. Exit fifteen."

"And what kind of vehicle is it?"

"It's a dirty old green Chevrolet with a smoking exhaust."

"We're on it. Tell us what vehicle you're driving."

"We're in a bus, like a Greyhound bus."

Silence from the other end.

"Hang on," Harry called. She swung off onto the ramp, blaring the horn as she took the corner and slowing to thirty for the stop sign before blasting through that.

Jim turned to her. "Where did he go?"

"He turned left. I got him," she said, and swung the big bus into a left-hand turn, blaring the horn all the way.

Cars screeched to a halt.

Big-eyed faces peered out through windshields.

And up ahead, through a haze of smoke, the green Chevrolet.

He turned and watched a street sign rush by. "We're heading up a hill on Colorado Avenue," he yelled into the phone. "You got that?"

"What kind of vehicle are you in?"

"I just told you, we're in a bus, like a Greyhound bus."

"Is this some kind of joke?"

He stared at the smoking exhaust and realized they might actually be gaining.

"We're in a big bus with Colorado State University written—oh shit, he's turning off."

"I told you once, sir, this is going out live on our scanner."

"I got him," Harry said.

He held on as Harry took the corner, the big vehicle leaning way over, and he said a silent prayer before it slammed back on all fours just in time to see—sonofabitch—the exhaust smoke trail around the next corner.

"He just made another—"

"Hang on," Harry said.

The big bus careened into the turn, horn blaring, bystanders scrambling onto the sidewalk as the bus swayed toward them.

"I think we just passed some college students." He caught sight of another street sign. "We're heading down the hill on Pine. Back into the center of town."

"Yes, sir, we're blocking off the Interstate."

He turned to Harry. "They're blocking off the Interstate."

She nodded, blaring her horn at the sparse Sunday traffic.

Jim watched as the thickening smoke, the car hardly visible through it now, took a right at the bottom of the hill. "Where the hell is he going?"

"I think he's panicking. Just trying to lose us. Probably doesn't realize you've got the police on the phone."

"Right." He turned back to the phone. "He's not taking the highway; he's heading downtown."

"Yes sir, we have him in sight from the Interstate."

He grabbed on as Harry swung them through a right turn and felt the wheels leave the ground, but the big bus righted itself and charged across a small bridge over the Purgatory River. "We're on Commercial Street—he's making another turn."

"I got him," Harry said, her air horn stopping cars in their tracks as she swung into a left turn.

Sonofabitch.

This was getting monotonous.

He watched Ju Jo's Pub rush by.

It would be a joke if Dodee wasn't trapped in the trunk.

If she was trapped in the trunk.

Sonofabitch, suppose she wasn't?

Suppose she had gone into the motel lobby and the wind had blown down the easel?

The Chevrolet grabbed another right and Jim held on, waiting for Harry to career after him.

Screw it.

If the police wanted to hang him for an innocent mistake, they could. Better that than take the chance the guy in the big cowboy hat would harm her.

They charged through the turn in time to see the black smoke take another right.

"He's gaining on us?"

Harry shook her head. "We're gaining on him. I can't understand it, unless his engine's breaking down. Hang on."

She had to slow way down, horn blaring, to make the sharp turn. She eased it around a white SUV and Jim grit his teeth for the crunch of a fender, then let out his breath when they passed and picked up speed down the street.

"We're on Main Street now," he yelled into the phone.

"Roger, we're heading up Animas," came the voice on the other end. "We'll block him off."

The Bloom Mansion and the Bacca House swept by.

"Is this thing ever going to end?"

Harry nodded toward the windshield. "I think his engine's blowing up."

Jim stared at the billowing exhaust smoke. More of it now. He heard sirens, but saw no police cars. Then the Chevrolet took another right corner, not finished yet, and Jim hung on for a controlled crash.

"We got him," the voice on the phone reported.

191

Harry swung to the left and then sharp to the right, sweeping through a wide turn.

"He just passed us heading for the information—holy shit."

A cop car straight in front of them, blaring its siren, filled with slack-jawed bug-eyed faces, yanked to the right while Harry jammed on her brakes, blasted her horn, bounced onto the sidewalk and sped down the hill without the screech of metal on metal.

"Holy shit, you are a bus."

"Careful, there," Jim said, unable to resist, "this is going out live on the police scanner."

"Yes, sir."

He turned to Harry. "It was a miracle you didn't smash into them."

She glanced at him and back to the road. "When this is over I have to go to the bathroom."

Now they were sandwiched between following sirens and the smokescreen ahead. They passed under the Interstate and out into one massive cloud of black smoke, then broke out into clear air.

What the hell?

And in front of them the green car coasted off left and bounced to a stop in front of the Dairy Queen.

The door flew open. Big aviator glasses popped their way. Harry slammed on her breaks and the guy tear-assed off between the gas station and the Dairy Queen as the tires screamed against the pavement, and the big bus shuddered, and shook, and finally staggered to a stop five feet from the dusty old Chevrolet.

Jim turned and looked at Harry looking back at him. "You can drive my race car anytime."

She swung open the door and he leaped down and raced to the car, grabbed the keys from the ignition, charged back to the trunk and yanked it up.

For one moment two panicked big blues stared up at him, mouth open, wheaten hair disarrayed, then her whole body relaxed in one long exhale, and she looked beautiful.

Thank you, God.

"You okay?" he asked, taking her hand.

"I think I am now."

He lifted her out and wrapped his arms around her.

"I thought I lost you, lady," he said, barely getting the words out as a sob betrayed the emotion that suddenly overtook him.

"I thought I lost me, too," she answered, openly sobbing with her head next to his.

"I love you, Dodee."

"I love you too, sweetheart."

He glanced around to see they were surrounded by police. "You guys did a great job," he said, choking back another sob.

"Where's the driver of the car?" asked a tall, swarthy man with a big star on his chest.

Jim pointed toward the Dairy Queen. "The last I saw he ran behind that building."

The man, brass name tag of Iglesias, badge that said Sheriff, waved his hands and four cops set off, splitting in twos to take each side. Iglesias turned a concerned face back to them, heavily lidded blue eyes contrasting with his swarthy complexion. "You okay, ma'am? You want to go to the hospital?"

Dodee shook her head. "I'm okay. I'm fine." Then she turned to Jim. "Hold me."

He put his arm around her waist and snuggled her in close.

"You sure you're okay, ma'am? We can get a doctor—"

"No, no." She wiped the tears from her cheeks. "I'm really okay, now. He said he didn't want to hurt me."

Iglesias hooked a big thumb in the general direction of the man's disappearance. "The driver?"

She nodded. "He said he only wanted to know where the falcon was." She turned to Jim. "He thinks you have the notebook. He knew you were there when the shaman was killed."

"Whoa," Sheriff Iglesias said. "Let's take this one step at a time. You say a shaman was killed?"

Jim held onto her as he explained the events in Denver, in between interruptions by Dodee as she added things he forgot, and by Iglesias's cell phone as the chase on foot wore on.

During one of the phone interruptions Dodee turned to Jim and mouthed, "The paintings?"

He shook his head.

They had enough real problems without going into that.

Iglesias pointed to the Chevrolet. "And how does this fit into the picture?"

"He said he was after the falcon," Dodee said. "Or the notebook, which is supposed to lead to the falcon."

"Sounds like this guy told you a lot. When did he do all this?"

"Not a lot. He said, 'Get in the trunk. I don't want to hurt you. We know your boyfriend picked up the notebook from the shaman. All we want to know is where the falcon is.'"

"We? He said, 'we'?"

She stared at him for a moment, then nodded. "Yes, I think that's right."

Iglesias squeezed his lower lip between thumb and forefinger, then picked up his cell phone. "Be alert. There could be someone out there picking him up." He turned back to Jim. "And this falcon thing is?"

"Something called the Mayan Falcon, made from gold with diamond eyes. It's supposed to be a legend, but apparently somebody thinks it's real."

"And this guy"—he pointed to the green car again—"just came out of the blue?"

Jim shrugged. "I think he's been following us since Friday when we were in Pueblo. I noticed him again this afternoon when we were sitting in Ju Jo's Pub. A tall man got in the car with him and then they drove off."

"Why didn't you call the police?"

Jim held out a hand in another shrug. "Because I couldn't figure out why he would be following a bunch of Elderhostelers, much less Dodee and me."

"What's this Elderhosteler business?"

So he went on to explain about Elderhostel.

The sheriff squeezed his lower lip between thumb and forefinger again. "You say there was another man? Was he in the car when you were chasing him?" Jim shook his head. "What did he look like?"

"Tall. I just got a brief glimpse of him." He turned to Dodee as the sheriff got another phone call. "You okay?"

"I think I'm all right now," she said, some of her old confidence kicking in.

Harry came out of the Dairy Queen spooning ice

cream from a Blizzard cup and Iglesias turned his half-mast eyes to her. "And how do you fit into this picture, ma'am?"

"I drive the bus," she said, pointing to it with her long spoon. "We're sponsoring, that is, Colorado State University is sponsoring this Elderhostel. When Jim said Dodee had been kidnapped, we took off after the car."

Iglesias cocked his head and stared at her. "You drove the bus?" She nodded. "You were the one swinging through the corners like that?"

She smiled. "I also drive race cars."

He gave his head half a shake. "I can believe it."

She turned to Jim and Dodee. "Can I get you guys a Blizzard?"

He looked at Dodee and shook his head when she did.

Harry turned to the tall man with the sheriff's star and gave him a smile with the full charm of her youthful face. "And how about you?"

"No thank you, ma'am, but thanks for the offer."

"Sheriff," Dodee said, "should I be worried this man will come back?"

"Nope. I'm sure he'll be spending the night in one of our luxury jail cells." He reached into his pocket and brought out a leather folder and extracted some business cards, handing one to Dodee and Jim. "You can give me a call later if it will settle your mind, or if you think of anything else that might help us." He turned to Harry and gave her a card and a smile. "And perhaps you can make use of one, ma'am."

"Hey, cool," Harry said, and returned the smile.

Jim flipped the card in his hand. "Are we going to be able to finish this trip?"

The lips turned down in the swarthy face. "I don't see why not. You say you're coming back through here in two days? On the slim chance we need you for something else, we'll catch you on the way back. It's not like someone has committed murder. Right?"

Twenty-Seven

Dodee snuggled close to him in the right front seat of the bus, but craned her neck toward Harry as she drove onto I-25. "Thanks for coming after me."

"No problem. Besides, I come through Trinidad a lot. Might be cool to know that sheriff."

Dodee nodded. "I noticed that look you gave him."

Big grin in the overhead mirror. "Did you see his eyes?" Harry checked the side mirror before pulling out into traffic. "Blue eyes in that dark-complexioned face . . . sexiest eyes I've ever seen."

"Bedroom eyes," Dodee said.

"What do you mean?" Jim asked. "Because they were half closed?"

"Yes, sweetheart."

"You mean if I hold my eyes"—he squinted so he had to tilt his head to look at her—"like I'm half asleep, that's sexy?"

"No, sweetheart, you do that and you'll walk into a wall. Besides, you're sexy enough as you are."

Harry glanced at them in the mirror. "What do we tell them when we get back?"

Dodee shrugged and turned to Jim.

"As little as possible," he said. "If no one saw us racing out, you can tell them you ate at a restaurant after gassing up, and we can say we slept in."

"I wish now I had taken your offer of a Blizzard," Dodee said. "Think we can still get some dinner?"

Jim nodded. "They have a restaurant at the motel. Worse comes to worst, I'll buy you dinner. I'll buy you both dinner. You sure you've recovered?"

"Right now. Something might hit me in the middle of the night. The guy said he wouldn't harm me, and I believed him. I think. He said they only wanted the falcon."

"So how were they supposed to get it?"

She shrugged. "Maybe that second man you talked about was going to call you and be the go-between."

Jim gazed out the windshield as they rolled up the long hill on I-25, the Best Western visible on the left. "And you said he knew I was there when the shaman died? How did he know that?"

"Everyone knows you were with the shaman. It was all over television."

He nodded and stared out the big window again.

She was right about that. All he had been thinking of was someone who had seen him first hand, like—

"Sonofabitch, Hank Adamo." He looked at Harry through the mirror. "Dr. Longtree said he was a special case. You hear anything about that?"

She shook her head.

"Suddenly it all falls into place. He was there with a handlebar mustache. Why did he shave it off? Why did he pretend he didn't know me? And why did he suddenly show up to join the Elderhostel? Because he thinks we know where the Mayan Falcon is."

"How does this fit with the man in the Chevrolet?" Dodee asked.

"An accomplice. The guy kidnaps you and Hank tells me to fork over the falcon or it's curtains."

Her big blues turned to him. "Curtains?"

"Well, you know what I mean." He thought back to Ju Jo's Pub. Could Hank Adamo have been the second man in the car?

Harry gave him a quick glance. "But isn't Hank taking a chance you'll be able to identify him after that?"

"Unless"—he nodded—"unless he wasn't going to leave us around to talk about it. Hell, he was probably the one that mystery writer saw up on the roof. And if he pushed the shaman off, what's the worry about croaking one or two more?"

"I don't want to hear this." Dodee shook her head. "Now I will have nightmares."

The bus turned off the highway and circled around to the Best Western.

"Let's call the police, sweetheart, and tell them."

"Tell them what? All we got is a lot of supposition."

Harry swung into the parking lot and pulled up beside the pool. "If you want the sheriff, I'd be glad to call him for you. I just happen to have a cell phone and his number."

Jim scanned the row of rooms and the parking area and saw no one. He checked his watch. "I wonder if they're finished with dinner."

"We have a lecture afterward," Dodee said.

"Okay, here's what we'll do. I'll find out his room number and see if he's there. If not I'll sneak in and—"

"How are you going to do that?" Dodee asked.

200

Harry swung around in her chair. "Can you pick a lock?"

"No, he can't."

"Wait a minute. Give me a moment to think." He turned toward the lobby. "I'll tell them I'm Hank and that I locked my key in the room. I'll get another key with the room number on it, and go in and check it out."

"And what are you looking for? Something that says, 'Hey, I'm a bad guy'?"

"Maybe I'll find a picture of him with his handlebar mustache. Or maybe he's got information about the Mayan Falcon. Wouldn't that tell us something? Then we call the sheriff."

"And if not?"

"One step at a time." He turned to her. "What I need you to do, Dodee, is stand in the doorway of the lobby and wave if you see Hank coming. And you," he turned to Harry, "give me three blasts on the horn if you see her wave."

"You want me involved?"

"After racing all over Trinidad, don't you want to see the outcome?"

Dodee shook her head. "Call the sheriff, sweet   "

"I'm checking the room out." He hopped up. "You want to help, fine. Otherwise, I'll go alone." He climbed down the stairwell and Harry opened the door.

He started for the lobby in the chill night air, evidence of Trinidad's higher altitude over that in La Junta. Dodee caught up and handed him a penlight. "You might need this."

"Okay," he said, pocketing it.

"Suppose they know you're not Hank Adamo?"

He faltered a step, then continued. "Longtree picked up the keys. They wouldn't know Adamo from Adam."

"Then suppose they just have a block of rooms and don't know what Hank's number is."

He looked down at her. "Why are you giving me such a hard time?"

"I'm just trying to cover the bases. Suppose they want to ask Longtree what room he assigned you?"

He nodded.

Yeah, suppose.

He grinned. "I'll just put my hand in my pocket and suddenly find I had my key all along."

"And they're going to believe that?"

"Yeah, I'll pretend I'm an old fart who's losing his memory."

Now she grinned.

He shook his head. "Don't say it."

He entered the lobby alone, dark wood walls, dining area off to the left, but a bigger room in the back where he heard the sound of cutlery on china and smelled roast beef that sent his mouth watering. A dark-haired woman with a pony cut stood filling out a card at the front desk.

"Hi, I left my key in the room. Hank Adamo. Would you have a spare I could borrow for a moment?"

"You know the room number?"

He shrugged. "I think I'm starting to lose it."

"Hank Adamo," she said, typing the name into a computer. "One twenty-two." She reached behind her, came up with the key, and handed it over.

"Thanks. I'll bring it right back."

He walked out into the cool air, flashed the plastic key to Dodee and continued on.

Room one twenty-two. Right next to their room. What were the odds of that? Or had Hank asked for it? Maybe to listen in on their conversations?

He rapped on the door with the back of his knuckle. No answer. He did it again and scanned the still-deserted parking lot. He knocked once more, louder, then checked the picture window.

The drapes were drawn, but he saw light at the bottom. So much for needing the penlight. He glanced around again, slipped the plastic key in, and clicked the lock. He cracked the door and listened. Only the guttural roar of a diesel climbing the grade out on I-25 disturbed the night.

"Hank?" he called through the crack in the door. Nothing. "Hank, are you in here?"

No Hank.

He shoved open the door, rushed in, closed it behind.

O-o-o-h shit.

Hank lay between bed and dresser. Eyes staring into eternity. A pool of blood had leaked out of a gash in his throat, filling the room with a coppery smell.

He yanked open the door, rushed out, and breathed deeply of the cool night air. He glanced around the parking lot again, then he shut the door and started for the bus.

Time to call in the sheriff.

Only, how would he tell him how he knew Hank was dead inside his room?

He whirled around, went back into the room, and parted the window drapes. Then he wiped off both door handles with his handkerchief and headed for the bus.

Dodee caught up with him as he reached it. "That was quick."

Harry opened the door. "What did you find?"

203

"Hank Adamo."

Dodee's eyebrows rose. "He was in—"

"Just his body."

Harry caught her breath. "A dead body?"

"Most bodies are. I think it's time to call in your sheriff."

"What do I tell him?" she asked, dialing.

"Tell him we discovered—tell him I think I saw a body in the room next door to us."

Harry talked into the phone, smiled once as she listened, then told the sheriff that Jim thought he had found a body. She snapped off the phone. "He's on his way."

Dodee touched Jim's hand. "How you going to explain you knew he was dead?"

"I saw him though the window."

He turned back to look at the room, then he jumped from the bus, hurried across the lot to it, and looked through the parted curtains.

Shit, all he could see were feet.

Just great.

He hurried back to the bus and looked from Harry to Dodee. "Okay, I saw his feet on the way to the room—"

"Hank's room is farther away from the lobby than ours."

"From the bus."

"So is the bus."

He took a deep breath and let it out. "Okay, I mistook his room for ours and peeked in to see who had turned on the light." He looked at her and she shrugged. "I saw the feet and hurried to the lobby to get his key."

"Which you asked for by his name."

"Shit. Well, I recognized Hank's shoes so I knew it was him. But when I got to the lobby I forgot the number—"

"Why didn't you tell them to call an ambulance?"

"I got to thinking maybe he was only lying there taking a snooze."

"On the floor?"

"Exercising. So before I got everyone upset, I got a key to check him out before calling an ambulance. After all, I am an EMT. When I opened the door and saw him, I ran to the bus"—he turned to Harry—"and had you call the sheriff." He came back to Dodee and palmed-up his hands. "How's that?"

"Slim story."

"You got a better suggestion?"

"Tell the truth?"

He looked back to the room.

But if he had innocently gone in to check on Hank Adamo, what would they say when his fingerprints weren't on the door handle?

He heard a siren out on I-25 and scanned the parking lot entrance.

Did he have time to rush across and grab it?

Right, and be frozen in the headlights when they slammed around the corner.

He turned to Harry. "What do you think?"

She nodded. "I'm with Dodee. The truth is cool."

He turned again to the room.

Oh sure, all he needed was to tell the police he only wanted to search the room when he found the body.

He turned back to see them both staring at him, and shrugged.

"Yeah, you're right. Whenever anybody gets into trouble with the police, it's because they try to make up a story that keeps falling apart. I'll just come out with it."

Except, how does he answer when they ask how come his fingerprints aren't on the door? And with the curtains now open, what happens if they ask why he entered the room when he could see Hank's feet?

Great, just absolutely great.

Twenty-Eight

He watched the police car pull into the lot and followed Harry and Dodee out of the bus.

Show time.

The car pulled up to them and the Sheriff got out on the passenger side, a second officer standing by the open door at the driver's side.

"We meet again," Iglesias said, smiling at Harry. "What's it about this time? Someone say they think they saw a body?"

Both Harry and Dodee turned to Jim.

He took a breath and let it out, then led the way to the room next to theirs. He slipped in the key and opened the door, suddenly realizing that his fingers were now on the handle.

Hoo-rah.

At least that part would check.

He stepped aside for the sheriff.

The swarthy Iglesias took one look inside, blinked, then turned to them. "Yes, sir, I'd say you definitely saw a body." He partially closed the door. "Don't touch a thing." He started for the car. "Rico," he called to the second

207

officer, "get on the horn, and get the state crime lab in here." He turned back when he reached the car. "Don't touch a thing."

Jim nodded and smiled at the others. "Don't touch a thing."

"What's so funny?" Dodee whispered.

"Tell you later."

With his fingerprints on the door handle, all his options were back in play: He had come out of the bus, had seen the light on . . . and take it from there.

Iglesias came back from the car, half-mast eyes taking them all in. "Want to tell me what went on here?"

Both Harry and Dodee turned to Jim again.

"When we got back here, I saw the light on and thought it was our room. We're next door," he said and motioned to it. "I peeked in, saw feet on the floor, realized it wasn't our room, and wondered if the guy was hurt."

Dodee's eyebrows arched and Harry's jaw dropped.

Ah, shit, he'd never get away with it. He took a deep breath and let it out.

"That's not actually what happened. This is a little complicated."

Now the brows arched above Iglesias's bedroom blues. "Take your time."

"On the way back up here I got to thinking, how did the guy in the Chevrolet—"

"Dick Stubbs."

"You caught him?"

"Not yet, but we have the license plates. Seems to fit the description you gave us. You were saying?"

"Right, on the way back we were trying to figure out how the guy—Dick Stubbs—knew I was there when the

208

shaman plunged off the roof. We got to thinking"—he caught Dodee's cocked head and folded arms—"I got to thinking, how did he know who I was? That's when I thought of Hank Adamo." He nodded toward the unlatched door. "I'm pretty sure I saw him there with a handlebar mustache. Then when he showed up a day late for the Elderhostel, I recognized him as the same guy without the mustache."

"You're going to get around to telling me about the body?"

He took a breath and let it out.

Here goes.

"Well, Dodee thought that Hank might not be the guy with the mustache and so I thought I'd check out his room before confronting him."

"You mean, like playing detective?"

He glanced at Dodee and back to Iglesias. "You want me to go on?" Iglesias nodded. "I went to the desk, told them I was Hank, and came back and opened the door. He was lying on the floor as you see him."

Two police cars and a state police van came swinging into the parking lot with an ambulance close behind. Iglesias waved them aside. "We'll take this up later. Don't go far."

"Can we get something to eat?" Harry asked, pointing toward the motel lobby and Iglesias nodded.

They crossed the parking lot as the Elderhostel group started out the door.

"Jim," Martin Martin said, "you missed a fine lecture."

"And a good dinner," Helen Martin said.

Dr. Ward Longtree rushed up. "What's going on here?"

"Hank Adamo is dead," Jim said. "The police are investigating it."

Max Solnim's magnified eyes glared out from behind his thick glasses. "Dead, you say?"

"How did it happen?" Claire Renquist asked.

Everyone crowded around now.

Jim held up his hands. "We probably shouldn't say anything. The police want to question us when they're finished."

"Question us?" Betty Baskins asked, pudgy face turning toward the police cars. "What for? I hardly knew him. John, you talked to him a lot."

The retired priest also shrugged. "No more than anyone else."

"Ladies and gentlemen, please," Dr. Longtree said, lifting his chin to take them all in. "Let us not speculate on what has transpired before we know the facts. May I ask you all to return to your rooms and when I ascertain what is happening I shall inform you." He turned to Harry as they dispersed. "You were not at dinner?" He looked at Dodee and Jim. "Where were you?"

Harry shook her head. "It's a long, long, long story." She motioned to the lobby door. "Think we can still get something to eat?"

"If not, I'm sure you can order from the menu." He motioned toward the police. "I better assess our chances of getting underway tomorrow."

They sat in the lobby dining room and the motel manager brought them each a plate of potatoes and gravy, green beans, rolls, and two pieces of chicken.

"I'll never be able to eat all this," Dodee said.

Jim picked up a knife and fork. "That's okay, you have a friend."

"You can eat at a time like this?"

"Maybe that's why I can eat, because I'm so nervous." He downed a forkful of potatoes. "How did I do with the sheriff?"

Harry looked up at him. "I thought for a minute you were going to tell him the story you made up."

"So did I," Dodee said.

He shook his head. "Give me a little credit. I knew better than to try that."

Iglesias came in as they finished and stared down at the table. "Looks like you all had a nice supper."

Jim nodded. "You want me to see if I can get you some?"

"No-o-o thanks." He pulled out his notebook, swung a chair around to the table. "Let's see if I got this right. You went into the deceased's room to see if he was the same person you saw when the shaman plunged to her death. Is that about it?" Jim nodded and Iglesias nodded back. "You know that's breaking and entering?"

Jim took in a deep breath and let it out. "I had a key."

"Oh, yes. See"—he pinched his lip between thumb and forefinger—"how come the desk clerk just gave you the deceased's key?"

"Dr. Longtree collected all our keys when we were unloading the bus and gave them to us outside. I figured she wouldn't know who was who, so I told her I was Hank Adamo."

The sheriff nodded and pinched his lip again. "The other thing is, why did you just barge into the room?"

Jim stared into the swarthy face, trying to read what Iglesias was getting at. "I didn't just barge in. I sort of sneaked in, and as soon as I saw him, I got the hell out."

"But why—"

"It didn't take a genius to see he was dead."

"No, why did you go in? You could see his feet on the floor and knew something was wrong. Or didn't you look in the window?"

Jim glanced at Dodee and Harry, then into the sheriff's half-mast blue eyes. "I tried, but the curtains were closed."

The half-mast eyes opened wide. "Someone opened the curtains?"

"I opened the curtains."

"Oh." The eyelids drooped. "Now why would you do that?"

He looked at Harry and Dodee again. No help there. When he turned back, Iglesias was still staring at him.

"I figured I was going to get into trouble for opening the door—like you said, breaking and entering—but we had already called you about the body, so I parted the drapes to pretend I saw him in the window. But then I decided just to tell the truth."

"Did you touch anything else?"

"No, well, the inside of the door handle, but I wiped that with my handkerchief. That's when I was thinking about making up a story."

Iglesias turned to Dodee. "And I suppose you can corroborate this?" She nodded and he turned to Harry. "You too?"

"Well," Harry bit her lip, "except we helped him decide to tell the truth."

Iglesias nodded a couple of times, glanced at some Elderhostelers passing through into the back dining room, and came back to Jim. "I should lock you up, you know that? I'd be justified. You know the only reason I'm not? Because the coroner set the probable time of death as the same time you all were terrifying my citizens, playing Richard Petty in a forty-foot bus."

Dodee leaned forward on the table. "Then the guy in the Chevrolet couldn't have done it."

The sheriff cocked his head at her. "You going to start playing detective now?" She placed both hands over her mouth. Iglesias smiled and shook his head. "Lord, save me from old folk."

"But if it wasn't the guy in the car—"

"Dick Stubbs."

"If it wasn't Dick Stubbs, it must be someone here in the . . ." She let it trail off.

Iglesias turned back to Jim. "You said you saw someone get in the car with Stubbs this afternoon."

Jim nodded. "He was tall."

"And?"

"And? That's it. I didn't get a look at him. Just saw him get in the car. I thought it might be Hank Adamo. I guess not."

"Anyone with you?"

"Dodee. And John Walsh."

The sheriff turned to her. "Tell me you got a good description of him."

"I didn't even notice the car."

"How about this John Walsh? Did he notice anything?"

Jim shrugged, then gazed into the half-mast eyes. "You still haven't caught Stubbs? He can tell you who it was."

"Well, thank you, sir, for that little bit of information." He turned as Longtree stopped by the table.

"I have managed to gather all our group in the back room, as you requested. Have you made a decision about us proceeding tomorrow?"

"You're the leader here?"

"Temporarily, yes. The coordinator took ill, but he plans on meeting us in Santa Fe tomorrow, should you allow us to leave."

Iglesias yawned and pushed back his chair. "First I need to talk to everyone on the trip. Let's see what develops before we tackle that." He got to his feet. "You three stick around in case I have any more questions. And you," he glared at Jim, "stay out of police business." He turned to go, then turned back, leaned his hands on the table, and gazed into Harry's eyes. "I didn't mean that crack about terrifying my citizens, although I don't think Richard Petty could have done as well in a forty-foot bus."

She grinned. "I'm cool."

He nodded and headed for the back room.

By the time the crime lab finished up with Hank Adamo, and Iglesias finished up with the Elderhostelers around two in the morning, there was no assurance they would be able to continue the trip.

Jim put his arm around Dodee and they headed for their room. "I think the sheriff should be concentrating on finding Dick Stubbs, rather than talking to us." He opened the door and followed her in. "He can tell them who the other man was."

"I'm not crazy about sleeping right next door to where Hank was killed," Dodee said.

"Want me to ask for a change of rooms?"

"I'm too tired to move, sweetheart."

He put his arms around her. "You okay? I mean from the kidnapping business."

She nodded against his chest. "Just tired."

"Maybe we should hold off our coming attractions until tomorrow night."

"You don't mind?"

"Frankly I don't know if I can stay awake until I can get into bed."

"Oh, damn. Today's Sunday?"

"Not anymore."

"You were supposed to remind me to call my girlfriend in Denver."

"Don't forget to call your girlfriend in Denver."

"You're flying out Thursday afternoon?"

"That's the plan."

"Because she wanted me to stay over with her. Remind me to call her tomorrow."

"Don't forget to call her tomorrow."

That got him a poke in the ribs.

He brushed his teeth, put the chain on the door, and crawled under the covers. She scooted over and nestled beside him, arm over his stomach.

"Comfortable?"

"Um," she said, voice drifting up from somewhere down near his armpit. "I'm just glad to be here next to you."

"Well, I'm glad your glad because I'm glad you're here."

"Lots of 'glads' in there. Thank you for saving me today."

"Thank Harry. She was the one who chased Stubbs all over kingdom come."

"Why would anyone want to kill Hank?"

"I thought we were so tired we were going right to sleep."

215

"Sorry." Quiet from down below for a few moments. "Erynn saw it coming."

That snapped his eyes open. "What do you mean?"

She popped up on one elbow. "Remember when we met this afternoon, when I told her I was twenty-nine and she told you not to let me travel off with someone? She knew it was going to happen."

"Oh, come on, Dodee, that's so nebulous—"

"And she said Hank was walking around under a black cloud. Remember?"

He didn't answer; no way to win that argument.

She rested her head back on his arm. "It keeps coming back to the shaman and the missing notebook, doesn't it? And the Mayan Falcon. That's what Stubbs was after."

He stared into the darkness. No way to win that argument either.

He turned toward the door, tempted to get up and check the night chain, but he knew he had set it.

The sooner they got out of Trinidad, the better.

Except, it wasn't Stubbs who killed Hank Adamo.

While they had been racing around town, that guy had been right here. Next door.

But if he wanted the falcon, why kill Adamo?

Twenty-Nine

In the end, since all the Elderhostelers had alibis for the time Hank Adamo had been murdered, Iglesias allowed them to continue on the trip. But because of the late hour they got to bed, it wasn't until mid-morning that Harry drove out of the parking lot, turned south on I-25, and pointed the bus's headlights up the long climb to the top of the pass to Santa Fe.

Dr. Longtree blew into the mike.

"Ladies and gentlemen, it's unfortunate that the events of last night will color our sojourn here, for truly Trinidad is a pleasant little village. People are settling here from Santa Fe because Trinidad is more idyllic and economical, and has a thriving art colony. Would that we had more time to view it."

Jim shook his head.

The whirlwind, Indy-Five-Hundred-Tour had been enough for him. They still hadn't caught Stubbs, not to mention that little matter of Hank Adamo.

He heard a small tinkling and turned to see Erynn Sunflower sitting across the aisle in a new New Age peasant dress. "Colorful duds."

"Thank you. I like to wear some browns and greens to keep me in touch with Mother Earth." She gazed down at it. "And, of course, red for passion." She bit her lip and leaned across the aisle. "Did I tell you I have a twenty-one-year-old lover?" she whispered, and blushed, not something he often saw in a fifty-five-plus face. "He's very romantic." He glanced at her dress again. "And then, of course, I have to counterbalance the passion with the cool blue of intellect so things don't get out of control."

"That's more than I wanted to know and was afraid to ask. Except for the bells in the hem?"

"That's to make a joyous sound to encourage any spirits who might be hovering nearby to come and communicate." She leaned forward to look past him to Dodee. "Have you thought anymore of what we talked about?"

Jim turned to Dodee, who smiled and shrugged.

What the hell had they been talking about?

"Santa Fe would be a good place," Erynn said. "Ancient spirits running around there. Think about it."

"I will."

He stared at Dodee, but she avoided his gaze.

"What do you think about Hank Adamo?" Erynn asked. "You said there was something strange about him."

"Me?" Jim stared at her. "You were the one who said he had a black cloud hanging over him."

Dr. Longtree blew into the mike again.

"Ladies and gentlemen, because of our delayed departure we shall journey straight into Santa Fe, with stops for restroom facilities and our box lunch. By taking this route we shall miss the planned visit to Rancho Rayado and the St. James Hotel in Cimarron, sometimes referred to as the Ghost Hotel."

Jim smiled at that.

Talk about ancient spirits running around Santa Fe, what would Erynn have done had they stopped at the Ghost Hotel?

"Perhaps on the return journey," Dr. Longtree continued, "time will allow for the possibility of detouring to visit those localities. However, we will make one fast stop right up here." The bus slowed as it reached the mountain top and pulled off onto a small side road. "Ladies and gentlemen, this is Raton Pass, the last major hurdle on the trail to Santa Fe. Reaching here was a prodigious achievement for those making the trek. Once they made it over this rise, it was, if you'll forgive the expression, all down hill."

Groans and laughter from the Elderhostelers.

Jim helped Dodee from the bus into a fair breeze blowing across the pass, but warmed by the mid-September sun. Clouds hung in the high sky, which would mean rain back in Calvert County, Maryland, but here?

They followed the crowd to an overlook of loose gravel with only a two-by-four separating it from a gully of grass and small pines sloping back down toward Trinidad. Off on the horizon he could see the twin Spanish Peaks, and Fisher's Peak off to the east.

Dodee put her arm around him. "Pretty, isn't it?"

"What was that business with Erynn?"

"What bus—"

"The business in Santa Fe where the spirits-are-stronger business."

"Erynn wants to see if we can make contact with the Indian shaman. She thinks we won't get any peace until we find out what the shaman's spirit wants."

"Oh boy." He shook his head. "And she's going to help us?"

"It couldn't hurt, sweetheart."

"That's bullshit, Dodee. If we start fooling with that stuff, the notebook, and the Mayan Falcon, we'll only end up in major trouble."

She turned and put her hands on his shoulders. "I think trouble has already found us, and I think I know why Hank Adamo was killed."

He waited for her to go on, but the big blues just stared at him. He threw out his hands. "Well, you going to tell me?"

"I'm trying to figure out if I should."

"And I'm trying to figure out if I should take you across my knee and spank you."

She smiled. "Later, sweetheart."

"Damnit, Dodee—"

"I don't think they meant to kill Hank Adamo. I think the killer was looking for something and Hank came back to the room at the wrong time."

"The Mayan Falcon? What makes you think Hank knew—"

"I think the killer was in the wrong room."

That popped his eyes open. "What makes you think the killer meant to enter our room?"

"Think about it, sweetheart. He and Stubbs were looking for the Mayan Falcon. With me kidnapped and you chasing me, he had the room to himself."

"That doesn't work. I don't think Stubbs would have touched you if he'd had any idea I'd be tear-assing after him."

"No, I think the plan was for Stubbs to kidnap me and

then his partner would contact you about the notebook or the falcon, but when he saw you take off after me, he thought he had a clear shot at ransacking our room. The only problem was that he entered the wrong room."

Dr. Longtree took over the PA system again when they got underway. "Ladies and gentlemen, when we arrive in Santa Fe we will be lodging at the Plaza Resolana, a Study and Conference Center belonging to the Presbyterian Church. The facility is one we could afford on our limited budget and still be close to the Plaza downtown. All of you will have private bathrooms, that is, commodes and sinks, but some will have to walk down the hall for showers. No alcoholic beverages are allowed and there are no televisions."

"Damn," Jim said, "there goes my Redskins game."

He stared out the window as they ground out the miles, checking out the grassy plains for something of interest and finding only prairie falcons sitting on telephone poles, mule deer and cattle grazing, prong horns prancing about, and a lone golden eagle pouncing on an unseen meal in a wash by the side of the road. The scenery picked up as the afternoon wore on and they neared the city, pine trees and occasional houses breaking up the monotony, and traffic increased as well; they were no longer king of the road. They came in on a street called Paseo de Peralta and passed by some statues of elephants, ostriches, and a water buffalo on a grassy corner, oddly out of place in Santa Fe. Then Harry circled a traffic island and brought the bus back to the animal statues, turned right and pulled into a parking lot next to a tan adobe building with a long veranda and painted fleur-de-lis crosses on its wood trim. A bronze, engraved sign embedded in its adobe wall announced:

PLAZA RESOLANA, STUDY AND CONFERENCE CENTER. Five wide brick steps with large marigold-filled ceramic pots at the ends led up to the veranda. Two heavy wooden doors at the entrance had odd-sized rectangular windows so placed that they gave the impression of Native American symbols. One of them flew open and a paunchy man with sand colored hair strutted out. A wide grin split his ruddy face and Federico Rudavsky, Ace, threw wide his arms.

"Welcome to Santa Fe. What kept ya?"

"Hey, look who's back with us," Narcisco Ramos called, a cigarette already lit in his mouth.

Ace waddled down the steps and the Elderhostelers gathered around like he was a long-lost friend.

"Welcome back."

"How you feeling?" ·

"When did you get here?"

"I got in late last night. Came through Trinidad yesterday and looked for the bus, but I couldn't find you."

"Yeah, well," Jim said, "that's because Harry and I were racing in the Trinidad Grand Prix." He told him the story of Dodee's kidnapping with added bits from Harry and Dodee spicing the narrative, and ended with Hank Adamo's murder.

Ace turned down his lips and shook his head. "That's terrible. I hardly knew the man before I got sick, but you hate to see something like that happen."

"It made for an exciting evening," Jim said.

Harry nodded. "With all the horns and sirens blaring and the twirling lights of the police cars, I can't believe you didn't see us."

Ace shrugged. "Well, you're all here and tomorrow's a new day. Like I said, welcome to Santa Fe." He raised one hand filled with room keys. "I've got your room assignments when you're ready."

Jim helped Harry unload the luggage, then picked up their bags, turned to the building, and stopped short at the sight of the small letters at the bottom of the bronze sign.

Great, just great.

A PROGRAM CENTER OF GHOST RANCH—PRESBYTERIAN CHURCH (U.S.A.)

Ghost Ranch.

Erynn and Dodee didn't need to go to the Ghost Hotel.

They had the Ghost Ranch right here in Santa Fe, right where Erynn claimed a lot of ancient spirits were running around.

Just when he thought he was leaving it behind, here he was, back in the world of oooOOOooo.

Thirty

He followed Dodee down a long hall in the Plaza Resolana, cut right in a cross hall halfway down, and came to their door at the intersection of another long hall, and entered a cheery room with two double beds separated by a night table and lamp, a desk and hanging closet opposite, and a small lavatory into which Dodee immediately disappeared.

Jim parted the drapes, flooding the place with late evening sun, and looked out at the animal statues.

"Why do you always open the drapes?" Dodee asked, drying her hands as she came out of the bathroom.

"I like natural light. I'll close them if you like."

She shook her head, came up to stand beside him, fluffed her hands through his hair, then pulled his head down to hers.

He kissed her soft lips, her tongue welcoming his, touching and caressing, triggering a response down below. He broke off the kiss. "You're saying you want me to close the drapes?"

"Love in the afternoon?"

"Like the movie with Audrey Hepburn and Gary

Cooper. Except the afternoon's over. How about love in the evening? Or, more accurately, love in the transition from evening into night. How does that sound?"

"Never make it as a movie title, sweetheart." She looked at her watch. "We have a choice of running a race now and perhaps not making it to dinner, or waiting until bedtime for a more casual stroll in the park."

"Later. I might be up for a casual stroll, but I'm not ready for a race at this altitude."

"How about huff and puffs with Max in the morning?"

He glanced at the ceiling and let out a breath.

"You know," she said, "you don't have to go with him."

"Yes, I do. The guy could croak out there with no one around to give him CPR. At ninety-three, he's a heart attack ready to happen. I think."

They went down to dinner and tagged onto the end of the chow line as it reached the buffet table, leaving no doubt that had they tried for a foot race, they would have gone hungry.

Jim loaded a plate up with mashed potatoes, broccoli, and meatloaf. He turned to get a salad and bumped into a man coming the other way—with the guy at six foot three, two hundred and sixty pounds, Jim felt like a sports car meeting an eighteen-wheeler.

"Excuse me," he said to a multicolored, patchwork-quilt shirt.

"No, excuse me," the man said in a deep, gravely voice, take James Earl Jones and throw in a bucket of beach sand. "Didn't know you were going to turn around."

"I thought I was last in line."

The man gave him a yellow-toothed smile, wrinkling

225

the laugh lines around bushy eyebrows. "I shouldn't have been following so close."

Jim picked up the salad, added a piece of coconut cake, and wound through tables to sit next to Dodee, across from Ace and—sonofabitch—Erynn Sunflower.

"Ace was just telling us that they still haven't caught Stubbs," Dodee said.

"How did you find that out?"

"Harry talked to the Trinidad sheriff," Ace said.

"You mean she called him?"

Ace shrugged.

Dodee smiled. "Or he called her. There seems to be a little chemistry there."

"May I join you?" interrupted the James-Earl-Jones-with-a-bucket-of-sand voice. The big man gave them a yellow-toothed grin. "Everything seems to be full up."

Ace motioned to the empty seat next to him. "Be my guest."

He sat down and pulled the napkin-wrapped cutlery out of the pocket of his patchwork-quilt shirt. "Dining room's crowded tonight." A prominent wart lived on one side of his chin and another by a deformed right ear. "I guess it's from the bus that pulled in this afternoon."

"Ah," Ace said, shaking his finger, "that would be us. We're here on an Elderhostel, studying the Santa Fe Trail. I'm the coordinator, Ace Rudavsky."

"Aaron Burr." He gave them another yellow-toothed smile. "No relation to the historical figure."

When he turned his head Jim saw that his left ear was deformed as well, as if in time past he had been a boxer or a football player, big and broad enough to be either, eroded now with a paunch in middle age.

"You here on business?" he asked.

"Sort of. I'm a Presbyterian minister."

So much for the football-slash-boxer theory.

Erynn stabbed a stalk of broccoli. "Dodee, did you see what was on the sign out front?"

She shook her head.

"This is the program center of Ghost Ranch. Can you imagine a more portentous omen for trying to get in touch with our spiritual friend?"

"Spiritual friend?" Aaron Burr's bushy eyebrows perked up. "That sounds like something in my field."

Jim shook his head. "You don't want to hear this."

But the bushy brows remained arched as he settled his gaze on Erynn.

"Well," she said, "an Indian woman, a shaman, was killed last Tuesday and ever since she's been turning up in Dodee's paintings. I believe she's trying to make contact with Dodee."

"What are you planning to do?" Aaron asked. "Hold a séance?"

She nodded and fingered the large crystal hanging from her neck. "Dodee was painting at the time of the shaman's death. And Jim was with the shaman's body right after it. I think her spirit made the leap from Jim to Dodee, because she's a receptor, but it is Jim she really wants to contact."

Jim cut a piece of meatloaf with his fork. "There's got to be a logical reason for her popping up in the pictures."

Aaron turned to him. "Are we talking about the shaman who tumbled off a roof in downtown Denver last week?"

Ace jerked his wrist around and looked at his watch. "Gotta go." He stood up, clinked his glass, and called out. "Listen, folks, all of you with the Elderhostel. Listen up.

227

We've been asked to help out the kitchen crew, so please take your tray to the back, scrape your plate into the garbage, and place your dishes in the racks. We have a lecture in fifteen minutes in the room just past the desk. Be there or be square."

Dodee turned to Jim. "I have to go back to the room first."

"Go ahead. I'll take care of the trays."

He carried them back to the kitchen, placed everything in their proper place and waited for her on a curved couch formed to an inside wall separating lobby from the entrance. Eventually she came back up the hall.

"What kept you?"

"I needed to go to the bathroom and I tried to call my girlfriend. No answer."

They entered the conference room and sat in the back as Ace introduced a teacher at the Santa Fe Community College and a recognized historian of the city, Oliver Alnan, square shoulders, red hair tied in a ponytail, and flat stomach covered by a striped yellow-and-navy rugby shirt.

Alnan lectured them on Santa Fe, getting them to pronounce it by its historical name of Santa Fee. He told them that the Spanish had arrived about 1609, about ten years before the English arrived on the east coast. He also gave them a different picture of Kit Carson, a legend in his own time, but whether he was hero or villain depended upon which side of the cloth you viewed him.

"From the Navajos' prospective, he was an army general who had orders to shoot every male Navajo over the age of fourteen, and between eighteen sixty-two and sixty-three, he brutally scorched the tribe, much like Sherman did on his march to the sea. The Navajo people are filled with a hate for him that lasts to this day."

Alnan fingered his red ponytail, as if deciding how to proceed.

"History is never painted in black and white. For instance, archeologists in the nineteen-thirties came upon what possibly may be the ancient remains of the first men who came across the Bering Sea land bridge to this continent. They called them the Anasazi, meaning 'the ancient ones,' and carted their bones back to the Smithsonian Institute in Washington for further study."

He nodded his head as he looked over the room.

"But, hey, no one asked the Native Americans how they felt about it. They regarded the Anasazi as their ancestors. How would you like your mother's grave dug up and everything she was buried with, including her bones, carted off to the Smithsonian Institute? So you know what the Navajos did? They sent a contingent to Washington and demanded the bones be returned to them so they could be re-buried with dignity and respect."

Alnan took a drink of water and fingered his ponytail again.

"The Smithsonian weighed scientific research against the religious beliefs of Native Americans and in the end, good sense prevailed. This led to the Native American Grave Protection and Repatriation Act, which is now law. The bones were returned home a couple of summers ago, to a reservation some fifty or so miles down the road, and—in a spot known only to the tribal elders—placed in a common grave."

At the end of the evening, Alnan told them he would lead a walking tour through Santa Fe the next day.

Jim and Dodee signed up and then strolled hand in hand back to their room. He put on the night chain and while she went into the bathroom, he slid her black sketchbook case under the bed and sat back against the headboard. He suddenly remembered the Washington Redskins had played that night and wondered how they made out. He had never considered himself a big television man, but now in a place where they didn't have one, he realized how much he had grown used to it. Instant news from all over the world, like the score of the Redskins game.

Dodee came out in a yellow nightshirt emblazoned with DOGS HAVE MASTERS, CATS HAVE STAFF.

"You telling me you have a cat?" he said.

"Uh-huh. One of the undiscovered things you don't know about me."

She sat on the bed next to him, put her arms around his neck, and gave him a long, sweet kiss that tasted of toothpaste. She smelled of soap and vanilla perfume, and under the nightshirt was only warm skin.

"Don't be too long, sweetheart."

And she gave him another kiss to hurry him along.

Five minutes later—bladder emptied, teeth brushed, face shaved and splashed with PS For Men—he reentered the darkened bedroom and started to crawl under the covers when he heard her giggle behind him.

"You're in the wrong bed, sweetheart."

He spun around and climbed under the cool sheets to a spot her body had warmed, and encircled her in his arms. And they went on that casual stroll they had talked about, unhurried, with easygoing familiarity, like comfortable old shoes, until they suddenly picked up the pace, breaking out into a mad footrace for the finish line, arriving in a dead heat, struggling to catch their breath, then easing down with soft moans into each other's arms.

"Thank you, sweetheart," she whispered sometime later.

"Any time." He stared at the ceiling for a moment. "Well, not any time, but any time I'm up to it."

She entwined herself around him.

"Are you perfectly comfortable?"

"I'm getting there."

"Don't say anything."

"About what?"

"About anything." He caressed her breast. "You're forever saying something, like about who might have killed somebody, and then falling off to sleep and leaving me wide awake to think about it."

She snuggled in closer. "There's nothing to discuss. Not until they can track down Stubbs in Trinidad."

He nestled her head on his chest, and closed his eyes. There was nothing to discuss. Like she said, not until Stubbs showed up in Trinidad.

Except Stubbs was probably long gone out of Trinidad.

Hank Adamo's killer had probably picked him up and lit out while everyone was running around at the motel.

Except, where had they lit out for?

He popped open his eyes.

If Stubbs and the killer still believed he and Dodee had the notebook, if not the actual Mayan Falcon, and knew of their itinerary, guess where they had probably lit out for?

Can you say Santa Fe?

Thirty-One

He awoke to the sound of tapping on the door.

What the hell—oh, shit.

It came again and he disengaged from Dodee's body and eased out of bed.

How the hell had Max found his room number?

He opened the door and peeked through the night chain gap at Max Solnim in a yellow cap and thick glasses, wrinkled face beaming.

"Ready for huff and puffs?"

"Meet you in the lobby in five minutes."

"You got it."

Jim put on the shorts, shirt, and socks he had worn on the morning walks, starting to smell ripe now—major laundry time needed—pulled on his walking shoes, grabbed his water bottle, crept out of the room and headed down the hall.

This was getting to be a regular pain in the butt.

He should let the old bastard go out and croak by himself.

But it did have one redeeming grace when it was over: The residue of stress from the previous day *had* been sweated away.

He found the old bastard limbering up on the front veranda as birds flittered and twittered about the trees and the veranda's roof beams, happy to be awake and alive.

Screw 'em.

They charged down the street, across the Paseo de Peralta, and turned right, and by the time they reached the end of the long block that curved around to another street, Jim was barely keeping up.

How high was Santa Fe? He felt like he was climbing Mount Everest.

He took a swallow from his water bottle to ease the dry air coursing through his lungs.

Meanwhile old bastard Max strolled jauntily along.

Ha, maybe it was a prelude to a coronary. What the heck, at ninety-three, hadn't he overstayed his visit to the planet?

Or maybe, with a little luck—please God—he would misstep off a curb, break his ankle, knock off his thick glasses, and an eighteen-wheeler highballing for Las Vegas would flatten him.

Max turned to him. "Hey, found out some interesting stuff on the Mayan Falcon."

"You did?"

"Hooked up my laptop and went out on the net. Show you when we get back."

"Watch your step on the curb."

They rounded the round corner of the long block, skirted past the animal statues, and turned into the Plaza Resolana's driveway with Jim's butt scraping the asphalt as he began his cool-off.

At least, after a shower, he'd be ready to conquer the day.

He gazed up at Narcisco Ramos standing at the top of the stairs, puffing away on a cigarette.

On the other hand, there was something to be said for just muddling through.

He staggered inside, found the coffeemaker, poured himself a cup.

"Morning, Jim," John Walsh said, sitting alone at a four-person table in the lobby.

Jim lumbered over and flopped into a chair beside the retired priest.

"I'll be a sonofabitch if I understand it." He held up his hand. "Sorry there, John—"

"What don't you understand?"

"We just went for a forty-minute power walk and I was puffing like a ten-pack-a-day chain-smoker."

"It's seven thousand feet above sea level here. A lot different from Maryland."

"But Max was hardly winded. And he's ninety-three. And from Massachusetts."

John flicked his dark eyebrows and grinned. "He's from Massachusetts, yes, but for the last fifteen or twenty years he's lived in Cloud Croft, New Mexico, nine thousand feet above sea level. He's used to this altitude."

Jim stared in John's light blue eyes. "I'm gonna kill the old bastard."

"After what happened to Hank Adamo, you might not want to say that too loudly."

Max popped out from around the corner. "Here we are." He set a paper on the table and dropped his yellow cap on it. "Let me get a cup of coffee."

Jim lifted the cap and studied it, titled "Mayan Falcon" across the top, but the rest appeared to be written in chicken scratches or Indian sign language. "What is this, secret code? Hieroglyphics?"

"I told you it first surfaced in Mexico, which, of course, is where you'd expect to find a Mayan artifact." He plopped down in a chair next to Jim with a cup of decaf. "Except, and this is strange, the statue has a remarkable likeness to a prairie falcon, not something normally found in Mayan territory."

"What does that mean?"

"Don't know." He took a sip of coffee and picked up his paper. "It was s'posed to be sent to Spain, but the Conquistador who found it, Don de la Hara Guzmon, was murdered and the falcon disappeared. The next time it showed up someone had carried it up the old Camino Real to Santa Fe." Max looked up and grinned. "Right here in River City."

"It's still here?" John asked.

He shrugged. "The man who was s'posed to have it"—he ran his finger down the paper—"this is all conjecture, you understand. Stuff of legend, but if it is, it's got research legs. Anyway, the man who was s'posed to have it, who brought it up the Camino Real, one Don Juan de Peralta, a descendant of Don Pedro de Peralta, the founder of Santa Fe, was murdered one night in his sleep and the falcon went missing." Max's crevassed face came up, the watery blue eyes magnified by his thick glasses. "So far so good."

Jim rubbed his chin. "That's it?"

"That's what we already knew." Max sipped from his coffee. "The next mention I came up with had to do with the Santa Fe Trail. A gold prairie falcon with two diamond eyes was mentioned in a trading invoice that left on a caravan for St. Louis a hundred years later. This invoice is s'posed to be in the Palace of Governors Museum downtown. Whatever, the wagon train never made it. We have to assume that it was lost in an Indian raid by the Cheyenne or the Apaches, because the next time we have anything that even resembles it is during the Indian Wars. A young army lieutenant from Georgia, one Beauregard St. Simian, was reported to have taken an artifact from a Navajo chieftain. This is not fact, but what is? On the other hand, we do know Lieutenant St. Simian resigned his commission about this time, unusual in a West Point graduate."

Jim blinked. "You're saying he had the falcon?"

Max's lips turned down and he nodded. "No doubt in my mind."

"So what happened then?" John Walsh asked.

Max shrugged.

"That's it?" John's eyebrows shot up. "After leading us on?"

Max touched his finger to the side of his nose and winked as some Hispanic women dressed in uniforms entered the lobby and headed for the kitchen. He waited until their voices faded, and lowered his squeaky voice. "That's it, for now." He folded up his paper. "You know, when I first heard about this, I thought it was made of the same dream stuff as the Lost Dutchman Gold Mine, but if Moondance Wolf and possibly Hank Adamo died because of it, maybe we shouldn't be bantering this around."

Jim nodded. "You going to keep searching?"

Max shook his head. "I might poke around the Palace of Governors while I'm here in Santa Fe, but after that I've got my own research to do." He stood up and put on his yellow cap. "If I come up with something, and don't see you tonight, I'll catch you for huff and puffs in the morning."

Jim watched him saunter down the hall and turned back to John Walsh. "Sonofabitch. Did I just get sucked into another power walk?"

The retired priest grinned. "I'd say you've been had."

He went back to his room, silently grabbed some fresh clothes, and hopped into one of the common showers. When he came out, squeaky clean and wide awake, he was ready to conquer the world, provided he had backup from Genghis Khan's Golden Horde. He returned to his room and found an apparition standing before him, tasseled wheaten hair, squinty blues, limp arms hanging zombie-like at her sides.

"Coffee?"

"Right."

He pulled on a T-shirt, barefooted it down to the lobby, and returned with two coffees, sipping one along the way.

She took the coffee in her right hand, wrapped her left arm around his neck, and gave him a long kiss. "Thank you."

"Welcome to the land of the living, lady." Then he clenched his teeth. "You know where that old bastard is from?"

"Which old bastard would this be, sweetheart?"

"Max Solnim. He's from Cloud Croft, New Mexico." Her eyebrows arched. "That's nine thousand feet above sea level. He's used to even more altitude than this. No wonder he was be-bopping around while I was ready to croak."

She smiled. "One of life's major mysteries solved."

"Speaking of mysteries." He told her what Max had found out.

"So maybe the Mayan Falcon really exists?"

"Maybe."

He gave her another kiss and held her close, staring over her shoulder to the world outside the window.

And maybe Max was right. Maybe they shouldn't be bantering the Mayan Falcon around. Maybe someone would end up thinking it existed, and maybe figure he and Dodee had the clues to find it.

And while he was stretching a string of maybes together, maybe he better keep his eyes open as they strolled around downtown.

Thirty-Two

After breakfast, he and Dodee followed the same path along the Paseo de Peralta that he and Max had taken earlier that morning, only this time they moseyed along hand in hand, down to a statue at the end of the block where they found John Walsh.

"You two taking this walking tour?"

"Why we're here," Jim said. "You ever been in Santa Fe before?"

"Once, years and years ago, but I don't remember all that much."

Dodee hugged herself in her short-sleeved blouse. "I think I should have brought a jacket."

"It will warm up before we're finished," John said.

Jim walked over to the statue.

One man sat on a horse, wide-brimmed hat turned up on one side, Aussie-style, with an outstretched arm pointing off in the distance. A second man, also with a wide-brimmed hat, stood beside the horse, hand on a walking stick, looking in the direction the first man was pointing.

Some more Elderhostelers drifted up, eleven in all by the time Oliver Alnan showed, ten minutes late. He started out by telling them about the statue of Don Pedro de Peralta, the guy on horseback, and informing them that Peralta's standing friend actually held a Spanish yardstick. The statue depicted them laying out the town plaza.

"But guess what?" Oliver Alnan said. "Don Pedro is pointing off into nowhere; it's the horse's rear end that's pointing downtown. That's a little inside joke here."

Alnan led them around a half-circle corner to South Federal Street, then held them up.

"By the way," he said, pointing back in the direction of the statue, "if you're wondering why the road curves here, and down at the other end of the block it does the same thing, it's because at one time this was a huge racetrack where they bet on horses. Isn't that interesting?"

Alnan led them in and out of the post office and into the Federal Courthouse showing them murals depicting Santa Fe, of more interest to Dodee than to Jim.

When they came out, he gazed back down the street to see a tall, broad man hurry into the post office, and realized only after he was gone that it was the Presbyterian minister from the night before, Aaron Burr, wearing the same multicolored patchwork-quilt shirt.

They moved on to City Hall, which was built on an ancient Indian holy site, and continued downtown to the Palace of Governors, now a museum where they kept some of the old city records, one of the few buildings still standing after the Indians kicked out the Spanish for thirteen years. Around the corner, but still part of the museum, he showed them a covered walk where only Native Americans were allowed to display and sell their goods, and they even had to be licensed, ensuring that everything was handcrafted and authentic.

Alnan led them across the Plaza marking the heart of the city to the End of the Trail Monument.

"This is the last of some two hundred signs the Daughters of the American Revolution have placed, marking the trail. For all those who started out from St. Louis or Franklin, Missouri, to follow the Santa Fe Trail, enduring the hardships of open prairie, cold and heat, breakdowns and Indian raids, this signaled the end of the nine-hundred-mile trek; their goal had been won."

He led them south along Old Santa Fe Trail Street, the actual street where the Trail came in, pointing out that to go east to Missouri they first had to go south to get around the mountains.

From there he took them to the Loretto Chapel, a narrow, high, gray-stoned gothic-styled building with a statue perched atop its A-shaped roof.

"I remember this place," John Walsh whispered as they entered the building with its high, vaulted ceiling.

Alnan gathered them around a cordoned-off circular staircase, which continued two full turns up to a balcony at the top.

"This is no longer a church building. At one time it was a chapel where girls going to Catholic school across the street came to Mass. The school burned down in nineteen sixty-seven. But when they were building this chapel in the eighteen-seventies, they realized they didn't have a way to get from the nave to the choir loft without losing a lot of pew space, which they couldn't afford. They thought about using ladders, something the Native Americans in the region had used for years, but while it might have worked for boys and men, for girls and nuns in skirts and habits it wasn't an option. So the nuns did what all nuns do when they have a problem, they prayed."

Jim eased around to the other side of the stairway and caught sight of the big, football-lineman figure of Aaron Burr slipping out the exit.

What was that about?

Was the guy following them?

Or was he getting paranoid?

"What they did," Alnan said, "was pray a novena, a prayer that's said every day for nine days, and on the night of the ninth day, a carpenter appeared who said he was the one who would build them the staircase. He worked on it for four months and what he ended up with was this spiral staircase, making two full turns, without a central column, and no handrails. The handrails you see here have been added in the renovation, but the original stairs depressed under the weight of the climber and then sprung back into place. This staircase has been studied by scientists and engineers and been the subject of many television shows, all trying to figure how it was done. Over two hundred thousand people visit this staircase every year. It is a remarkable piece of woodwork from an engineering, mathematical, and scientific standpoint. If you call it a miracle, so much the better."

John Walsh raised his hand. "Wasn't there also something about the wood?"

"Oh, right." Alnan nodded and pointed to him. "For many years no one knew what kind of wood it was, and only recently, after some researchers did a molecular test on it, did they discover it was made of spruce, but of a species of spruce no one can find, not here or anywhere else in the world. And they can't find out anything about the carpenter. He never charged the nuns anything for it, there were no outstanding bills in the local lumberyards, and no one thought to find out the carpenter's name before he left, and he was never seen again. Isn't that interesting?"

They went out into the bright high-altitude sunshine and started up the street.

"You saw this before?" Jim asked John Walsh.

"I told you I had been here many years ago."

Dodee slipped her arm under Jim's. "Did it already have handrails on then?"

"Oh, yeah. Just like it is now. From what I read, the nuns always believed it was St. Joseph who came as an itinerant carpenter to answer their prayers."

"You believe that?" she asked.

He shrugged. "But I do know that if He decided to send St. Joseph down here to build a staircase that has all the experts stumped, He's not going to get an argument from me."

They continued on, crossed Alameda Street, and Alnan stopped them to look down on a small, flowing stream.

"This is the Santa Fe River. I know to you from the East this is only a creek, but out here where any water is precious, this is called a river, and it is this water that got Santa Fe established."

Jim gazed down at it, and on one grassy bank saw a spot of yellow and tapped John Walsh. "There's one of your dandelions."

He smiled. "See, we are not alone, and we are loved."

Alnan led them on another couple of blocks to the church of San Miguel, the oldest church in the United States, dating from the last quarter of the sixteenth century, older than Boston, Philadelphia, Plymouth, New

243

York, Savannah, Charleston or any other city in the United States. After this, Alnan pointed out a few restaurants where they might have lunch before thanking them and ending the tour.

Jim and Dodee followed John Walsh inside the old adobe church building, long and narrow with a wood beam ceiling and a wooden altar full of paintings and small statues. They made a quick tour and left John Walsh kneeling in prayer.

Jim led Dodee out into bright sunshine and searched the street for the broad figure of Aaron Burr, but the big guy was nowhere to be found.

Maybe he *was* getting paranoid.

Still, it was hard to believe every time he turned around the guy was there. Well, twice, but each time the guy looked like he was trying to duck out of sight.

And what about his name? What mother in her right mind would name her child Aaron Burr?

Thirty-Three

They strolled back in the general direction of the Plaza, popping in and out of art galleries along the way, and ending up in one with a wood carving in its courtyard, a grizzly bear and a small Indian boy standing face to face as if in some spirit communication. Inside were five rooms filled with paintings and sculptures, mostly Native American and western scenes catering to Santa Fe tourists.

"You studying the paintings or—"

"Yes, some. Always looking out for new things and techniques. If you want to be a successful artist you always have to be aware of how others work, just like if you want to be a writer, you have to read to find out how others write. I also study galleries for the same reason, to get ideas for displays."

He looked over the room, trying to see it as she did. "Your gallery this big?"

She rolled her eyes. "Since Alison has taken over the management we're getting there."

"That good or bad?"

"Good for business, but a lot of work for us."

They exited through a second door, onto a different street. "Wait a minute."

He left her, hurried to the corner, and peeked around it.

Aaron Burr stood across the sun-bright street, next to a tree. If Jim had looked out the front door rather than from a different angle on a different street, Burr would have been hidden in the tree's shadow.

Forget about paranoia.

He strode back to find Dodee talking on her cell phone. He looped his arm through hers and guided her down the street.

"Finally got a hold of my girlfriend in Denver," she said, replacing the phone in her handbag. "What was that business of going to the corner about?"

"Just trying to figure where we were."

They strolled down San Francisco Street with Dodee looking into shop windows while Jim checked their tail, but either they had given Aaron Burr the slip, or he hadn't been following them in the first place. They came to a small mall just past the Plaza and he pointed to a Blue Corn Cafe sign.

"Why don't we go in and get some lunch?"

"Because we're hungry, or because you want to get us off the street?"

He blinked at her. "What do you mean?"

She took his arm and they entered the building. "There has to be some reason you keep looking behind us, sweetheart. You think we're being followed?"

"Now what makes you think I keep—" She stopped dead in his path, big blues leveled on him. "Okay, okay. I saw someone a couple of times this morning and, while it's probably a coincidence, I thought I'd keep an eye open."

They followed a sign in the shape of a hand with a finger pointing up, and climbed a flight of stairs to the second floor.

"You think it's Stubbs?"

"No, this was a big guy."

"Big as the man who had dinner with us last night?"

"Actually it is the man who had dinner with us last night."

"The Presbyterian minister? Aaron Burr?"

"That's another thing. Don't you think that sounds phony? What kind of mother would name her child Aaron Burr?"

She batted her big blues at him. "Oh, I'd say she was a—"

"Don't say it."

"—Jim Dandy mother."

He opened the door and gave her a small push into the Blue Corn Cafe and Brewery. He felt like he had entered at the side because the windows were off to the left and to the rear, the cafe having been built in a corner of the building.

"Want to sit in a booth?" Dodee asked.

But he passed them up, wound through a flock of tables to one by a window. He held a chair for her, and then sat down opposite, gazing down on an intersection of two streets.

"Not bad, huh," he said, folding his hands on a painted table, red chili peppers on a white background. Natural wood beams gave a touch of rusticity to the room, and walls painted white enhanced the light.

"I'm glad you suggested this," she said. "I suddenly realize I'm hungry."

"I'm starved out of my mind."

A young, rail-thin waitress appeared with two menus.

"Can I get you something to drink?"

"The sign says Blue Corn Cafe and Brewery. Does that mean you make your own beer?"

"Yes sir, we have End-Of-The-Trail brown ale, we have—"

"I'll have that. We're about at the end of our trail."

"Iced tea?" Dodee asked.

"We have regular and prickly pear iced tea."

"Oh." Her big blues opened. "I'll try the prickly pear."

They scanned the menus and when the waitress returned with their drinks, Jim ordered a bowl of tortilla soup and enchiladas *especiales* while Dodee ordered a tortilla burger.

He took a big swallow of End-of-the-Trail Ale and nodded. "Not bad." He turned to the window, and scanned the streets below.

"You still looking for Aaron Burr?"

"I'm not saying he was following us. I'm just saying it seemed odd that on three occasions when I happened to turn around, there he was."

"Why would he be following us?"

"Why was Stubbs following us? And what about Hank Adamo? If the killer was Stubbs's accomplice, and Stubbs hasn't been found, where is he?"

"You think the killer would be brazen enough to come to dinner and call himself Aaron Burr?"

He took another sip of beer and turned to the window. "To answer your question, do I think I'll find him down there, the answer is no. After the slip at the art gallery it would take a miracle for him to find us."

She placed her hand on his. "Do you believe in miracles?"

Her big blues shifted sideways and he followed her gaze, then immediately jerked back to her, but it was enough to give him a snapshot of the rail-thin waitress taking an order from a big man in a patchwork-quilt shirt.

"Still think I'm imagining a Presbyterian minister following us?"

"It could be a coincidence."

He wobbled his head. "Oh, yeah."

The waitress brought his tortilla soup and delivered a Miller Lite to Aaron Burr.

"That's another nail in the Presbyterian minister's coffin," he whispered. "He just ordered a beer."

"I think ministers can drink. John Walsh drinks."

"John Walsh is a Catholic priest." He took a spoonful of soup, chicken base with onions, peppers, shredded chicken, and a touch of heat. "Catholics have never been shy about taking a drink."

"Well, he may or may not be a Presbyterian minister, but one thing he is."

He paused with his spoon at his mouth. "What's that?"

"Coming this way."

Jim blinked, then glanced up at Aaron Burr, forty feet tall, standing beside the table.

"Mind if I join y'all?" he asked in his gravely, deep bass voice.

"Oh, yes," Dodee said, "please join us."

Oh, yeah, great.

Welcome to our table said the fly to the spider.

But Aaron Burr had already pulled up a chair before Dodee offered the invitation. "Nice place, isn't it?"

"I haven't tried the food yet," Dodee said, "but the prickly pear tea is delicious."

"Good soup," Jim muttered.

"Heard you two just came in from Trinidad," he said, the wart on his chin bobbing as he talked.

Dodee nodded. "Yesterday. Have you been here in Santa Fe long?"

"Did y'all hear anything about that commotion up there? A bus ran amuck through the town?"

Dodee glanced at Jim.

He shrugged and turned to the man.

Time to go on the attack.

"I notice you're drinking a beer."

"I notice you're drinking one yourself. What kind is that?"

"End-of-the-Trail Ale."

"Oh, like end of the Santa Fe Trail. That's what you're studying, isn't it?"

Dodee's brow wrinkled. "You mean our Elderhostel?"

"There was also a murder in Trinidad, wasn't there? Know anything about that?"

Jim finished up the soup and pushed his bowl to the side.

"You're drinking a beer," he said again. "I thought Presbyterian ministers weren't suppose to drink."

Burr gave him a yellow-toothed grin. "Are you the ministerial police?"

"No, but I keep wondering why every time I turn around, there you are."

Burr raised one shoulder and let it drop. "I'm just making conversation here." He turned to Dodee. "So what about the murder up there?"

Dodee pressed her lips together and trained her big blues on Jim.

"Why do I have the feeling this conversation is more like an interrogation?"

The man took a mouthful of Miller Lite, filling out his cheeks, then swallowed it, then stared at Jim with a half-closed right eye. "You're very shrewd. I was hoping you'd just answer my questions without getting involved. Guess I can't do that, can I?"

Jim shrugged. "I never believed your name was Aaron Burr, either."

That brought another yellow-toothed grin. "Oh, but a name like Jim Dandy is okay?" He reached into the breast pocket of the patchwork-quilt shirt, pulled out a leather business card holder, and flipped it open to give them both a swift glance at a badge, then folded it back to give Dodee a long look at the other side before showing it to Jim.

A Federal Bureau of Investigation identification verified the man, by picture and printed name, as Brian Doubt.

Thirty-Four

Jim glanced at the man's face and back to the picture, convinced they were one and the same. "Why did you go through this charade?"

"Mind if I ask a few questions first?" Brian Doubt put away his identification. "And maybe get some answers this time?"

Dodee smiled. "Aaron Burr. You can come up with a better alias than that."

Another grin. "Really, if my skulking skills weren't so rusty, would you have questioned my name? I find that if I use something outlandish, especially one that's historic, people won't question its authenticity because it is so outlandish it has to be true." He glanced at Jim. "I think Aaron Burr is a Jim Dandy name."

He groaned. "You're not winning any points here. Can I ask why you're questioning us?"

"You can ask. Will I tell you?" He scratched his chin by the wart. "Because your room was next to Hank Adamo's. You also found the body. And you were also there when Moondance Wolf took the high dive. Adamo saw you there."

Jim pointed to Dodee. "I told you."

The waitress came with their food, enchiladas for Jim, the tortilla burger for Dodee, and two Brewery Burgers for Brian Doubt.

Jim dug into the enchiladas, hot, spicy, full of cheese. "I recognized Hank Adamo in spite of him shaving off the handlebar mustache."

Brian Doubt paused with his Brewery Burger halfway to his mouth. "Handlebar mustache?"

"Looked like an old-time bartender in the Yukon."

Brian bit out a hefty chunk of burger and chewed it with his right eye half closed. "Why would he have a handlebar mustache?"

"Maybe he just stopped shaving his upper lip and it came by itself."

"Very funny." He reached into his pocket and placed a tape recorder on the table. "You're sure he had a handlebar mustache?"

Jim turned to him. "Yes. You're saying it wasn't real?"

"Never saw him with a mustache."

Dodee put her tortilla burger down. "You knew him?"

"Know of him. Hank Adamo works—worked—for the Bureau of Indian Affairs. That's why we are involved, because he was a federal agent. Adamo was supposed to meet with Moondance Wolf." Brian turned to Jim. "You know anything about that?"

"I don't know anything about anything." He scooped up a piece of cheese-gooey enchilada. "I told the Denver police I saw the woman plunge from the roof and ran down to see if I could help. I had just arrived in Denver an hour before. I didn't know the woman. I didn't know what she was about. I didn't know Hank; I never saw

253

him before that day he was sporting the handlebar mustache."

Another yellow-toothed grin. "That's pretty emphatic." He polished off the first of his two Brewery Burgers. "Maybe you saw something that didn't register at the time?"

Jim gazed across the restaurant and thought back on the scene outside Duffy's. "I saw Hank come running out of the building. Then he disappeared. Ah, but he made a comment when I moved the chain—" He turned back to the FBI agent. "I moved a chain bunched around the woman's neck to check for a pulse."

"Okay."

Jim took a bite of enchilada, once again visualizing the scene, and shook his head.

"No artifact of any kind?" Brian asked.

He shook his head again.

"How about the notebook? A witness said you picked up a notebook?"

"I never saw it, no, although everyone seems to think I did, thanks to the damn lady on television." He gave Brian Doubt a sideways glance. "You too?"

He rubbed his chin, then turned to Dodee. "What about the shaman showing up in your paintings? Anything to that?"

She shook her head. "I can't explain it. Erynn Sunflower thinks the shaman's spirit is trying to contact us. She wants to do a séance."

Brian Doubt scratched his chin by the wart. "Maybe you should do it."

"Oh, yeah," Jim said, rolling his eyes, "I'm sure that's going to tell us a lot."

"Never know what shakes out of these things." He took a swallow of beer. "Somebody thinks you two know about an artifact called the Mayan Falcon. Ever hear of it?"

Dodee nodded. "We never stop hearing about it."

Jim told Brian what he knew of the falcon's history. "The last anyone knows, a young army lieutenant had it—Beauregard St. Simian, I think—and he was heading for Missouri."

"How did you find that out?"

"From Max. Max Solnim, he's on the Elderhostel with us."

Dodee wiped her mouth with her napkin. "He's a professor of Native American History."

"No, Ward Longtree is a professor of Native American History. But Max's writing a book on Native Americans."

Brian half closed one eye. "Max Solnim? What's he look like?"

"Like a bald mountain with a lot of crevasses. This thing actually exists then?"

Brian raised one shoulder, let it drop, and gobbled up the last of his Brewery Burger. "We think we know that Moondance Wolf had a notebook with information on the whereabouts of the Mayan Falcon. Someone broke in and searched Raymond Wolf's storage area looking for it. We searched it as well and found nothing. Adamo thought you picked it up and so arranged to get himself on this Elderhostel to follow you. But, if you don't have it—"

"Let me repeat myself." Jim held out his hands again. "I don't have it."

Dodee placed a elbow on the table. "How do you know the person who broke in didn't find it?"

"Because if he did, he wouldn't have sent Dick Stubbs

255

to kidnap you." He partially closed his right eye again. "Did Stubbs say anything to you?"

"He said they only wanted to know where the falcon was."

"Really?" The FBI agent's brows knitted. "He didn't say he wanted the falcon, but wanted to know where it was?"

The big blues blinked a couple of times. "Yes. He said he wanted to know where it was."

"Where it was." He folded his arms, sat back in his chair, and raised his chin. "And Adamo is killed right next door." The half-closed eye focused on Jim. "And you didn't take anything from the body?"

"I didn't even touch him—"

"Moondance Wolf. You didn't find—"

"Listen to me. I don't know anything about anything. I didn't know the woman, didn't know Hank Adamo—"

"Okay, okay," he said, holding up his hands. "Maybe you don't know anything about anything, but somebody thinks you know something about something." He pulled out a business card and a pen. "I'm giving you my cell phone number." He handed it to Jim. "Be careful. These guys are still out there." He stood up. "They're obviously taking this Mayan Falcon thing seriously. They've killed at least once in trying to get hold of it. I don't think they'd stop at another."

"Well, thanks a bunch, you've made our day a whole lot brighter."

"Oh, I'll be out there skulking around and keeping an eye on you. That's why I gave you my cell phone number. Keep in touch."

Jim watched him go. "Why don't we round up our stuff and get the first plane the hell out of here?"

Her big blues leveled on him. "And never find out what it's all about?"

"I can live with that."

She shook here head. "Sweetheart, we only have two days left—"

"And it only took a few hours for you to be kidnapped and Hank Adamo to be murdered."

"But Brian said he'd keep an eye out for us."

"Oh, that makes me feel a whole lot better."

"You don't like him?"

He looked at the card. Federal Bureau of Investigation and Brian Doubt's name and phone number were in embossed print, the cell phone number in black ink. "I guess he's competent enough." He stood up and held the chair for her. "You can tell he's a government employee."

"How's that?"

He waved the check in front of her face. "He made sure he ordered before joining us. His per diem might cover his own lunch, but you can bet the government wouldn't spring for him buying ours."

They strolled back to the Plaza, circled it, and Dodee stopped him outside the entrance to the Palace of Governors.

"Didn't Max tell you there was a trading invoice for the falcon in here?"

He frowned. "That was a hundred and fifty or two hundred years ago."

"But if the invoice is real, wouldn't that tell us the falcon is real?"

He shook his head, but followed her inside, entering into a smallish room with postcards and painted cards and beaded handbag examples of Native American art. He

257

waited while she talked to one of the clerks, then tagged along when she motioned him to a back door.

"We have to talk to the curator."

A dark-haired woman with a dark complexion gave them a dazzling white smile as they entered. "May I help you?"

"We were told to talk to the curator about looking at some old invoices for a research project."

"Invoices," came a strong male voice from a second office. A tall man with blond hair appeared in the doorway, a pair of granny glasses hanging on the tip of his nose. "What are you looking for?"

Dodee turned to Jim.

Oh, sure. She leads the way into the lion's den then introduces him to the animal's fangs.

"We heard there might be an old invoice documenting an artifact—"

"The Mayan Falcon?"

"You know about it?"

He removed his granny glasses and turned to his secretary. "I don't believe this." He turned back to Jim. "You're the fourth person to ask me about it. Today." He leaned against the doorjamb and folded his arms. "And a woman was here last week. We gave the woman permission to research the stacks because she was a Ute, but since then we've discovered some of those records are missing."

"So there was an invoice?" Dodee asked.

The curator flopped a hand over and back. "Didn't know anything about it a week ago, really don't know anything about it now. But you can bet after today I'm going to be researching it."

They started back to the Plaza Resolana, their home

away from home. He was tired, his feet complained of pounding the pavement, and his eyes whispered it was nap time.

Dodee took his arm. "Think we should call Brian Doubt and tell him about this?"

"Why? We haven't learned anything."

"We've learned that four people have come here looking for the invoice. Maybe we should go back and ask them who they were."

"No. Call Brian and let the FBI figure it out if you want, but I'm going back to the shack. Besides, one of them was probably Max."

When they got back to the Plaza Resolana he stopped at the registration desk. "Can you give me Max Solnim's room number?"

"Max Solnim?" the woman asked. "He checked out this afternoon."

"Checked out?"

"Yes, sir."

He turned to Dodee. "What do you make of that?"

"Think he found out something?"

He shrugged and turned to see Martin walking toward him. "How you doing, Martin Martin?"

"Just Jim Dandy."

"You haven't heard anything about Max have you?"

"No. A small group of us are getting together to go out to dinner. Some place close by. Want to come?"

He looked at Dodee, who nodded. "Count us in."

They headed for the room.

"What could he have found out?" she asked. "Max, I mean."

"Don't know, but it's an ill wind that blows no good."

She looked up at him.

"No more huff and puffs."

They met for dinner in the lobby, Martin and Helen, Ace, John Walsh, and Claire Renquist. They crossed the Paseo de Peralta, cut through by the post office, and strolled to Osteria D'Assisi, an Italian restaurant with crowded outside tables, and entered a dining room with a large kitchen opening onto it. A waiter pulled three tables together by a window, gave them menus, and rushed off to get them water.

John Walsh sat opposite Jim and Dodee. "You two didn't happen to go over to the capitol building after you left me, did you?"

"We headed back toward the Plaza," Jim said, putting on his reading glasses and studying the menu.

"It's filled with art and sculpture. Could have spent the whole day in there."

"We stopped at some commercial galleries," Dodee said. "Then we ate lunch at the Blue Corn Cafe."

"I saw the sign for that," Helen Martin said. "Was it any good?"

Jim nodded. "I had an End-of-the-Trail Ale that wasn't bad at all." He put down his menu. "Has anybody seen Max?"

John nodded. "I saw him this afternoon. He rented a car and checked out."

"Of the hotel?" Ace asked from the other end of the table, brow wrinkled on his ruddy face.

"Yeah. He left. I assumed you knew about it."

"Nobody told me. Where was he going?"

John shrugged. "He was in a hurry and didn't want to talk."

Jim bit the side of his lip. "Think it had anything to do with our discussion this morning?"

"About the Mayan Falcon?"

The whole table fell silent.

"What about the Mayan Falcon?" Ace asked.

"Just that Max was looking into it," John said. "Wait a minute." He turned to Jim. "When I came into the lobby, Max was getting himself a cup of coffee. I noticed a paper on the table and looked at it. Suddenly Max rushed over and snatched it away."

"You didn't happen to see what was on it?"

He rubbed his big nose for a moment, then a smile split his Irish face.

"Beauregard St. Simian. Didn't Max say he was the last one to have the Mayan Falcon? The note said, 'Ex-lieutenant Beauregard St. Simian lost everything in a card game to Wild Sam Sheridan, and called him out for being a cheat. Wild Sam met St. Simian on the street in Cimarron and dropped him in front of the St. James Hotel."

Thirty-Five

Jim helped Harry load suitcases in the chilly morning as everyone boarded the bus for the trip back to Trinidad. Ace came down the steps as they finished.

"Ready to go?"

"I haven't seen Dr. Longtree," Jim said.

"He went back to Fort Collins yesterday. He had work piling up at the university." Ace turned to Harry. "Okay, Pardner, round 'em up and move 'em out."

They took Paseo de Peralta to I-25 and headed south, following the Old Trail as the mule skinners had one hundred and fifty years ago.

Jim leaned in close to Dodee. "Say we trekked across the plains in our Conestoga wagon, traded two or three tons of stuff, and now we're heading south to go east, back to Missouri. What about your Santa Fe Trail now?"

"You still don't think it would be an adventure?"

"Maybe on the way out when we didn't know what was over the next rise, but on the way back? Knowing the months of grinding out fifteen miles a day on the blistering plain, rationing water and fixing wagon breakdowns? How do you feel now watching Santa Fe pass out of sight as you slap your oxen on the rump and shout giddy-up, or oxen ho, or move your bloomin' arse, whatever you say to oxen."

"Hee haw."

"You anxious to make that wagon trip now? Or are you ready to opt, thank you very much, for Delta Airlines?"

"You mean, no more cuddling on the buckboard, no more noonering it when the wagons are brought to a stop in the heat of the day?"

He looked out to the pine trees passing by on the hilly countryside. With only one night left, it might not be the time to rid Dodee of her romantic notions. Not if he wanted some of that buckboard and noonering stuff.

"We're going into hyper-drive, folks," Ace's voice crackled out of the PA system. "Harry's going to take us up to warp seven. In the meantime, some of you have asked if we can stop off in Cimarron on the way back, since you missed it on the way out. We're going to try to do that. We want to stop off at the Pecos Pueblo National Park, then at Fort Union National monument, and if we skip Rayado and don't mind getting into Trinidad later in the evening, I think we can squeeze in Cimarron."

John Walsh leaned across the aisle, opposite sides of the bus from the first day out. "Anyone tell Ace they wanted to go to Cimarron?"

Martin Martin leaned forward from the seat behind. "I don't know, but he already said we were going last night at dinner."

Jim blinked at John Walsh, watched his lips turn down on his freckled face, and turned to Martin. "I don't remember that."

"Sure, right after he found Max had checked out of the hotel. Did you tell him you wanted to go?"

Jim shook his head. "In fact, I'd just as soon skip Cimarron."

Dodee swung to him. "Why?"

He sat back in his seat and leaned into her. "I think that's where Max went. And maybe those guys who've been dogging us. I don't want any part of it, thank you very much."

They stopped off at Pecos Pueblo National Park for a walking tour up a blustery hill where the Pueblos built their houses, one attached and on top of another, the area where they had gardens, the river with water nearby, and the hogans, steam pits built into the ground for ceremonial cleansing. They ended up at a church the Spanish built in 1717, now only a ruin with high adobe walls rounded off and eaten away by wind and rain, and back down to the parking area where Harry and Ace had broken out the sodas and lunches.

Jim picked up two boxes while Dodee got two sodas and led the way to a lone table in the lee of two junipers. She sat down with her back to them, looking out onto the parking lot.

"What treasures do we have today?" He sat opposite her and opened the box on a roast beef sandwich, a bag of chips, an apple, and two cookies. "Awright. If you don't want those cookies, I might be able to relieve you of them."

"Might?" She smiled. "Might?"

"Mind if I join you?" John Walsh asked, standing by the table.

Dodee held out a palmed-up hand. "Of course, John. Why would you think otherwise?"

He grinned. "I thought you two might have come over here to be alone."

"We came over to get out of the wind."

John sat down, silently blessed himself in a little prayer, and opened his box. "What have we got today?"

"Roast beef sandwich," Jim said, taking a bite of his. "And cookies that are probably poisoned, so if you want to get rid of them—"

"Don't listen to him," Dodee said.

"Speaking of food poisoning," John said, taking a bite out of his sandwich, "Ace seems to have recovered. He ate last night like he had to make up for lost time."

Jim nodded. "He can really pack it away."

Dodee's eyebrows rose. "Oh? And who was it who just asked us about our cookies, sweetheart?"

"Change the subject. I'm from Brazil where the nuts come from."

John pointed to him. "*Charlie's Aunt*?"

"Right, that was the play. *Where's Charlie* was the movie with Ray Bolger. I saw it when I was dating my wife." He shook his head. "A long time ago."

Dodee held a potato chip between two fingers. "What do you think of Max leaving so suddenly?"

John flicked his eyebrows. "I thought you two were the ones who knew everything."

"Forgive the expression, John," Jim said, "Father John, but we don't know shit."

He laughed. "That's fairly graphic." He ate some of his sandwich. "I think Max left because he found something out about the Mayan Falcon and is running off to chase it down. Half the bus is talking about it."

"Really? No one told me anything."

"Me either," Dodee said.

"That's because you're involved. Like the Emperor's new clothes."

Jim shook his head. "Right. And if they find out Wild Sam Sheridan dropped Beauregard St. Simian on the street in Cimarron, everyone will be popping out in falcon fever."

John Walsh grinned. "They already have." He took a bite of his sandwich. "There're two schools of thought: One is that the shaman's spirit is trying to tell Dodee where the falcon is, and the other," he looked to Jim, "thinks you have the shaman's notebook."

"Well, you can tell them I never saw it, don't have it, don't know if it exists. And Dodee's not being contacted by the shaman's spirit." He turned to her. "Right?"

She pressed her lips together.

Jim glanced skyward. "Oh, boy."

"Any news on your kidnapper?" John asked Dodee.

She shook her head. "We haven't seen a television in a couple of days."

John rubbed his big nose. "Isn't Harry now friends with the sheriff in Trinidad?"

"Good idea. Maybe we can ask her."

Jim nodded. "It would be nice to know he's locked up before we get back there tonight."

John tossed a couple of chips near the junipers and a chipmunk dashed out, grabbed one, and scooted back into the brush. A black and white magpie snatched the other and flew off, only to have one of its brethren swoop down to contest its prize.

"They act like they're starving," Dodee said.

"Probably are. With winter coming on there aren't as many tourists around."

Jim ripped open his bag. "Do not feed the animals. They become dependent and lose some of their natural skills. When the food supply is gone, they die." He popped the chips into his mouth.

"One thing I've learned about death, with all the sick I've attended, and funerals I've served," John tossed some more potato chips toward the junipers and turned back to them, "it's that even in the best of health, we're only a whisper away."

Thirty-Six

Jim gave Harry a hand loading the unused sodas and ice water into the bus's hold. "Have you talked to Sheriff Iglesias lately?"

She smiled. "You worried about my love life?"

He shook his head. "I'm worrying about my love life, especially heading back into Trinidad. Any news about Dick Stubbs?"

She lowered the compartment door and looked up. "Sorry, didn't think about that. I'll call later and see if he'll tell me anything."

"I'd appreciate it."

He climbed on board and sat down next to Dodee, and looked over the parking lot as the bus moved out.

Brian Doubt, his friendly FBI agent, had promised to keep an eye on them, but if he was skulking about out there, Jim couldn't see him.

"Okay, folks," Ace said, mike to his mouth as he stood in the aisle, "I want to thank you all for taking care of my popcorn while I was in the hospital. This means my wife won't be a self-made widow this winter."

Laughter rippled through the bus.

"Our next stop is Fort Union National Monument, where we'll be able to get a good look at the old wagon trail and get some idea of what it was like to serve in the army out here during the Indian wars. After that we'll swing by Rayado where Lucien Maxwell and Kit Carson settled. If we have time we might try for a quick stop. Had things gone as scheduled we would have done all of this on the way down."

The PA clicked off as Ace cleared his throat, then clicked back on.

"People have been asking me about Cimarron. The Santa Fe Trail ran right through Cimarron. It was also the center of a lot of wars that developed in the area, like the Lincoln County war, which was the start of the Billy the Kid legend. There's a museum there, the Aztec Mill, that was established in eighteen sixty-four. There's also the St. James Hotel, where people have seen the ghosts of old cowboys like Billy the Kid, Bat Masterson, Jesse James, and Pat Garrison, who all stayed at the St. James in its heyday. The hotel is still in operation and you can tour it. So, while it will put us late into Trinidad, it's well worth the trip."

John Walsh turned to Jim when the PA system clicked off. "Looks like we're going to Cimarron, whether we want to or not."

"Looks like."

Dodee leaned close and whispered, "Suppose it's someone on the bus?"

"Suppose what's someone on the bus?"

"We thought Stubbs's accomplice had mistakenly broken into Hank's room, but suppose it was someone already on the bus?"

He glanced around.

That kind of thinking could make it anybody. Someone comes on the Elderhostel for fun, watches that damn television interview, catches falcon fever, and becomes an opportunity killer when Adamo returned to catch him.

The problem was, half the bus had falcon fever.

Which left the retired priest as the only one he could trust. Except, how did John Walsh know Harry and the sheriff of Trinidad were friends?

Welcome to paranoia-land.

They pulled off the Interstate and headed through prairie grassland with only a few cattle to give relief to the flat terrain. At a bend in the road they came across the ruins of brown adobe buildings standing stark against a lead-gray sky. They turned into the entrance and around a circular drive to—what else?—an adobe Visitor's Center.

"This is Fort Union, folks," Ace said. "We'll be here just long enough to make a tour of the place and use the facilities."

They followed the others and stepped out under a dirty sky and into a brisk breeze that had the promise of winter in its teeth. They used the facilities Ace had mentioned, then hiked out alone through knee-high prairie grass to where the old trail skirted the fort.

Jim gazed in both directions, having no trouble seeing, even now, the depressions left by sixty years of the Conestoga covered wagons rolling on one after another.

Dodee turned, pulled his arm over her shoulder, and stood in his lee as the wind whispered over grass. "It's a little creepy out here, looking over these tracks made so long ago. Like ghosts are still walking the trail looking for a place to rest."

"You sound like Erynn."

"Can't help feeling that way, sweetheart."

He turned to scoff at her, but the thought died stillborn in the rustle of the wind and the undulating grass, the skeletal remains of soldier's quarters open to the gray clouds, and the tracks stretching to a somber horizon.

They climbed back on board and Harry pushed on down the hill to the Interstate and turned west off it an hour later onto Highway 58, winding through grasslands and scrub evergreens.

Ace climbed out into the aisle.

"We'll be coming up on Rayado where Lucien Maxwell, from Illinois, settled with Kit Carson in eighteen forty-eight. He established a ranch out here from various land grants, either as gifts from his wife's family connections or purchased from the original owners, to end up with one million seven hundred thousand acres, over twenty-five hundred square miles, about twice the size of the state of Rhode Island. Not a bad little spread. The ranch house is still up here and we'll stop for a brief visit—"

"Let's just go by," called out a voice from the back of the bus.

"Yeah, let's go on," added another.

And a third joined in, "It's already starting to get dark."

Ace clicked the mike. "Some of you want to go on? We can do that. Let's take a vote. All those who want to pass it by raise your hands." Jim raised his hand along with almost everyone else in the bus, and Ace nodded. "Okay, we'll pass it by and pick up some time."

Dodee turned to Jim. "You doing okay?"

"My rear end is getting tired and I'm just about Santa Fe Trailed-out. I think we're all getting ragged."

Ace came back on sometime later. "If you look off to the left you'll see Rayado. It was a place to buy fresh animals and supplies and repairs for those coming along the trail to make the last run into Santa Fe."

"What's that off to the right?" Betty Baskins asked.

"On the right we'll be coming up to the Philmont Boy Scout Ranch museum—"

"No, it looks like a fire way out there."

Jim leaned over to see a wave of smoke darkening the already deepening horizon.

"Don't know what that is," Ace said. "Looks like someone is burning something."

A short time later, they slowed at the intersection of routes 64 and 58, just a spot in the road, a couple of stores, a few ramshackle buildings, and a trailer camp that made up Cimarron, New Mexico. Harry turned right and then right again and eased the bus into a small parking lot in front of a two-story, well-kept, light-gray building, black trim around the windows and a small windbreak shed protecting the entrance. Two men in state police uniforms leaned on a hitching rail as Harry pulled to a stop and opened the door.

They had arrived at the St. James, sometimes known as the Ghost Hotel.

Thirty-Seven

The two officers straightened up and started for the bus. Ace popped out into the aisle. "Everybody remain in your seats and let me see what the police want."

Jim stared out the window at the pantomime of Ace and the uniformed men. One of them, heavyset without being really fat, looked at Ace from under the brim of a pointed hat. He shook his head when Ace pointed north, the direction they had been traveling. When Ace pointed toward the east, the man shook his head again and pointed west.

"What do you think?" Dodee asked.

"Something to do with the roads."

Ace held out his hands and the man nodded and Ace nodded back. Then the two officers walked toward a police cruiser while Ace entered the hotel.

"What do you think?" Martin Martin asked, echoing Dodee's question.

Jim shrugged. "From all the pointing, I'd say the police were lost and asking for directions."

John Walsh grinned. "We all need direction once in a while."

Helen Martin leaned forward. "Maybe it has to do with the smoke we saw."

Ace climbed on board and picked up the mike. "Okay, folks, we're going to be here awhile. The Interstate north is closed by a brush fire, so our choice is to go back out to the highway and sit in traffic, or stay here until everything clears. The bad news is, I've called ahead to the Best Western and canceled dinner. The good news is I've arranged for us to have dinner here, but they need a little time to set up. Meanwhile, you can sit in the lobby, or tour the hotel where they have old-time pictures of notorious Wild West figures. There's a museum down the street that's probably closed, but the old jail is right around the corner by a trailer park."

They climbed off the bus and Dodee turned to Jim. "Want to tour the hotel?"

He motioned to the line of people waiting to get in the doorway and turned in the direction of the trailer park. "Let's go look at the old jail while we still have light."

"Wait a minute." She climbed on the bus and came back a few minutes later and showed him a penlight. "See, told you they'd come in handy."

They started down the street in the gloom of the gathering night. The wind blew fresh off the shadowed foothills of the Sangre de Cristo Mountains, bringing with it a hint of pine and sage. Dodee snuggled into the lee of his body.

"This is not the best idea you've had, sweetheart. It's cold and getting dark and what will we see?"

"The old jail. You've been talking about how romantic it would be to come across the plains in the covered wagons. Thought you'd want to see where you'd end up if you tried to ply your wares."

"They didn't lock up ladies for plying their wares in those days."

"But you're no lady." He grunted when she poked him in the ribs. "Sonofabitch, when will I learn?"

They came upon a square, concrete-and-stone building and walked around to the other side where a wooden door provided a square, bared peephole to the inside. Dodee shined her penlight flash into the dark interior to reveal four bare walls.

So much for her handy-dandy penlight.

She clicked it off and started for a brass plaque on a stone pedestal, then jumped back with a small scream as a giant shadow slipped around the corner of the building.

"It's only me," came a James-Earl-Jones-with-a-bucket-of-sand voice out of the murk. Brian Doubt gave them a yellow-toothed grin. "The grand skulker."

Jim looked up at the six-foot-three FBI man. "Where did you come from?"

"I've been around."

"Have you found Hank Adamo's killer yet?"

He scratched his chin by the big wart. "Not yet. Any news about the Mayan Falcon?"

"Yes and no. Max Solnim rented a car and checked out of the hotel last night. One of the Elderhostelers got a peek at a paper he had and it talked about some cowboy—"

"Wild Sam Sheridan," Dodee said.

"Right, old Wild Sam, won the falcon in a card game, guess where?" Jim spread out his arms. "In good old downtown Cimarron."

"Then it looks like we're in the right place. I think once you leave the area you'll probably be safe. I'll stay behind and see what I can stir up. Hear anything about them catching Dodee's kidnapper?"

Jim shook his head. "Not yet. The bus driver is supposed to call."

"Okay. In the meantime, you still have my card. Give me a call if anything pops up or you get into trouble. Now you better get back to the bus." Brian Doubt slipped around the corner of the jail and disappeared.

Jim put his arm around Dodee and they started back to the hotel.

"You didn't tell him we're having dinner here," she said.

"He didn't wait. Skulked off as swiftly as he skulked in. Like one of the hotel's ghosts."

"He's not a ghost. He ate with us in Santa Fe. Ghosts don't eat."

"They don't? How do you know?"

"It's in the Bible somewhere." She changed sides with him to block the wind. "We can ask John." She stretched out her gait to match his, making her bounce alongside.

"You having fun, lady?"

"You call this fun, punk," she said through clenched teeth. "Tonight I'll show you fun."

"Oh, you think so. Maybe I'll show you fun."

She looked up at him, smiled and shook her head. "Nope, I'll show you fun." She matched him for a few more steps. "But before we get to all this fun, sweetheart, let me ask you something. If Brian Doubt is investigating Hank's murder, wouldn't you think he'd keep in touch with Sheriff Iglesias in Trinidad?"

"What makes you think he's not?"

"Because he asked if you heard anything about catching Stubbs."

Jim stopped and turned around. He saw only the deserted street, hardly visible now in the onrushing night, helped along by the overcast sky. "Maybe it was just a throwaway question like, how ya doin'. Or maybe he thought we heard something since he checked in."

Right, and maybe they should watch their backsides.

They entered the hotel and took a step back into the time of the Santa Fe Trail. Chandeliers lit the old-time lobby, only the candles had been electrified. Pictures and game animals—deer, elk, buffalo—hung on the walls, black drapes on the windows. Sofas gathered around a low circular table, a velvet-tufted settee huddled against the far wall, along with an upright piano and two easy chairs.

Dodee stood beside a curved wooden registration desk at the entrance. "This would be a fantastic movie set."

"Guys in rough clothes and rundown boots walking around with forty-fours strapped to the waist and saying, 'Howdy, Pardner.'"

Only the cowboys and cowgirls lounging around the lobby that night had gray hair, hearing aids, and glasses, and were damn lucky to be able keep their eyes open, much less be ready to slap leather.

"Are you with the Elderhostel group?" asked a woman from behind the desk, smooth skin, lithe body, perky boobs.

"Yes," Dodee said, "we went to look at the jail."

"You're welcome to go through the hotel if you like." While she looked fifteen, her demeanor placed her in the twenties. "Dinner will be in ten minutes."

Jim placed a hand on the desk top. "We the only ones here? Our group?"

She nodded. "We have a big party coming in this

weekend, although this is normally the slow season. We only had two guests last night."

He motioned to the animals on the wall. "How old is the buffalo head?"

"Old. Same with the elk. At least since the thirties, I think."

"I like this place. It has—" He jerked around to her. "One of the guests last night, could it have been Max Solnim?"

She opened a hardcover ledger book and leafed through until she found the last entry. "Yes."

"Is he here now?"

"No, he, ah"—she shrugged, clearly uncomfortable—"he's not with us tonight."

"What do you mean, not with us? Left the hotel? Out for the evening. Dead?"

"No, he's not dead. At least, I don't think . . ." She looked around, held out a hand, let it flop, and lowered her voice. "He was taken by helicopter to a hospital."

Dodee put a hand on the counter. "What happened?"

"He hit his head," she whispered. "We'd prefer to keep this quiet." Her eyes scanned the lobby before coming back to him. "We don't know what happened. We found him unconscious outside his room." Her voice was just above mouthing the words. "We do have some strange goings on around here, but no one's ever been hurt by them before."

Jim stared into the young woman's eyes. "Them?"

"You know." She grimaced and mouthed, "Ghosts."

Jim smiled and turned to Dodee. "This sounds like a fun place. I bet Erynn is beside herself with all the spirit cosmic energy."

Dodee's lips screwed to one side. "This might be the place—now don't get angry—for her to do a séance."

"Dodee—"

"Isn't that what Brian told us? To try to draw someone out?"

"I never heard him say that." He swung back to the woman. "Did you have a Native American stay here about a week or so ago?"

"I'm sorry, I really shouldn't give out that infor—"

"Tell me again," he said, in a voice that carried, "about my friend. What did you say happened—"

"Okay, okay." She opened the book. "Last week. What was his name?"

"A woman."

She jerked her head up. "Had a strange name, like Star or Moon—"

"Moondance Wolf," Dodee said.

"Yes, that's it. She spent one whole day doing historical research, didn't stay overnight. A week ago Tuesday, as I remember."

"Anyone with her?"

"Not that I know of."

He looked into Dodee's big blues. "A week ago last Tuesday would fit."

"Okay, everybody." Ace stood in the door of the dining room. "Dinner is served."

Jim turned back to the young woman. "Ever hear of Wild Sam Sheridan?"

"I guess so. It's the name of one of our rooms."

Thirty-Eight

They ate dinner at a white-linen-covered table with Erynn Sunflower, Claire Renquist, and John Walsh. Pork chops, home-fry garlic potatoes, and asparagus with a creamy sauce.

"Good food," Jim said, digging in.

John nodded. "One of the better meals, if not the best we've had on this trip."

Erynn Sunflower held up a home-fry in her fingers. "Too bad we don't have more time here, Dodee. This would be the perfect spot to call your shaman, right here where the spirits are lurking about."

Oh, boy, here we go again.

Erynn popped the home-fry in her mouth. "You can just feel them. When I wandered through the halls it was like those old cowboys and fancy ladies were standing right there talking to one another."

"Did you read the brochure?" John Walsh asked and flicked his eyebrows a couple of times. "This place has been on that television show, 'Unsolved Mysteries,' and been written up in papers and magazines. There's one story that a cleaning lady was supposed to have gone into a bedroom that had belonged to an owner's dead wife; the cleaning lady 'felt' the woman criticizing how the bed was being made. When she left to get some towels and came back, the bed covers had been pulled off."

Claire nodded. "And a man working late at night heard voices down the hall, only when he went to see who it was, no one was there. And a guest once saw some cowboys sitting around playing cards even though no one else was staying at the hotel."

Erynn spread her chubby hands on the table and lowered her voice. "I can feel their presence. Hear the murmuring of their voices. We could call them out if we only had more time."

The clinking of a glass rang out in the room.

"Okay folks." Ace stood in front of a mirrored credenza and some potted plants, and clinked his glass until the conversation died. "I have some more good news, bad news. The bad news is that it will be at least another two hours, more like three, before they'll open the Interstate. The good news is we canceled our reservation in Trinidad and booked us all in here for the night. It will mean a longer haul into Denver tomorrow, but we can leave earlier in the morning."

Dodee leaned over and whispered in Jim's ear. "I'll be right back."

As she headed for the lobby, Ace clinked his glass again.

"The good thing about staying here is that this is a world-famous hotel. It was founded first as a saloon in eighteen seventy-two by Henri Lambert, personal chef to Abraham Lincoln and Ulysses Grant when they occupied the White House. And you can tell by what you ate tonight,

281

that they've never lost their touch for putting out a superb meal down through the years, even on short notice."

That brought a round of applause.

"The hotel itself was started in eighteen-eighty and some of our more famous Wild West characters stayed here: Bat Masterson, Doc Holliday, Jesse and Frank James, both Billy the Kid and Pat Garrison, Wild Sam Sheridan, Kit Carson and Lucien Maxwell."

Ace looked back at his paper.

"Buffalo Bill Cody and Annie Oakley planned their Wild West Show while staying here. Wild West fiction author, Zane Grey, stayed and wrote here, and so did Lew Wallace, working on *Ben Hur*. And Frederick Remington, western artist and sculptor, stayed here and did some sketching in the nearby hills."

"Yeah," Batty Baskins called out, "but if you read the notices on the walls, some of these famous people checked in, but ain't checked out."

That brought a ripple of laughter through the room.

Dodee slipped back into her seat. Jim stared at her, but she turned her attention to Ace.

"That's the other thing about this hotel. People have seen ghosts here. No one has been harmed by them, but they have raised some goose bumps. You can understand why there might be a few lingering around when I tell you that twenty-six men were killed within these two-foot-thick adobe walls. So"—Ace shook his finger at them—"you better make sure your doors are locked tonight, heh, heh, heh, but will that keep out the ghost of Billy the Kid?"

Erynn glanced around their table, her glasses picking up the overhead light, giving her eyes a surreal glow. "I can promise you it won't."

Oh, boy.

Talk about oooOOOooo.

Ace clinked his glass again. "There is a new annex to the hotel where they have telephones and television if some of you would rather stay there. The old hotel has fully restored rooms with original antiques, but the only entertainment you'll have"—he brought his hands up under his chin and rubbed them together in a washing motion—"heh, heh, heh, is a visit from the likes of Doc Holliday, or perhaps a conversation with Jesse James."

Erynn swung around to them. "I'm staying in the old hotel."

Claire shrugged. "Depends on my roommate. I'm not worried about ghosts, but it would be fun to stay in an antique room."

"Maybe so," John Walsh said, "but the only spirit I'm aware of is the Holy One, and while I welcome His visit anytime, He'll find me watching television in the new section."

Jim nodded and turned to Dodee. "We're also opting for television and telephone."

"Guess again, sweetheart."

He glanced toward the lobby and back to her. "Is that where you went when Ace was talking?"

She leaned in close and lowered her voice. "I asked if we could have Wild Sam Sheridan's room. It's being repaired, but she put us in next door."

He shook his head.

She smiled. "You said you wanted to have some fun tonight."

"No, you said you were going to show me some fun. This is not the fun I bargained for."

Harry crossed the room and pulled up a chair between them. "I just talked to my friend in Trinidad."

Dodee swung to her. "The sheriff?"

She nodded. "They haven't found Dick Stubbs, the man who kidnapped you. Pard says, that's Sheriff Iglesias, he says the FBI is assisting them. The FBI thinks Stubbs is part of a two-man team that has been stealing artwork throughout the Southwest for the past couple of years."

"And they have no idea where he is?" Jim asked.

"Pard said the FBI put out bulletins all over the place, but they're concentrating their attention on Santa Fe."

He nodded. "You know, maybe I'm glad we're not going into Trinidad tonight, just in case."

"But it must be a disappointment for you," Dodee said to Harry.

She shrugged. "We don't know each other that well yet. Besides"—she touched her nose ring—"Pard wants me to get rid of this." She stood up. "He certainly doesn't know me well enough to ask for that."

Dodee turned to Jim as the dining room cleared out. "Should we call Brian Doubt about Stubbs?"

"Don't you think he already knows?"

"He didn't this afternoon." She pulled out her cell phone and handed it to him.

"Oh, when you say we should call him, you mean me." He took out the FBI guy's card and dialed. "We may not have a link—"

"Special Agent Doubt," came a gravely voice.

"Hi, this is James Dandy." He stared into her big blues. "Dodee wanted me to call and tell you they haven't found Stubbs yet, but they're looking for him in Santa Fe."

"Yeah, I knew about that."

"Oh, you already knew about it," he said, giving Dodee a phony grin.

"What I don't know is why you're still here in Cimarron."

"We're spending the night at the hotel." The other end went silent for so long Jim thought he had lost the connection. "Hello?"

"I'm here. We should meet. How about in the bus sometime after the hotel has settled down?"

"Are we in any danger here?"

Another silence from the other end, shorter this time. "I don't want to talk about that over the phone. But if it will ease your mind any, I'm around and I'll be keeping my eyes on you."

"Uh-huh."

"How about that New Age woman who wanted to do a séance?"

"You actually think—"

"Do it. I don't believe that stuff myself, but the thing is to get all the players out in the open. Meet me on the bus when it's over and let me know who attended. Agent, out."

Jim blinked as the connection was broken.

Agent out?

Who the hell says "Agent out"?

And with Brian "Agent Out" Doubt keeping an eye out for them, how come he didn't feel a whole lot safer?

And what about that business of getting all the players out in the open?

What was the game?

And who said he wanted to play?

Thirty-Nine

He picked up their bags and followed Dodee, and again he had the impression of stepping though a time warp into a long hall with a pressed-tin ceiling, dim chandeliers, and framed pictures of desperadoes—Billy the Kid, Bat Masterson, Wyatt Earp—hanging on busy, red-and-white wallpaper of alternating stripes and Indian symbols. The worst part of it was, squinting his eyes and using only a little imagination, the Indian symbols could be grinning skulls.

Just what he needed to go along with the séance Erynn Sunflower was cooking up.

An antique roulette table, about three-by-six feet, lived in the stairwell to the second floor a third of the way down the hall to their room, while a stuffed cougar mounted on the wall above it looked ready to pounce.

It promised to be a fun evening, yeah buddy.

He carried their luggage into the Pat Garrett room. A wrought-iron double bed rested against a green, fleurs-de-lis patterned wallpaper, two big pillows with a throw in between. A white, mantled, fireplace with a dark grate, a dresser with a mirror so low he had to kneel to see his face, and two straight-backed chairs rounded out the room. Two doors led off it, one to a closet, the second to a shared bath with a club-footed bathtub and a commode with a tank up near the ceiling for flushing.

Dodee eased past him into the bathroom and tried the connecting door to the next room.

"What are you doing?"

"It's locked," she whispered, easing past him again and going back into the hall.

Now what?

He crossed the bedroom and peeked out in time to see her try the door to the next room. She turned to him, shrugged, hurried back.

"It's locked."

"What did you expect?"

"That's the Wild Sam Sheridan Room. I wanted to see if it was being repaired like they said. We can find out later on."

He blinked at her.

"After we meet with Brian Doubt."

He blinked at her again.

"You can sneak behind the desk and get the key."

"And why, pray tell, would I do that?"

"Because it's the last link to the Mayan Falcon. We should at least take a look at it after all we've been through, don't you think?"

"No. What I think is that we should lock the door, bar the windows, hop into that bed, bury ourselves under the covers, and hope we see tomorrow's sunrise without someone trying to bump us off."

Her lips spread in a little downward smile. "Bump us off? Isn't that a little melodramatic?"

"Not if we're tying to stay alive until the end of this Elderhostel."

"We have to hurry." She turned to the mirror and fussed with a few of her wheaten curls. "We meet in Erynn's room at a quarter to nine. She's going to call in the spirits."

"The only spirits I'd like to call in are the kind I can pour from a bottle." He looked at his watch. "Why a quarter to nine?"

"She wanted to wait until midnight, but I told her no one would be awake."

He stretched out on the bed. "I don't even want to be awake at a quarter to nine." He grinned. "We could have some of that fun stuff you promised to show me."

"We have to go." She added a fresh touch of lipstick. "Isn't that what Brian Doubt said?"

"Screw 'em. And I'm beginning to doubt Doubt." He took a deep breath and let it out. "So who's going to be there?"

She straightened up and worked her lips together, spreading the color. "I don't know." She looked at something on her blouse, picked up the towel, and started rubbing it. "Erynn invited a whole bunch." She headed into the bathroom. "Maybe it will help us narrow down who killed Hank Adamo."

"I don't care who killed Hank Adamo. I only care that they don't kill good old Jim Dandy. And Dodee Swisher, for that matter. Besides, we're not the police. It's not our job to find out who killed who."

She poked her head around the jamb, put her finger to her lips, and disappeared.

He sighed, crawled off the bed, and lumbered across the room to find her ear pressed against the connecting door. "What are you doing?" he whispered.

"I thought I heard a noise in there."

He took her by the hand, led her from the bathroom, then shut and locked the door on his side.

"Didn't you hear what I just told you? I only care that they don't kill old Jim Dandy and Dodee Swisher. Stay out of it."

A half an hour later they stepped into the dimly lit hall, turned right at the roulette table, and mounted the stairs. The glass eyes of a snarling bear head gazed down at him from the wall as he climbed, its skin flattened like a cartoon Wily Coyote just squished by a steamroller. They turned right and continued on through a pair of double doors at the end of the hall.

Candles flickered on either side of a small pendulum clock placed on top of a fireplace mantle, giving a soft glow to the darkened room. The Martin Martins sat on a double brass bed scrunched in the left-hand corner. Ace Rudavsky and Claire Renquist sat at the opposite end of the room on easy chairs with a darkened window in between. Narcisco Ramos, running his fingers over his lips as if he were dying for a cigarette, rested his butt against a mirrored dresser set in the corner to Ace's right.

"Here's our main spirit receptor now," Erynn said.

She sat cross-legged in her peasant dress on the tail end of a cougar skin flattened on the floor, probably run over by the same steamroller as the bear in the hall, its still-attached head glaring up at Jim with a mouth full of teeth.

"Come in, Dodee," Erynn said, round face and glasses turned up to them, big crystal dangling between the wine-jug breasts. "I wonder if anyone else is coming?"

"Why don't we get on with it?" Ace asked.

"Right," Martin said, the brass bed squeaking as he got up. "Any more and we'll have to move to the lobby."

"Very well then," Erynn said, spreading her arms to indicate a circle around the animal skin, "if we could all take our places."

Jim sat at the cougar's head, right where its large teeth could gobble up his testicles if it leaped to life, not a happy thought. He looked into Ace's shadowed face. "I'm surprised to see you here."

"Wanna see this shaman woman if she shows."

"Quiet, please," Erynn said, then lowered her voice. "We will sit here in silence for a few minutes, eyes closed, until the spirit chimes call to us."

Jim closed his eyes and listened, but all he heard was the slow ticktock of the pendulum clock on the mantle. He felt like a kid playing a game of Spin the Bottle, but his body was too old and creaky to be cross-legged for long. If the spirit chimes, oooOOOooo, didn't start soon, he was stretching out and taking a nap.

Bong rang the tick-tock clock.

Was that the spirit chimes?

Bong.

No wonder she wanted to meet at a quarter to nine.

Seven more bongs followed, and when the last had faded into the ether, and the silence had settled again to a rhythmic ticktock, ticktock, a high-pitched, wobbly sound emanated from Erynn's throat, like the ululating greeting of Bedouin women when their desert warriors returned home. She kept it up as minutes passed by, and stopped just short of Jim charging across room and throttling her.

"We are seated here in the midst of the cosmic force

calling out to the spirits we know surround us. We call on all to come to us, but especially Moondance Wolf. We call you to come to us, Moondance, let us hear your voice, communicate to us what you have been trying to tell Dodee over this past week."

More silence.

Tick. Tock.

He cracked one eye to peek at Erynn, but the sight of her glasses in the dark candlelight, looking like empty eye sockets in a skull, made him snap it shut again.

"And if you can't come to us, Moondance, send another to give us your message."

She had to be off her freaking rocker.

Tick. Tock.

And he had to be off his freaking rocker to be down on the floor with her.

Tick. Tock.

"Tell us who killed you."

Tick. Tock.

"Tell us where the Mayan Falcon is."

He opened one eye on that.

Then jumped as the door slammed behind him.

The bed creaked and he snapped around to see a woman pop up from under the covers, long black hair flowing around wide eyes and sallow cheeks to reach down to the tips of two bare, perky breasts. "Beauregard, you surely did scare the life out of me."

A pockmarked man, polished boots and blue military pants, strode to the dresser. "Go back to sleep."

"You come into bed with me, sugar. You paid your money, don't you want to see what I got?"

"Later." He yanked a drawer out of the dresser and set

it on the floor. "Wild Sam is beatin' me in cards, and there ain't no way he could do that without him cheatin'."

"Pay him no mind, Beauregard, and come to bed."

But Beauregard bent down to the empty drawer socket and drew out a foot-long wad of burlap. "I'm gonna catch that cheat."

"Come to bed, sugar, before you git into a fight and git yourself killed."

"Let him try, by God," he said, unwrapping a gold figure from the burlap and shaking it in the air, "let him try and he'll be kissin' the devil's ass before sunup."

Jim swung back to the bare-boobed woman.

But the bed was empty; the sheets smoothed down flat.

He jerked around to Beauregard, but he, too, had left the building.

"Sonofabitch!" he shouted. "That was something." He glanced around at the faces in the circle. "I thought this spirit thing was strictly bullshit, but that popped my mind open, I'll tell you that."

He glanced around again, at all of them staring at him.

"What popped your mind open, sweetheart?"

He jerked his thumb toward the bed. "That bare-breasted girl. And what about old Beauregard grabbing that package out of the dresser drawer?" He ran his hand through his hair, then grabbed a wad of it and held it up. "It felt like this stuff was standing on end."

He looked from face to face.

Wide eyes with slack jaws stared back at him.

"Oh shit. You all didn't see them?"

They all had not.

"What did she look like?"

"Who was the guy?"

"What was in the package?"

"Yes, what was in the package?"

Questions coming from all sides suddenly fell silent on the last one.

"Yes," Erynn said, "tell us, what was in the package?"

"Something gold and heavy and a foot long." He turned and pointed to the dresser. "And he had it hidden behind one of those drawers."

Forty

Six old folks and Ace leaped to their feet and charged the dresser. Martin Martin and Narcisco Ramos elbowed the others out of the way as they ripped drawers from the wood hulk and tossed them to the floor.

"Wait a minute," Jim shouted, "wait a minute."

They all turned to him, as if he were going to tell them they were searching the wrong dresser.

"In the first place, Beauregard took it out of the dresser, so why would it be in there?"

They looked at one another for a moment, then Ace turned to him. "Beauregard's ghost tried to take it out, but ghosts can't carry anything."

They all jerked back to the dresser.

"Wait a minute, wait a minute," Jim called again and climbed to his feet. "You're going to kill one another. Let one person—Claire, see if there's anything in there."

The men glanced at one another, jaws set and brows knitted, but they stepped aside.

"It's too dark," she said.

Jim stepped to the wall and flicked on the lights.

She stooped and peered into each slot, then stood and shrugged. "Nothing."

Ace eased her aside and searched for himself, even reaching in and running his hand around. And Narcisco Ramos did the same. And Martin Martin, as if to make sure, absolutely sure, the others weren't hiding something they could come back later and retrieve.

"Nothing?" Helen Martin asked.

Martin shook his head, then glared at Jim. "This is not some kind of a joke you're pulling?"

He held out his hands and let them flop. "I told you what I saw. At least what I thought I saw."

Ace glanced sideways at him. "You're sure it was in this dresser? Not some other place—"

"That dresser," he said, nodding toward it. "But this isn't real. These guys weren't actually here, otherwise you all would have seen them."

Narcisco Ramos scratched his jaw. "Forget about the dresser. He took it outta there." He turned to Jim. "We need to know where he took it."

Jim spread his arms in a shrug.

Narcisco nodded. "We needa ask him. Quick, let's do this again. Only this time, when we see him, we ask him what he did with it. Everyone back on the floor."

Jim grabbed Dodee's hand. "Not us. I've had enough of this stuff to last a lifetime."

"Sure, you've seen them," Helen Martin said. "Now you don't want us to see them."

"You're not cutting us out of something?" Ace asked.

"I told you everything. You can think what you want."

Dodee turned to him. "Maybe we should try once more?"

"Nope. This is too spooky for me. Hell, I could have been hallucinating. The power of suggestion."

Ace stared at him for a few moments, then dropped to the floor. "Okay, let's do it without him."

"Yes," Claire said, joining him on the carpet. "Let's get started."

Jim led Dodee from the room, shut the door, and started for the stairs.

Her big blues came up to him. "Sure you don't want—"

"Nope." He looked at his watch. "Besides, we have a meeting with Brian Doubt."

She stopped at the head of the stairs. "Why don't you go to the meeting and I'll stay—"

"Didn't you see what just happened in that room?"

"Only you saw them—"

"I'm not talking about the ghosts. I'm talking about the bare, naked greed. You want to be part of that?"

"Oh, I know, and no, I don't." She took his hand and they descended the stairs. "I guess I got carried away by the desire to see the thing."

They glanced both ways when they reached the hallway: deserted.

"What now?" she whispered.

"How about skulking across the lobby and seeing if Brian Doubt is out on the bus?"

They skulked across the lobby, but he stopped her in the shadowed vestibule. "Let's not tell Brian about the ghost thing."

She looked up at him, but in the darkness only the tip of her nose caught the light. "Why not?"

He kissed the tip of the nose. "The thing is complicated enough without throwing in an hallucination."

He opened the outer door and the cold, night wind buffeted them. She brought out her handy-dandy penlight and led the way to the bus; the door opened as they reached it. Jim helped Dodee up, then followed after.

"Nice to see you two still alive," the big FBI guy said from the driver's seat.

Jim stopped halfway up the stairwell.

"You left us out there to see if we'd get killed?"

"No, no, I'm just talking. I've had my eye on you. So how has the evening gone?"

Dodee sat in the first seat. "We had the séance as you asked."

"Good. What happened?"

Jim remained standing on the second step. "Nothing happened. Did you think the spirit of Moondance Wolf was going to pop up and tell us who killed her and Hank Adamo?"

The FBI man raised one shoulder and let it fall. "Been nice. What I was hoping is that somebody would think they saw a ghost and confess on the spot."

"Or shoot us on the spot to keep us from talking?"

"Nothing came out about the Mayan Falcon?"

"Oh yeah. Someone pulled it out of his pocket."

Brian Doubt swung around in the seat. "You saw it? You actually saw it?" Then his shoulders slumped. "Oh. You're kidding. Right. Dumb question. So, who all was there?"

"A bunch." How much could the FBI guy's eye have had on them if he didn't know who was there? Jim rested an arm on the stairwell railing and ticked off their names as Brian wrote them down on a slip of paper. "Are you saying these guys are suspects?"

Doubt rubbed his chin. "I don't know. It's either one of them, or someone we don't know about."

"Great. Talk about a definitive statement."

"I mean one who's not here, or we don't know is here." Another silence. "Maybe somebody else is skulking about." He turned to Dodee. "And no one mentioned anything about the Mayan Falcon?"

"Nope," Jim said, preempting anything Dodee might be tempted to say.

"Okay, go back to your rooms and call it a night." Doubt opened the bus door. "Call me if you hear of anything, otherwise I'll see you in the morning."

"We could look around if you want," Dodee said.

"No, leave that to me. Go to bed."

Jim helped her down and they hurried back into the warmth of the deserted lobby.

"Brrr," she said, "it's cold out there." She glanced back toward the bus and then to Jim. "I don't believe he can see us here."

Jim nodded. "See us here? I don't think he's even trying—"

"No, I mean the key." He blinked at her. "The key, the key to the room next door."

"Hey, didn't he just say he didn't want us snooping around?"

"And didn't you just lie when he asked about the Mayan Falcon?" She glanced around the deserted lobby. "Get it, sweetheart, while we have the chance. We can decide whether to use it later."

He heaved a sigh. "I want to go on record I'm against this."

"So noted."

So noted, yeah, right, big help that would be if they got flung in jail.

He circled the desk, ducked down behind it, and started going through the room keys. He turned as she scrunched in beside him, hotel register in her hand. "What are you doing now?"

"You find the key. I'm just looking to see who has checked in here during the last few days."

He gave another sigh, went back to the keys, one for every room, probably spares, and doubles on rooms that were empty. The Wild Sam Sheridan bedroom was a singleton. So who had the other?

"Look," she whispered, showing him the ledger, "Max Solnim stayed in that room last night."

"I thought you said the room was being restored."

"That's what the desk clerk told me. So how could Max have stayed there?"

And where was the extra key?

"Let's get the hell out of here."

He raised his head, made sure they were alone, then led her out from behind the desk and across the lobby. The hallway, dim before, appeared ever dimmer. Had some of the bulbs blown out in the chandeliers?

A shadow zipped around the corner of the staircase.

"Someone's down there," he whispered. "Someone or something."

"You mean like a ghost?"

"I don't know what I mean. We're getting back to our bedroom, locking the door, and that's it."

He took her hand and they skulked down the hall, pressed against the opposite wall, and peeked into the stairwell. No one. But who knew what lurked in the shadows? He hurried her on to their door and slipped in the key, and turned it with a clunk that reverberated through the building.

"Just a minute there, Pardner."

He swung around, ready to fight.

"I wanna see them cards again."

Holy shit.

Beauregard St. Simian sat at the far side of the roulette table, another man at the near end with his back to them, and on the green cloth between, amongst some turned-down playing cards, sat a foot-high gold statue, two diamond eyes gleaming in an overhead light that wasn't there.

The second man—Wild Sam Sheridan?—dropped his right hand to a gun strapped on his waist. "You callin' me a cheat?"

Holy shit again. He yanked Dodee into the room and slammed the door.

"What's wrong?"

"What's wrong? We damn near got killed, that's what's wrong. They pull their guns and we're right in the line of fire."

"What guns?"

"You didn't see them? Then you're lucky. Beauregard St. Simian and Wild Sam Sheridan right there at the roulette table. And the Mayan Falcon between them."

The big blues opened wide, then she swung around and opened the door.

"Damnit, Dodee."

But no one sat at the darkened old roulette table.

He closed the door. "They were there."

She shook her head. "No, not really there, any more than the falcon was. But at least now we know it exists."

"Yeah, right. If those guys and their bullets don't exist, what makes you think that statue does?"

"Because you saw it, just like you saw those men."

"And then I didn't see them. How do you explain that?"

"I don't know." She marched into the bathroom.

"Don't be too long. I feel a sudden need to empty my bladder."

"I'm not doing anything if you want to use it."

He looked in to see her pressing her ear to the connecting bedroom door. He raised his eyes to the ceiling and let out another sigh, then crept up beside her. "Hear anything?"

"I thought I did, but—" She shook her head.

Then—sonofabitch—she tried the door.

"What are you doing?"

"It's locked from the other side."

"Whadja expect?"

"We'll have to go in through the hall."

Oh shit.

FORTY-ONE

He made sure the connecting bathroom door was unlocked from their side. If Dodee insisted on going into Wild Sam's room, they might need a second retreat if someone came down the hall.

"I want you to know I'm against this," he said, but she was already gone.

Great, just great.

He hurried into the dimly lit corridor, glanced at the empty roulette table, and caught up with her next door.

"I want you to know I'm against this."

"I know, sweetheart. You got the key?"

He slipped it in and eased it a millimeter at a time until it clunked open, then hesitated as he heard a faint sound from behind the door.

"What are you waiting for?"

"I thought I heard something."

He listened for an eternity, then opened the door onto a black hole.

Dodee snapped on her penlight and played it over a jumble of junk: an overturned and ripped-open mattress; dressers pulled from the wall and their drawers tumbled onto the bedsprings; and an andiron from the fireplace was stuck between the closet door and the jamb, as if someone had thrown it out of the way to search the chimney.

He glanced back down the hall, saw a shadow move in the stairwell, and rushed Dodee inside.

She played the light around walls papered with the same pattern as in Erynn's room, passed the cracked closet door, paused at a picture hanging cockeyed on a nail, and continued around to the bathroom.

"Hold it there," he said, hurrying across and unlocking it. "At least we're ready for a quick getaway."

"What do you think?" she whispered.

"If this is their idea of a restoration, I hate to think of their demolition."

"Someone was looking for the falcon." The light flittered over a black attaché case, broken open with papers spilled out. "Max's, you think? The clerk said he hit his head."

"Yeah, like against a blackjack. Let's get the hell out of here. Whoever searched this place might be coming back for another look-see."

She brought the light back to the cockeyed picture and held on it. "Maybe there's something written on the back."

"You mean like a treasure map with a big X showing where the falcon is?" He crossed the room, unhooked the picture, and turned it over. "Wow, there's a map here with a big X showing where the falcon is."

But Dodee fixed the light on the spot where he had lifted the picture, on a curl of peeled-back wallpaper. "Something's written underneath."

He peeled it off, exposing a straight pencil line with

three half circles above, the middle one twice the size of those on the ends, as if they represented different phases of the moon. He peeled off more paper to reveal graphic symbols below the line.

He turned to her. "Indian writing?"

"I don't know." She picked up one of Max's spilled papers, used his attaché case for a desk, and started copying it.

He chewed on the inside of his lip and glanced around the somber room.

The noise he had heard when they entered? Real or imagined—

The hall door flung open, a flashlight big as the sun blasted him in the eyes, and his heart fell out of his asshole.

"Did you find anything?" Erynn Sunflower whispered.

Sonofabitch. Ten years of his life down the drain.

"Maybe," Dodee whispered back.

He sucked his heart back into place and started breathing again.

"I knew it." Erynn came in and shut the door. "I knew we'd find something once we contacted the shaman."

Dodee went back to copying the wall symbols.

The door flew open again.

"What have you found?" Claire Renquist whispered.

Sonofabitch.

What the hell was this, a party?

"Shh," Erynn answered as Claire eased in and shut the door. "We don't know yet."

Dodee held up the finished paper for them to see.

"What is it?" Claire asked.

"Who cares?" Jim said, striding to his connecting bathroom door. "Let's get the hell out of here before anyone else shows up."

Erynn put a hand to her cheek. "Some kind of writing?"

"Indian symbols, I think," Dodee said.

"Hey," he said, grabbing the doorknob, "we copied it, now let's get the hell out."

"I can't let you do that." A new voice cut across the subdued conversation as a beam of light from the closet blasted him in the eyes. If Erynn's flash was the sun, this was the whole damn galaxy. "I'll take that paper, if you don't mind."

It took a moment for Jim to place the voice. "Dr. Longtree? What are you doing?"

"Same as you." He came completely out of the closet, his cool General Custer look disheveled now, his cool blue jacket and yellow tie wrinkled and spotted, but there was nothing wrong with the cool gun in his hand. "I knew you'd lead me to the falcon. When I saw Moondance hit the pavement I thought it was over, but then that television woman asked you about the notebook—"

"There is no notebook."

"—and I found out you were coming on this Elderhostel, it was a simple matter of replacing Ace and tagging along."

"You poisoned him?" Dodee asked.

Longtree held out his hand. "I'll take that paper now."

"Wait a minute," Jim said. "You were the one on the roof with the shaman?"

The big flashlight swung back onto Jim. "I know what you are thinking. That I became obsessed with the falcon and killed her, but all I sought was evidence to support my thesis that commerce existed between the Mayans and the early Plains Indians. You know how many people laughed at me for that? And Moondance had the validation right there, with the falcon, and refused to let me have it. I tried to reason with her, pleaded, threatened, and when I caught her on the rooftop, I only wanted to frighten her, but she went flying over the side."

"Yeah, right, and Hank Adamo slit his own throat when you mistook his room for ours—"

"Don't be silly. I assigned the rooms. Do you not think I knew who was where? I searched your room when we were in La Junta."

"Then who killed Adamo?"

"I don't know. But when I found out he was with the Bureau of Indian Affairs, it confirmed my suspicion that, if not you, someone on this excursion had evidence of the falcon. When Maxwell Solnim suddenly turned up some research and raced up here, I followed. Unfortunately"— Longtree motioned to the rubble in the room—"this is where his research ended. He didn't find anything. I didn't find anything. But when I came back to search again tonight, look who shows up." His eyes narrowed as he turned back at Dodee. "Now, for the last time, I want that paper—"

The hall door banged open. "Ah ha!"

The big flashlight swung around and transfixed Martin Martin.

"Trying to cut us out, are you?"

Jim jerked open the bathroom door.

"Cut us out and keep the falcon for yourself?"

He grabbed Dodee and shoved her into the bathroom.

"I don't think so."

The big flashlight swung back to Jim.

He jumped in after her and slammed the door.

Two shots split the air and punched out two holes.

Sonofabitch!

He rammed the bolt home, snatched Dodee's hand and tear-assed through the bedroom and out into the hall.

"Stop," someone shouted when he reached the roulette table.

He swung around and Beauregard St. Simian rushed him. And passed right on through.

Holy shit.

He grabbed Dodee and lit out for the lobby after him.

"Stop," Wild Sam Sheridan called again, "stand and draw."

And Beauregard St. Simian swung around, pointed a .44 at point blank range between Jim's eyeballs, and cracked off a shot that jiggled his sphincter as it zapped on through without leaving a hole.

Then Wild Sam blasted off two shots from behind that whistled off into eternity.

Great, just great.

But another shot slammed into the wooden doorjamb and showered him with splinters.

He grabbed Dodee and burst into the lobby, dodging leather chairs and zigzagging around sofas, heading for the exit, but jerked to a stop as a straight-armed man leveled a gun in his face. He tackled Dodee as the gun exploded, crashing to the floor by the front desk.

"Stand and draw," Wild Sam shouted and another shot rang out.

Great, just absolutely great.

Then another shot tore into the pamphlet rack above his head and he dragged Dodee behind the front desk as another one smashed into the window, raining down glass shards upon him.

Just abso-fucking-lutely great.

He scrunched Dodee in the corner and covered her with his body while guns blasted all over the place, unable to tell phantom from fact, until a cannon exploded just over his head, followed by the soft thud of someone hitting the floor, and silence.

Then a knock on the countertop.

"You okay back there?" asked a deep, gravely voice.

He looked up to see Brian skulking-FBI-agent Doubt.

"You got the falcon?"

"No, we don't."

He turned to Dodee. "You all right?"

She nodded.

"But you don't have the falcon?"

"I told you, we don't," Jim said, helping Dodee up.

Brian marched over to where Longtree lay crumpled up on the floor, blood pumping out of a hole in his chest. He picked up Longtree's gun and stuck it in Longtree's face.

"Where's the falcon?"

"There is no falcon," Jim said, walking over to the wounded man.

"Then why was he shooting at you?"

Jim knelt beside Longtree and ripped the buttons off his shirt. "We need to stop the blood flow." He looked up to see the lithe desk clerk standing in a robe by the door to the dining room. "We need some towels here."

"What about the notebook?" Brian asked.

"Damnit, for the last time: There. Is. No. Notebook."

"Then why was he shooting at you?"

Erynn, Claire, and Martin Martin crept out of the hallway as the desk clerk hurried across with an armload of white towels.

"Good." He grabbed a couple and pressed them to the man's chest. "Dial nine-one-one and get an ambulance."

Brian Doubt stood up and turned to Dodee. "Why was he shooting at you?"

She showed him the paper. "We found this written on the wall in the Wild Sam Sheridan Room."

Brian stared at the note. "What is it?"

"Indian symbols. We think it must have to do with the Mayan Falcon. At least he thought so. He was shooting at us to get it."

"Hey." Brian shoved his shoe into Longtree's side. "What's this got to do with the falcon?"

Longtree's face contorted and his eyes opened for a moment before rolling back into his head.

"All right." Brian holstered his own gun and stuck Longtree's into his waistband. "An ambulance is on the way." He stared down at Jim. "You okay until they get here?"

"I don't think it's serious if we can stop the blow flow." He rocked Longtree onto his side and looked at the exit wound. "I could use some help here."

Erynn rushed over and held a towel compress against Longtree's back.

Brian nodded. "All right. I have some things to do before the police arrive."

"Wait a minute," Jim said, "I thought you were

investigating Hank Adamo's murder? Don't you want to ask about that?"

"Later. I'll be back. Oh, by the way." Brian swung around and slipped the paper out of Dodee's hand. "Evidence." He folded it up and stuck it in his pocket. "Tell the police what happened and that I'll get back to them," he called as he marched out of the hotel.

Forty-Two

They didn't get to bed until three o'clock, after Longtree had been carted off by helicopter and the sheriff had finished questioning everyone, so when morning broke, it took some hard pounding before he unglued his eyelids.

"Time to get up," Ace said through the door. "Need to load up and get on the road. You want breakfast, get up now."

They got up now and hurried to the dining room to sit with the bleary-eyed crew from the Wild Sam Sheridan room, Erynn Sunflower, Ace, the Martin Martins and Claire Renquist.

"I still find it all so hard to believe," she said, "Dr. Longtree was so refined, well educated—"

"One with a full professorship at Colorado State," Jim said.

"Yes, a professor, that actually tried to kill you."

Ace nodded. "And I find it hard to believe the bastard poisoned me."

Narcisco Ramos came in wrapped in his stench of cigarette smoke and plopped in a seat beside Erynn.

"Well," Ace said, "we'll load up the bus as soon as you're

finished eating. Harry will be taking you in. I'm going to hang here and rest up for a couple of days."

Martin Martin suddenly snapped erect. "You know, that's a good idea. I think we'll do the same."

"Ya stayin'?" Narcisco Ramos asked. "I'm stayin'."

Erynn stuck her index fingers under her glasses and rubbed her eyes. "I'm too tired to go on a long bus ride."

Claire paused with a coffee cup halfway to her lips. "Me too. Besides, I need to contact a few people around here about artifacts for my gallery."

The sheriff appeared in the lobby doorway with a red plastic file-case tucked under his arm. A short, thin man, weathered face, salt and pepper hair, scanned the room until he made eye contact with Jim and Dodee and motioned for them to come out.

"Excuse us," Jim said, and held the chair for Dodee.

"What's this about?" she whispered on the way to the lobby.

"If we wait maybe we'll find out."

The sheriff waved them to a leather settee, set the red plastic case on a small round table, and slumped in a leather armchair. He must have already talked to the desk clerk because she had a cup of coffee waiting for him.

"Thank you, ma'am," he said to her, took a sip, and looked across to Jim and Dodee. "Sorry," he said, motioning with the cup, "it's been a long night."

Jim nodded. "I can imagine."

He took another sip. "I'm wondering about the man who shot Longtree."

"How is he?" Dodee asked.

"Longtree? He'll be fine."

"He said he didn't kill the shaman," Jim said.

The lips turned down in the weathered face. "So he says. Either way, after last night, he'll be in the system for the foreseeable future." He took another sip and set his cup on the table. "Now, the man who shot him?"

"Brian Doubt." Jim nodded. "Saved our lives."

"You said he was a federal agent?"

"FBI," Dodee said.

"You know that? Got a good look at his badge and identification?"

"Well, yeah." He glanced at Dodee, who nodded, and back to the sheriff. "You're saying he's not an agent?"

"Not now, not ever."

"Maybe he's undercover," Dodee said.

"Nope. I called the agents helping with the investigation in Trinidad, and called the agency. No one ever heard of Brian Doubt."

"Then why was he trailing us?"

"You tell me." The sheriff turned to Dodee. "You said you gave him something for evidence?"

She glanced at Jim, arched her eyebrows, and pulled a piece of paper from her pocketbook.

Jim shook his head. "Don't tell me. You went back in the room and made another copy."

"Everyone did, sweetheart." She passed it to the sheriff. "These are Indian symbols we think lead to a valuable Mayan artifact."

"Actually," Jim said, "we have no idea what they are, except for a lot of superstition."

The sheriff looked it over, grimaced, and half shook his head. "May I keep this?"

Jim nodded. "You bet. Keep it."

"You can see the original on the wall in the Wild Sam Sheridan Room," Dodee said.

The sheriff stared at it a moment, then handed it back. "I'll get a photograph of the wall." He picked up his case, slid open a plastic zipper, and removed a picture. "After I talked to the agents in Trinidad this morning, they faxed me this. Recognize him?"

"Oh, yes." Dodee nodded. "He's the man who kidnapped me. So they caught him?"

The sheriff shook his head. "This is from a previous visit Dick Stubbs made to one of our institutions." He slipped out a second picture and laid it on the table.

Jim nodded. "That's Brian Doubt."

"The Brian's right, but the last name is Aaron. He's a suspect in a number of art and artifact thefts throughout the Southwest, sometimes linked with Stubbs, but aside from serving a year and a half for a B'n'E in his twenties, he's never been brought to trial. Looks like he bought the big one now. They found fingerprints linking him to the murder. The theory is that Adamo surprised Aaron rifling his room and Aaron killed him. At least, that's what the Trinidad boys tell me." The sheriff finished off his coffee and stood up. "Don't worry. We'll get him. In the meantime, have a safe trip home."

Jim led the way back to the breakfast table.

"I have bad, badder, and worser news for you." He waited until he had their full attention. "The FBI guy who shot Longtree is actually wanted by the FBI. They believe he murdered Hank Adamo. And, talking about the falcon, this suspected killer has a copy of the Indian symbols, a seven-hour head start, and two guns."

They sat in silence for a moment, then Ace shook

314

his finger. "Well, as I was saying, it's a long ride into Denver."

When it came time to board the bus, no one stayed behind. The PA system crackled and Ace's voice came out loud and clear. "Harry, take her home."

Jim slept most of the way, except for pit stops and a box lunch somewhere between Trinidad and Denver, but he woke up around Castle Rock. Dodee was sound asleep beside him, so he stared at the plains slipping by outside, and ran his mind over Beauregard St. Simian and Wild Sam Sheridan from the night before.

Where had they come from?

Was there some kind of time-link between then and now, where the present and the past brushed by one another? Like a light-link or light shift in desert mirages, creating an apparent swimming pool or water scene that really existed, but miles away from where it appeared.

He eased out of the seat and moved down the aisle to join John Walsh.

"You look well rested."

The retired priest smiled. "I should. I slept in the hotel's annex and didn't learn about the excitement until this morning."

"Did you hear about the ghosts?" When John's brow wrinkled, Jim told him about the séance in Erynn's room, the shootout between Beauregard St. Simian and Wild Sam, and about his theory of a time-link. "What do you think?" he asked when he finished.

John shrugged. "You're confusing paranormal with spiritual. Erynn might make a stab at it, but not me."

"But is it at least possible? Except, why would I be the only one to see it?"

He shrugged again. "You mentioned the ticktock of the clock? Maybe it had an hypnotic effect on you. Maybe you were hallucinating. Or maybe God just gave you the gift to see what no one else saw."

Jim nodded. "Like you and the dandelions?"

He smiled. "Yeah."

They arrived at the Comfort Inn at three-thirty in the afternoon. A lot of handshakes around. Most of the group had left cars and were anxious to get on the road in spite of the long bus ride. Very few made false promises about keeping in touch; they had joined together into a community for this Elderhostel adventure, and when they headed out on another, there would be a completely new cast of players.

Jim and Dodee entered the lobby with some of the Wild Sam Sheridan crew, Erynn, Claire, and the Martin Martins, Jim to wait for the bus to take him to the airport, Dodee for her friend to fetch her. He picked up the flower box with Dodee's painting from the front desk.

She tucked her arm under his. "I was thinking, I could call my friend and ask her to pick me up in the morning if you want to delay your flight a day."

"My ticket doesn't allow me to do that. I should have thought of it before I left home. Besides, you seemed locked in with your friend for tonight."

She stood on her toes and kissed him. "The trip went by too fast for us just being us. We need to pick out another Elderhostel in a month or so."

He nodded, already feeling withdrawal pains.

They carried their things into the hospitality room, where John Walsh poured himself a cup of coffee and came over to set it on a table beside them. "Looks like everybody's wound down," he said, motioning to the others sitting around in a daze.

"Hey," Martin Martin sat up and cried out, "look who's here."

Max Solnim, a bandage wrapped around his hairless head, stood there with all the crevasses on his etched face curving around a broad grin. "Glad to see you made it back," he said in his squeaky voice. "Heard you had an adventure at the St. James."

"Us?" Erynn said. "How about you?"

"Anytime you wake up from a bump on the head has to be a good day." He rubbed his chin and glanced at Jim from behind his thick glasses. "Sorry for cutting out on you when I found out about the falcon. At first I didn't really think anything about it. Spirit messages from a dead shaman? Then I rummaged around in Spanish and Indian folklore, and darned if I didn't find out that the last person to have it ended up at that hotel in Cimarron. Suddenly I went crazy to see that damn thing. Like I was possessed. But it serves me right, running after a pipe dream like that." He turned to Dodee. "How about you? That shaman woman still showing up on your sketches?"

She shrugged. "I haven't done any since I painted the boy on the bench."

"You know, I'd sure like to see them."

Dodee turned to Jim.

He shrugged, unzipped the black case, and pulled out the sketchbook and opened it to Dodee's pencil drawing of Kit Carson. He tossed it onto the table, banging into the Styrofoam cup and spilling John's coffee all over it.

"Oh, damn." He glanced up at John Walsh. "See if

there're some paper napkins." He flattened his hand and swept its edge across the pad, trying to Squeegee the coffee off the page, and did it again. "Damn, I'm sorry, Dodee." He swept it clean again.

"Don't worry about it, sweetheart, I don't need it anymore this trip."

"I shouldn't have put it there," John Walsh said, rushing up with the napkins.

"No, it was my fault."

"Don't worry about it, sweetheart. It's not that big a deal."

He sponged the sketchbook, flapped the pages to loosen them up, then folded it backward over a chair.

A horn blasted from the hotel's portico.

"Oh, Lord," John Walsh called out, "there's my bus." He gave Dodee a hug and shook Jim's hand. "Glad to have met you." He grabbed his bag and waved to the rest. "I'll say a prayer for your safe trip home."

Max Solnim turned to them. "Still like to see those pictures with the shaman."

Jim picked up the black leather case, unzipped the back pocket, and slipped out the painting of the boy on the bench, stared at it a moment, and blinked at Dodee. Then he yanked open the flower box and unrolled the second painting.

"I'll be damned."

He spread them both out on a second table for the others to see, the one with the horse statues from the Adams Mark and the other with the boy, but all traces of the painted lady were gone.

"What do you make of that?"

Erynn looked to Dodee. "It means you heard her message."

"What message?" Claire asked.

"About Longtree," Erynn said. "Now that he's in jail she no longer needs to be in the painting. She can now go on with the rest of her journey."

Jim stared at her a moment, and at the others, and then back at the paintings.

It was all bullshit.

There had to be a logical explanation.

But how to explain no painted lady in the picture? And the shootout between Beauregard St. Simian and Wild Sam Sheridan? There had been entirely too much oooOOOooo to suit him.

Claire traced the small scar on her face. "But what about the Mayan Falcon? Wasn't that what she was trying to tell us?"

Martin Martin turned to Max. "Did you learn anything about it in Cimarron?"

"I found the hotel, if that's what you're asking. And I found the room, booked it, in fact, but when I started searching, pow, the lights went out and I woke up the next day in a hospital."

"You didn't see the Indian symbols on the wall?" Erynn asked.

Max's watery blue eyes stared out from behind his thick glasses and he cocked his head.

"Can you decipher Indian symbols?" Claire asked.

Suddenly everyone pulled out copies of the wall symbols and shoved them in his face.

Max took Claire's and studied it, the line with the three half-circles above it, the one in the middle larger than the other two, representations of the moon's phases, and the strange symbols below. He turned the paper sideways, then upside down and back around again, then his shoulders slumped.

"This is a joke, right?" His brow wrinkled, hardly noticeable in his crevassed face. "This is a joke?" He glanced around at them. "It's a word puzzle. Lines missing. Got a pencil?"

Martin Martin handed him a pen.

He set the paper on a table and drew a couple of small circles in the large half circle, three straight lines in the smaller ones to either side, added lines to the symbols below, then held it up for all to see.

A face with two hands peeking over a wall and words underneath: *Kilroy was here, May, 1946.*

Forty-Three

Jim went to the restroom and when he came out everyone was gone. "Where did they go?"

"Over to the Moonlight Diner," Dodee said. "Want to join them?"

"No, I don't want to miss my bus."

He walked over to the sketchbook and started to close it, then stared at the damp page, and at the one underneath, and the one underneath that, and turned to glare at Dodee.

"What, sweetheart?"

"Come look."

The likeness of the Indian shaman emerged from the line drawing of John Carson, and the blank page underneath, and the one underneath that.

He grinned. "I told you there had to be a logical explanation. There's some defect in the paper. When you wet it, either with your watercolors or John Walsh's coffee, up it pops. It only looks like the shaman. The rest was the power of suggestion."

"And when it dried, it disappeared?"

He shrugged. "See what happens when you get this home."

"Then what's this whole thing been about?"

"It's been about letting ourselves get carried away by our imagination." He re-packed the sketchbook and the paintings in the case. "And about sticking our noses into places they don't belong."

He carried everything out to the lobby and placed them beside the door. Then they sat close together on the couch, he waiting for the airport bus, she for her author friend.

The author arrived first in a red SUV. Jim dumped Dodee's bags in the truck, met the woman, then took Dodee in his arms.

"I miss you already, lady."

"I'll miss you too, sweetheart." She kissed him. "I'll call you next week and let you know when I'm safely home."

"You better."

"We can plan another Elderhostel."

He kissed her, soft and long. The sound of a diesel broke in on them and he looked up. "There's my bus."

He grabbed his bag and she followed, giving him another kiss at the door. "See you later."

"I'll call."

He climbed the stairs, dropped his bag on a hotel-side seat and stood in the aisle, watching out the back window as Dodee and her girlfriend got into the red SUV. He bent down and followed them through the windows as the car pulled away, circled around the driveway, and disappeared behind the Moonlight Diner.

He flopped in the seat beside his bag and stared out at the hotel.

Part of him had suddenly gone flat. His kids were at home, and he would be happy to see them, but that didn't stop the emptiness.

The bus started up and he watched the hotel slip by.

Alone, by himself, the sole passenger.

Then, in a low spot of the lawn, up close to the hotel where it was protected from drying winds, he saw the yellow face of a dandelion smiling at him.

He smiled back.

AFTERWORDS

DANDELIONS

As you may have guessed, John Walsh's experience with the dandelions actually happened to me in the spring of 1981. Since then, dandelions have become part of the signs and symbols of my life. Whenever I go for a walk and see a yellow face, or a fluffy seed pod, I recognize it as a whisper of God's love for me. It is my gift. Given to me.

And now I give it to you.

So someday when you are walking in your own personal desert, or alone in some alley at the far corner of the world, and you look down and see one of these bright yellow flowers, or watch a child send a seedpod of magical parachutes sailing through the air, you, too, may hear the whisper of God's love, and know you are not alone.

Peter Abresch
—2003